For the Record

JULIANA SMITH

Contents

Dedication 1

Rachel's Playlist: 2

1. Chapter 1: Adam 5
2. Chapter 2: Rachel 10
3. Chapter 3: Rachel 19
4. Chapter 4: Rachel 25
5. Chapter 5: Adam 32
6. Chapter 6: Adam 39
7. Chapter 7: Rachel 53
8. Chapter 8: Adam 58
9. Chapter 9: Adam 63
10. Chapter 10: Rachel 70
11. Chapter 11: Rachel 77
12. Chapter 12: Rachel 82
13. Chapter 13: Adam 93
14. Chapter 14: Adam 98

15. Chapter 15: Rachel 102
16. Chapter 16: Adam 114
17. Chapter 17: Rachel 126
18. Chapter 18: Rachel 134
19. Chapter 19: Rachel 143
20. Chapter 20: Adam 155
21. Chapter 21: Adam 158
22. Chapter 22: Rachel 170
23. Chapter 23: Rachel 181
24. Chapter 24: Rachel 194
25. Chapter 25: Adam 203
26. Chapter 26: Rachel 209
27. Chapter 27: Rachel 217
28. Chapter 28: Adam 227
29. Chapter 29: Rachel 238
30. Chapter 30: Rachel 248
31. Chapter 31: Rachel 259
32. Chapter 32: Rachel 267
33. Chapter 33: Rachel 273
34. Chapter 34: Adam 280
35. Chapter 35: Adam 287
36. Chapter 36: Adam 295

37. Chapter 37: Rachel 301

38. Chapter 38: Rachel 305

39. Chapter 39: Rachel 319

40. Chapter 40: Adam 322

41. Chapter 41: Rachel 328

42. Chapter 42: Adam 333

43. Chapter 43: Rachel 341

44. Chapter 44: Rachel 348

45. Chapter 45: Rachel 352

Epilogue 359

Acknowledgements 362

To the girls who have a playlist for every mood. And to anyone who has had to take care of a family member. You have a rare and beautiful soul.

RACHEL'S PLAYLIST

Can't Take My Eyes Off You by Frankie Valli
Alone Again (Naturally) by Gilbert O'Sullivan
Got My Mind Set On You by George Harrison
It's Raining Men by The Weather Girls
Break My Stride by Matthew Wilder
Too Sweet by Hozier
You've Got A Friend by James Taylor
Starfish and Coffee by Prince
Float On by Modest Mouse
Come on Eileen by Dexys Midnight Runners
Sir Duke by Stevie Wonder
I don't feel like dancing by the Scissor Sisters
Goodbye Yellow Brick Road by Elton John
I Say A Little Prayer by Aretha Franklin
Happy Together by The Turtles
I Still Haven't Found What I'm Looking For by U2
Home by Edward Sharpe and The Magnetic Zeros

You Really Got a Hold On Me by Percy Sledge

Open Your Eyes by Snow Patrol

Dancing In The Dark By Bruce Springsteen

Fast Car by Tracy Chapman

Vienna by Billy Joel

My Life by Billy Joel

Wildest dream by Taylor swift

Time Of The Season by The Zombies

Magic Carpet Ride by Steppenwolf

More Than a Woman by The Bee Gees

Golden Slumbers by The Beatles

Burning for you by Blue Oyster Cult

The Way I Feel Inside by The Zombies

Sunday Kind of Love by Etta James

Be My Baby by The Ronettes

Until I Found You by Stephen Sanchez

Love Grows (Where My Rosemary Grows) by Edison Lighthouse

Close To You by Neon Trees

I Believe In a Thing Called Love by The Darkness

Kiss Her You Fool by Kids That Fly

I Will Survive by Gloria Gaynor

I Miss You, Blink 182.

The Rain Song, Led Zeppelin

Someone's Gonna Break Your Heart by Fountains Of Wayne

Homesick by Noah Kahan

With a Little Help from My Friends, The Beatles

Cats In The Cradle by Harry Chapin

Thank you by Led Zeppelin.

You Get What You Give by New Radicals

CHAPTER ONE

Adam / Now

Currently playing: Can't Take My Eyes Off You by Frankie Valli

***

It was an odd thing to wake up to, long strands of blond hair tickling my neck, and my chest feeling as though an elephant was sitting on it. But alcohol tended to have that kind of effect on people, I guess.

I let my eyes adjust to the sunlight slipping between the closed curtains in my hotel room. The peek of the luminous glow from the sun outside lit the room up just enough to bring back memories of the night before.

My suit pieces splayed out on the floor, my suitcase neatly tucked away in its corner by the dresser, the nightstand next to me, a white and gold lamp on top beside my phone with a dead battery, and finally a small ripped white dress lying right in front of me.

I sat up slowly from the bed, back tensing and pulling, a reminder that there was a reason I didn't drink anymore. I wasn't twenty-two and didn't have the recovery I once had. Each pierce of a headache allowed a new vision into the day before: my messy tumble down the hall, the rush to get to the room as soon as possible. The feeling of *finally* resting on my chest, the weight of *she's mine* heavy in my heart. This cat and mouse chase was over, and she was right by my side.

At the thought of her, my eyes dragged slowly all the way up to the curvy frame lying under the covers next to me. A white comforter pulled up to right below her chin, her round cheeks pulled into a half smile, shut eyes and long eyelashes fluttering slightly in her dream state.

Soul brighter than the sun shining itself, she lay there in my shirt, smiling in her sleep, entirely unaware of my presence. My gut twisted, a rush of cool air racing up my arms and leaving goose bumps in their wake. I was a grown man, one in the military at that. I'd faced situations that would cause most men to hide under their beds. Butterflies shouldn't be in the pit of my stomach at merely watching a woman sleep. But that didn't stop them.

It would be a lot easier to neglect that feeling in the pit of my stomach if she was anyone else. If she were a random woman I had picked up on a night out in Vegas. Someone I could spend a night with and forget the next morning before moving on as though nothing had happened. But she wasn't the type of woman you would do that to. She was the kind of woman that made you forget there were even other females out there. She was the type you held, cherished. The woman you savored and longed for because who knew how long you could keep her. Like the last bite of dessert or the last slow pull of your favorite cigar before it was snuffed out. A bright light in a dark world that I selfishly wanted to keep to myself.

The corners of my mouth tilted up as a tiny puppy-like snore left her swollen pink lips. The covers shifted as she readjusted, and I watched for a moment as her chest rose and fell, my shirt expanding with every breath she took. Hazy memories of the night before began to piece together with every minute passing by. I had offered a clean shirt to her before she passed out. She said no and claimed she wanted the one I was wearing under my suit. Said it smelled more like me. Like a lightning bolt to my chest, I felt this swell of pride. Before that, I walked hand in hand with her from the hotel bar to the elevator. She matched my height perfectly in her heels, leaning over to plant soft kisses along my cheek as the doors slowly shut. The feel of her in my hands, the way she called to me, how...*male* she made me feel? I was like a gorilla about to beat on his chest or something.

It all felt like a dream I had pieced together in my mind. And if the proof wasn't lying right beside me, makeup-free face and tousled blond hair across my pillowcase, I probably would have assumed it *was* a dream. Something my mind fabricated as a torture device to push me through the rest of the day.

My arm lifted to run a hand through my hair. I needed to check the time. Needed to make sure my brothers weren't blowing up my phone, wondering where I'd ended up last night or who I'd ended up with. But my phone was dead, and since apparently no one needed clocks anymore, the time was nowhere to be found in the room around me. Eyes snagging on the suitcase across the room, I lifted a hand from the sheet and slowly pushed myself up, prepared to walk lightly across the floor and grab my charger.

A small hand reached for mine before I could move, her long white nails softly dragging over the veins in my hand. My breathing sped up, heart pounding against my ribs, butterflies coming back even stronger. I turned my head back to her, expecting a wide-eyed blonde ready to make some cocky remark about *oops, we did it again*. Instead, I was met with her still sleeping form.

Her fingers laced over mine in the lightest touch. Feminine on top of masculine, soft over rough, purity over corruption. I watched for a moment more, knowing when she woke, we had things to discuss from the last week. Things she and I had been avoiding for far too long now. Things that were bound to hurt, but it was going to be the good kind of pain. The kind you knew made you stronger. Growing pains. I knew it was only a matter of time before they had to be let out. But I wanted this peace, this overwhelming light in my chest, to stay just a little longer.

It was when her fingers fully rested against mine that I looked down and noticed them.

A large diamond ring on her left finger, and a gold band on mine.

My pulse raced violently. The last clear memory I had before I succumbed to my drunken state seeped its way in, like I was getting an outside glimpse of my own life. It was me walking hand in hand with a certain blonde into a twenty-four-hour wedding chapel.

That was when the weight of the night before truly hit me. Rachel and I had gotten married.

CHAPTER TWO

Rachel/ Then

Currently playing: Alone Again (Naturally) by Gilbert O'Sullivan

***

You know the best thing about being an adult? You can go into a random bar you've never been to, order anything you want, and sulk as long as you like. Or until the bar closes, actually. But other than that, you have total free will.

I chose the perfect day to use said free will, considering it was the worst one I'd had in a while. Instead of drowning in my tears or eating ten Little Debbie cakes and screaming the lyrics of Genesis's "That's All" at the top of my lungs, I figured it was time to put on my big girl pants and sulk the way most adults do. With alcohol. I googled the best bar in Philly, took a quick trip down the road, plopped myself and my sequined mini skirt onto a barstool, and ordered what I thought would make me feel the most mature.

It was an incredibly stupid choice, considering I had never touched whiskey a day in my life. Growing up, all my favorite songs talked about women who could shoot it straight, and I always thought *oh yeah, I'm gonna be* that *girl one day.*

Holding my nose, because the smell alone was bound to cause a hangover, I forced myself to take one more sip of what tasted like great-grandpa's medicine cabinet mixed with a touch of hand sanitizer and a splash of bleach.

The liquid burned the back of my throat like drinking straight lava out of a fancy glass. The downright alien cough that left my mouth was proof enough that I wasn't meant for drinks that didn't have fun names like *sunrise shore*, or *peachy-Malibu wave.*

I cleared my burned throat, mumbling to myself as I tapped my finger on the rim of the glass. "Screw Carrie Underwood for making me think I had to shoot whiskey to be cool."

My apartment was filled with thrifted furniture, I wore heels that were taller than most women dared to touch, and my collection of records was like a shrine to the greatest artists of all time. I didn't need to order some dignified, manly drink to be cool. But it sure would have felt nice if I could, for one night, act like one of those girls who drank beer and knew how the heck a welder worked and what its purpose was. The quintessential cool-but-doesn't-know-it girl. That was everyone's favorite in the movies. Very early 2000s Megan Fox.

"Do you, uh, want mine?" A deep rumble one chair over from me sent vibrations up my spine and made the hair at my neck stand up. His voice sounded like rich dark chocolate. He sounded like the kind of guy who did order whiskey straight.

My neck craned to take the stranger in, and part of me was surprised I hadn't checked the guy out sooner. His tattoos caught my eye first. It was probably rude, since he was looking at my face, but I noticed both arms were covered in tiny art designs. Flowers, an old airplane that looked straight out of those movies our high school teachers forced us to watch, a couple of tribal ones. But my gaze mostly stuck to the one that looked like two little boys had scribbled it right there with a Sharpie. *Miles and Dallas.* Adorable. He was a dad. That was charming. Automatically, the next place I looked was his left hand, which was completely ring free and looked like an excellent place for me to rest my own hand.

He cleared his throat, and I realized it had been a solid minute since he'd spoken. I'd been too stuck on these doodle pads he called arms to notice. I looked up at his face and was surprised when I felt a lick of heat up my spine.

He wasn't really my type. I typically liked pretty boys, more handsome than able to physically lift me kind of thing. The kind of guy who had a golf membership and never used it, or who could go fishing but would never bait his hook. I liked control, and going out with a guy who was on the less-masculine side typically meant I had the upper hand.

This was not that guy. This man certainly baited his own hook. I doubt he had ever even been near a golf course. Rugged features, strong nose, cut jawline. His hair was a bit of a dark mess and scattered all over. Yet it worked perfectly for him. A tiny scar sat across his right brow, a stroke of white against his tan skin. There was a smudge of dirt along his chin, and I felt the urge to lick my thumb and clean it off. I would bet my money this guy owned a tool set. Or that he knew what an oil change consisted of at the very least.

Everything about him screamed *man.* He even had cargo pants on, something that had never done it for me. Who needed that many pockets? Then again, the guy was a dad, and I would think being a parent required snack pockets.

I finally landed on his eyes, dark green pools staring back at me. The one spot on him that looked soft, that looked longingly back at me. A boost of pride hit my chest at that.

"How do I know you're not going to poison me?"

He looked from his drink to mine. It was almost comical how his had a tiny umbrella in it. What business did Arnold Schwarzenegger here have drinking something frozen and pink with an umbrella in it? But then again, what business did I have drinking whiskey straight?

"I wouldn't poison my own drink." He lifted the glass to his full lips and took a sip as if to prove his point.

I shrugged. *Touché.* My mouth watered at the sight of the frozen cocktail. Sweat had formed on the glass, and it was melted enough to have a rim of liquid at the top that looked full of sugar and rum and everything nice.

"Okay, we can swap. But if I don't like it, you owe me something else."

He didn't smile, but his face twitched with slight amusement. Like he'd gone from a nine to a six on the *unapproachable grump* scale.

"All right," he rumbled and moved his pink drink my way.

I happily took it, and since the guy made me feel a little flirty, I placed my lips on the rim exactly where his had just been.

Smooth, sweet, cold relief poured down my throat and left a spread of warmth in my chest. Peaches and oranges danced in my mouth.

I sighed and took another sip. To my right, the guy's shoulders dropped. Either in relaxation or disappointment that he didn't have to get me another, I couldn't tell.

Unashamedly, I twisted my stool so I was facing the tattooed man. I smiled to myself when I saw that he was already looking at me. His eyes shifted from my drink to the bartender in the corner to my lips. I fluttered my lashes a little and gave my sweetest *I am but a fair maiden in need of rescue, sir knight* kind of look.

The base of his neck turned red right above his black tee, and I quickly found him even more endearing. The stranger turned back to his own drink, taking a swig of the whiskey and not even flinching.

"Heavy drink for someone who's not used to it." His voice poured over me.

My shoulders slumped, my heart falling into a sad rhythm. "My day felt worthy of it."

He tapped his finger against the glass, and I mocked his movement against my own. We each took a sip.

"Do...you want to talk about it?"

My eyes circled his face. He seemed mostly unapproachable, with his short answers and no hint of a smile anywhere to be seen. But then again, I saw his gaze drop to where my thighs met my skirt and stay there for a while, so maybe he was hoping to appear to be interested in my day. It was working. Well, that in combination with his scruff.

"You don't seem like the talking type."

At that, the corners of his lips pulled lightly and set back down. Like a small glimpse of light through the crack of a doorway.

"That's why I asked if *you* wanted to talk about it."

I laughed at that. This whole macho-man, big, tattooed, muscles, and strong jaw kind of thing was starting to work on me.

I crossed one leg over the other. "My favorite job in the world is considering closing up shop." My only job, really. One of the two things I loved and cherished most in this world. Half of my whole life had a fifty-fifty shot of being ripped out of my hands.

My fingers reached for my glass, and I took a larger sip in hopes of forgetting. Verbalizing it made me feel somehow better and worse at the same time. It was such a first-world problem, but I *was* still allowed to be upset, right? I mean, sure, things could have been a whole lot worse, but was I not at least a little entitled to be emotional about it?

Dad always said feelings were like water. They could bow and flex to their surroundings, but they could also be like a pressure washer, forcing themselves into your chest, flaking off all the loose bits in your heart and leaving only the steady stuff. It felt more like a pressure washer tonight.

"It feels stupid when I say it out loud." I scoffed, rolling my eyes at myself. "It's not like it's my family's place or anything. I just really love it there, and now...I don't know where I'll go if they do end up selling."

"That's not stupid," he grumbled, like he was fully prepared to argue with whatever part of my brain had caused me to believe it was. It was almost enough to make me smile again.

"Thanks, I guess." My shoulders slumped still, and I twirled the cute blue umbrella floating in my drink with my pointer finger.

A moment of silence passed.

"What is your, uh..." A line formed between his brows.

"Job?" I supplied.

"That."

I smiled, to him and myself both. "I work at a record store downtown. My job is everything and nothing at the same time. Some days I take in the new records, sort them by music genre, and then alphabetize. Some days I work the register and sweep the floors. I'm there alone a lot, and it's just, I don't know, my place, I guess."

More than that, Sip 'n' Spin was home in a lot of ways. It was bundled up with memories of Dad before his diagnosis. Before everything slowly fell apart around me.

The guy beside me didn't say anything. He didn't tell me everything was going to be all right or that there was something better out there for me. He merely nodded along and tapped his glass.

Feeling selfish for talking his ear off, I leaned in closer to the seat separating us.

"Why are you drinking tonight?"

"I just got back from being deployed to Germany. Felt right, I guess." He shrugged, and the expression he wore as he stared at his half-empty glass looked like it felt anything *but* right. I couldn't help but wonder where the mother of his kids was. If he'd slipped off a ring and hopped inside a bar in hopes that she wouldn't notice. I hated that it was where my mind immediately went, but it wouldn't have been the first time a married man had hit on me, and unless someone got down on a knee and popped the question my way, it wouldn't be the last.

Maybe I should've asked rather than giving the guy the benefit of the doubt, but I dunno...something about those blunt answers and to-the-point directions made it seem like he didn't possess the ability to even lie. He seemed like the type to tell you the 100 percent truth, even if it hurt. Or maybe especially when it hurt, judging by that scowl.

"Military?" I asked.

"PJ."

My head tilted. I was somewhat versed in military positions because of my dad, but I was by no means an expert. He retired when I was fairly young, and I was spared most of the traveling and extensive knowledge regarding positions and deployments. The only pj's I knew were pajamas. Specifically ones with Winnie the Pooh on them. Or when I felt frisky, my pink ones with tiny white bows. They made me feel like the princess of Genovia or something. Besides, if my apartment were to randomly catch fire in the night, I would prefer to have the hot firemen find me in pj's fit for royalty.

"Pararescue," he explained. "I fly in to save American forces when they're injured."

"*Oh.*" I nodded along, but I was imagining this giant guy hopping out of a plane and stitching someone up. A shudder worked through me. Screw the firemen.

With my head tilted to the side, I wondered if Dad had worked with pararescues. He'd never really mentioned that term before. Then again, he hadn't been injured to the point of needing one, I didn't think.

"My dad was a Navy SEAL!" My voice reached a few octaves higher than I was hoping for, but there were few people I could discuss these topics with, so I jumped at the opportunity.

He eyed me, and I continued. "You should hear some of the stories he tells me. Well, when he has a good day and remembers."

His jaw ticked. "I've seen some things. I know."

My lips turned up a little. I really liked this guy. No cutting corners, no small talk. Just very...real. What was the last thing I'd had that felt this real? The last person to be so blunt with me?

I sighed with that smirk and eyed his drink.

"All right, grumpy pants. Let's get you something with an umbrella in it."

CHAPTER THREE

Rachel / Now

Currently playing: Got My Mind Set On You by George Harrison

***

There was a man in my shower.

Or I assumed it was a man by the number of times products were knocked off the shelf and onto the tile, followed by a couple of low curses. That and the scent of the woodsy, axe man–filled steam seeping through the cracked door.

My hands reached for the baseball bat normally sitting beside my bed, only when my fingers reached just past the wooden frame, I realized it wasn't wood. It was a soft canvas, with sheets pulled so tight against the mattress it was a wonder they didn't snap in the night. So...not my shower, then. I looked around. The bed was facing a different way from what I remembered yesterday. So...also *not* my hotel room.

I groaned at the pulsing in my head. It was a sharp tapping, like a tiny caveman was in my brain, chiseling away. The only light visible came from the small sliver of exposed sun between the drawn curtains and a glow from the occupied bathroom door to my right. I glanced around the room, seeing a silky white dress I didn't recognize on the floor, a suit tossed around, and a navy-blue suitcase. It wasn't until I looked down and recognized the white T-shirt that the night before began to click into place.

My hands gripped the collar of the oversized tee, pulling it to my nose, and I breathed in. Woodsy pine soap, patchouli, and leather. Adam. Relief coursed its way through me, naturally settling my body. Of course it was Adam. Who else would I find in my shower on our trip to Vegas to help one of my best friends get married? I should have known this would happen. That's what I got for arguing with him on and off for the last few months. The sexual tension between us had to be cut with a chainsaw. Add some liquid courage and pretty Vegas lights into the equation, and chances were X equaled me ending up in his bed.

Resting against the sheets, I closed my eyes, envisioning the night before. I strained to piece memories together, walking through the night step by step.

Trying my best to not be angry. Then seeing him in a suit and tie at Liam and Marigold's wedding and forgetting what I was mad about in the first place. Flirting with him all night, hoping to break him enough to bring him up to my room. Silently begging him to put an end to all the awkward silence we'd endured on the plane ride here. Him playing along, pretending as though I had an eyelash on my cheek and he needed to delicately hold my jaw to get it off. Offering to take me to my room until I placed the lightest kiss on his cheek. The hurried tumbling down the hallway. How sweet he was. How he always made me feel like the most important woman he knew. How his rough hands were always so careful with me.

How are you so beautiful?

Made for me. You are made for me.

That pretty smile. Always gets me.

Each comment from the night before snuck its way into my memory. Half of me wanted to kick my feet and squeal like a fifth-grade girl. The other half wondered whether, when he got out of the shower, he would take it all back again. Were we going to end up exactly where we'd left off? Unsure of the future and our friendship?

I reached for my phone, seeing almost a hundred missed texts from the rest of the Wells family. None of them asked where Adam and I had gone, thankfully. I wasn't quite prepared to let my best friend and her entire family know that her brother-in-law and I had been secretly close friends for years. Or that we'd ended up in a hotel room together after somewhere between seven and ten drinks. Truthfully, if it had only been two drinks, we would have ended up right back here.

We'd been too close to imploding over the last few days. The tension between us had been riding higher than it ever had, and we were reaching a mending or breaking point. This felt a lot like mending.

The shower water stopped running, and I jolted up. *Shoot, shoot, shoot.* I thought I would have another minute to process this whole thing. Adam wasn't someone I could casually hook up with, then go about my day. I mean, we had a *history*. My fingers ran through my hair in a desperate attempt to settle the wild strands. I wiped my knuckles under my eyes, hoping to clear my face of any leftover mascara. Except when I pulled my hands back, I only saw black smudges smeared. Great, I was going to give the poor guy a heart attack when he got out.

I could pretend to be asleep. I wasn't really good at faking things, though. Even as a kid, my dad could see right through me with any tiny white lie.

Faking this wasn't the answer. No. I was an adult now. I owned dryer sheets and updated my car tag on time. I was going to handle this like a real woman, headfirst.

The knob turned, and then the door opened. Steam filled the doorway as Adam appeared in my line of vision. He was dressed in only black sweatpants, his hair still wet, and his tall, slim, tattooed figure surrounded by steam. A golden glow shone behind him, illuminating the room even further. I half expected a choir of angels to sing and a halo to fall upon his head.

I was going to pass out. Right here, right now.

"Sorry." Adam cleared his throat and used a single hand to scratch along the muscles near his belly button. "Left my shirt out here." He pointed to the gray tee laid out over the bench in front of the bed.

My chest pounded, and heat formed in the pit of my stomach as I unashamedly watched him lean over the bed and put the shirt on. I took in every inch of bare skin until he was properly covered. And because I had lost all feeling from the neck up, some rational part of my brain thought it would be a good idea to raise my pointer finger and jokingly taunt. "Yeah, don't do it again."

I could practically see his secondhand embarrassment. The wince across his face as his jaw tightened and his gaze went from me to the apparently ripped dress on the floor by his feet. This place looked like a zoo. I wondered just how much he remembered of the night before, or if the whole thing was a blur to him like it was to me.

An uncomfortable silence floated between us, which was even more odd, considering Adam and I didn't do uncomfortable silence. Never awkward or weird. We'd always been real with each other. We were both all too easy to understand, even though I usually did most of the talking. It was one of my favorite things about him. He was always black and white with me. I never had to wonder, because he made it perfectly clear to me. Until the last two weeks or so.

Adam took a seat facing away from me on the bench, his shoulders slumped forward and his back tense.

I sat up farther, the white comforter lowering as I raised my knees to my chest and wrapped my arms around them. "Are you mad that we did it again?"

"No." He didn't hesitate for a second.

The amount of reassurance that flooded my veins was almost pathetic. I could handle confused Adam, but not regretful Adam. I couldn't take back last night, and if it meant us somehow attempting to get along again, then I would have done it all over again.

I leaned farther, scooting closer to the end of the bed. "Adam, are you freaking out? It's okay if you are."

With his head pointed down, he shook no. "No." He paused for a moment. "Not at all."

My curiosity was piqued. "Really? Because it kind of seems like you are."

"I feel like *you're* going to freak out."

My head tilted to the side, and I eventually slid all the way to the bench and sat on my knees next to him. I silently pressed as I stared at him. He wasn't prone to using his words, and after so many years, I could usually read him pretty well. But right now? I was completely lost, even as I tried to read the creases in his brow like they would whisper an answer to me.

Adam sighed again, his fingers digging into his temple. "Keep in mind, this is easily fixable."

I pulled back a little to take him in. "You're scaring me."

He continued, his gaze stuck on the floor. "Whatever you decide, I will go with, okay?"

"Adam...did I get you pregnant?"

I knew something had to be wrong because he didn't even flinch. There wasn't a single hint of a smile or a small pull of his lip. He always liked my jokes. Even if it had taken a couple of years for him to admit that verbally.

Adam lifted his fingers to mine, fidgeting and shakily raising my left hand in front of my face. My confusion sank even further when I saw an enormous diamond ring on my hand.

"No...I am definitely not pregnant. But we did get married last night."

CHAPTER FOUR

Rachel / Then

Currently playing: It's Raining Men by The Weather Girls

***

The guy moved so he was one stool closer to me. So technically right next to me. As in less than a foot from me.

Something that was painfully obvious as my body became hyperaware of his presence. The clean scent of laundry mixed with a masculine woodsy scent was barely light enough that each time he lifted his drink, I got the tiniest whiff. I kept searching for more tattoos. Unashamedly watching as he'd move his arm and his sleeve would reveal a peek of more. I wondered just how far up they went and if they spread across his chest. I pictured an eagle or something on his back, or maybe a giant axe. In my mind, his whole body was permanently painted like an Old Spice ad.

My interest was clear to him. I was sure of that.

I wasn't exactly the kind of girl to flirt openly with a stranger, especially one with kids. But I also wasn't the girl who passed up a good opportunity when she saw one. Besides, the most action I had gotten in the past several months was buying a pack of Brawny paper towels and dipping my fingers into the plastic, ripping the film shirt and imagining it was real. So a girl could ogle if she decided to, and I did.

Our eyes were at the same level, so he wasn't shorter than me. A huge plus in my book. I liked to wear heels, and since I was naturally on the taller side, it was nice to find someone with enough height that my heels didn't offend their ego. Not that I was picturing myself and this complete stranger walking down the street together hand in hand or anything.

The whole single dad thing hadn't ever really done it for me before, but then again, neither had fictional men on household products. I supposed I had reached a new low. Although if *this* kind of man was what I considered low, then maybe I needed to change course on my standards.

"How old are your kids?" I appealed, taking a sip from my swirly straw of drink number...three? Sure, let's go with that. My whole body faced him while he spun his stool to face me every few minutes, our knees bumping occasionally.

A low, husky rumble left his throat, as if he was questioning me back.

It was kind of humorous; the more he drank, the more he grumbled. It was an odd contrast to me, since the more I drank, the more I laughed. Like alcohol had some kind of funny bubble juice in it.

"Your kids." I searched his forearm, craning my neck closer to his personal bubble. "Miles and...Dallo-no, Dallas. How old are they?"

"Oh." He cleared his throat with a grimace before rubbing a hand along the stubble on his chin. "They aren't my kids. They're my nephews. And they turned seven a few months ago."

"So, no kids?"

"No kids." He nodded, and my smile grew wider.

Nephews. Even better. I lifted my chin, exposing my neck and pulling my shoulders back.

"Hmm. You must really love them to get a tattoo of their names."

He grunted, but this one was a little lighter. An affirming grunt. Over the last hour or so, I'd been getting very good at speaking caveman. Our bartender delivered each of us one more full glass. The guy next to me looked at the drinks, as if waiting to make sure I was all right with one more. I was all right with ten more. I just wanted to remain in his company a little longer. It had been a while since I had someone to talk to.

I had friends. Well, friend. Singular. One. But Layla was off living her life, chasing her coworker around like a lost puppy, hopelessly in love, growing at her job, and who was I to get in her way? I could have gone back to our apartment tonight, made a weak homemade version of the drink I was having now, and watched *13 Going On 30* for the fifth time this week. But what good would that have done? If Layla was worried about me, she'd fuss over me instead of visiting her not-so-little crush, and then she'd regret it the next day.

I was sure to have no regrets about Mr. Brawny here. Not with his big hands or the way he listened intently to everything I drunkenly slurred, and especially not with how good he smelled.

This night had turned out much better than I thought it would be.

The thought of any alternative somehow made me giggle again. Then the thought that I'd giggled over essentially nothing caused me to snort. Which made me laugh more.

"Are you...okay?" Brawny asked with a hint of concern in his voice. Even that was hysterical at this point.

Mid-laugh, I opened my squinted eyes enough to see that his lips were turning blue from the last drink I'd made him try. He insisted he didn't like blue raspberry, to which I'd said that notion was preposterous. He replied that blue raspberry, and I quote, *wasn't even a real flavor*. I said something along the lines of *I'll show you a real flavor* and pushed the drink in the guy's face, not missing the way his expression lightened slightly after. His brows didn't look so heavy, and I liked that. Made my tummy do a little backflip.

"Your lips are blue," I stringed together between laughs.

His green eyes lifted up a bit, staring at my mouth. "You should see yours."

Oh. Yeah, I didn't think mine would be the same. Probably worse, actually. But I'd had two pink drinks since my blue one, so those canceled each other out on the color wheel, right? I thought that was what my color analysis lady had once said. Then again, she also told me I couldn't rock a pastel yellow dress, so what did she know, really?

Reaching my hand out, I grabbed my phone and used the black glass as a mirror. Sure enough, blue lips stared right back at me. Which was even more funny, causing me to lean my head back and laugh.

Putting a little too much trust in my barstool, I threw my whole body into the laugh, back arching with my head toss, leading me to almost falling onto the floor. For a split second, the front legs of my stool lifted off the ground an inch, and I saw my life flash before my eyes.

I let myself envision it for a brief moment: Me humbly falling without ruining a centimeter of my makeup. Someone shouting to call nine-one-one. Brawny here would stand and rip open his flannel to show a firefighter shirt beneath it. "*I'll take care of her*," he'd boast with certainty in his gravelly tone. His jaw would clench. My chest would heave, whatever that meant, and he would wrap his arms around me. Then he'd leave his black and red flannel with me for warmth, despite the hot summer night. Strong, tattooed muscles would lift me off the floor, and in a vivacious turn, he would rush me out of the door and into his—

My fantasy was cut short because my stool did not fall back any farther. It was caught by my newest friend. His hand pressed firmly into the back of the chair, catching me before my humble, graceful fall. Two of his fingers rested above the chair, on the exposed skin of my upper back.

"Be more careful," he grunted.

My lids dropped halfway, and a slow pull of a smile reached my lips. I pointed a finger at him, my freshly painted nail almost caressing his not-flannel. "*You* are a protector," I proudly diagnosed.

A sarcastic snort left him, like a dragon puffing out steam. "Habit," he grumbled.

I let out a *tsk* and shook my head, but then the room spun, so I stopped and recalibrated my focus on the scar above his brow. "No, you can be one of a few things. A protector, a provider, a nurturer or a...what's the last one? Calculator?"

"That doesn't sound right." He raised the brow under my stare.

"Either way." My hand waved between us. "You're a protector. I'm a nurturer. We would make great babies."

With my blond hair and long eyelashes and his handsome, strong features, I was willing to bet we would raise an army of perfectly beautiful babies.

Brawny choked, coughing and beating at his chest. Maybe babies weren't first-date talk. Not that this was a date.

I reached a hand out to his broad back, giving rough jabs with my palm like I'd learned in the CPR class I'd taken in high school. The memories of late-night *The Office* binges hit me, and I began beating his back to the tune of "Stayin' Alive" by the Bee Gees. A classic. I certainly would need to pull out the vinyl soon. Hit number 189 on *Rolling Stone's* greatest hits of all time. Part of me got a little caught up in the beat, not realizing the guy was no longer choking.

He glared over at me with a confused frown and cleared his throat, straightening his back under my touch. Glad I could help. I guess all those late nights laughing at Kevin Malone came in handy.

"I wasn't choking. You caught me off guard." He corrected my self-fulfillment, sending a sad little *womp-womp* to my chest.

"Sorry." For the baby mention. Not the CPR thing. That felt worth it. "Didn't think I'd scare you that easily."

His shoulders did a small rise and fall, as if that humored him. It was like watching a puppy use head tilts to show his emotions. I was slowly figuring this guy out.

"I don't scare easily," he proudly proclaimed with another sip of whiskey.

An idea, not necessarily a good or bad one, popped into my head at that, and a proud smirk smeared across my face. I licked my lips and leaned into him, staring directly into his forest green eyes.

"Prove it," I whispered just loud enough for him to hear over the music around us.

Not tearing from my view, his eyes bored into mine. He leaned forward until our lips were mere inches apart. My chest heaved under his stare. I dropped my gaze to his mouth and back, shocked to see a confident sneer from him.

He growled a low mutter, something about *I shouldn't*, before his full lips pressed against mine and one hand went to my hair.

CHAPTER FIVE

Adam / Now

Currently playing: Break My Stride by Matthew Wilder

***

She wouldn't stop laughing.

It had been all of five minutes since I broke the news about the diamond on her finger, and all she had done was laugh.

I usually liked her uncontrollable giggles. It brought a tiny bit of sunshine into my mostly quiet days. It was always nice to hear, like wind chimes in the spring air or the sound of a puppy eating. Cute. I wasn't exactly a comedian, but knowing I somehow always managed to make her chuckle was something I proudly clung to.

But this laugh didn't feel like sunshine, or rainbows, or everything good in life. It felt like a homing beacon of death.

Every minute or so, she would settle down, her shoulders slumping and chest heaving as she let out a comical sigh. But then her attention would go back to the rings on our fingers, and she would burst into fits of giggles again.

"Rachel." I gritted my teeth.

She sniffled, wiping a tear from her eye and slowing her breathing. "Sorry, sorry." She let out a breath in a *phew* and then lifted her chin up and poked her chest out. "Nah, that didn't happen. We probably went through one of those dreams where people hallucinate the same thing. Like that group of guys who all saw spaceships in the woods. Or was it Bigfoot? Honestly it could have been a sasquatch. But what's the difference between a sasquatch and Bigfoot, really?"

"Rachel." I lowered my tone.

"Yes?"

"We got married."

"How are you so sure?" she questioned in this sugary-sweet tone that made it incredibly hard to stay frustrated with her.

"I remember every second of it."

Well, most of it. There were a few blurry moments between leaving the wedding chapel and arriving at the bar. Then the trip back to my room that felt like long, slow blinks. But the rest all fit together.

She waved a noncommittal hand at me. "No, no, no. Last night, Marigold and Liam got married and ran off. Everyone else went to go see shows, and your parents took the boys to some arcade and climbing thing. I told you I felt like having a drink, and you did your little growly grumble and followed me. I had a few glasses—"

"An entire bottle."

"—of whiskey, and then we joked about how I was sick of going to weddings."

I nodded along, dipping my chin in an attempt to force those doe eyes to look at me. "And then I said 'what about when it's your own?' And then you said you want to get married now so you can be a housewife and take care of plants all day and stare at your records and—"

"—dance in fuzzy socks in the kitchen to Stevie Nicks—*ohmygosh*. We got married." Her green eyes widened in shock as she rapidly blinked.

My hand lifted to the back of my neck as I moved my eyes to stare down at the floor. I didn't want to see how disappointed she was. Maybe it would be best if I just left.

I stood from the bench, feeling a little faint because of the giant empty pit in my stomach. She needed time to process, and she probably couldn't do that when I was in her face. She could have my room. I would come back later. It was fine—

A small tug behind me made my shirt pull tight around my stomach. I turned to look down, finding Rachel staring up at me with those big blue eyes. My legs instantly crumpled, forcing me to take my rightful seat next to her.

Her chest hitched a little. "But why did you ask *me*?"

"I don't remember that one part." My throat cleared. "Just the rest."

Rachel's eyes moved back to her ring. She twisted it with her thumb underneath, watching as the overhead light caught it. Her head dipped to one side, and she squinted. "Where did you even find *this*?"

Did she not like it? I thought she would. I wasn't an expert on rings. Or people. Or anything that wasn't my job. But when I saw it, I had this feeling of *yeah, that's my Rachel.* I wasn't exactly good at reading situations either. I was better at looking at things from afar. That was hard to do when you were constantly with each other like we had been for the last few years.

I looked down to the swirled design on the navy-blue carpet, my eyes dialing in on a gold circle. "There was a jewelry place a couple of doors down from the chapel. I grabbed the rings and told you to get a dress."

At the word dress, she perked up, her neck craning to see the crumpled and ripped pretty white fabric in a ball on the floor. Her eyes went wide again at the sight, her chest picking up pace and her thumb twirling her ring back and forth even faster.

Desperate to steady the shaking in her fingers, I splayed my hand over her dainty one. Her pearly white nails were barely visible under my grasp. "I told you this was fixable. Don't freak out."

"Fixable?" Rachel's voice was a shriek now. She stood up, her hands flailing. "Adam, I am *your wife.*"

It was probably the wrong time for it, but her emphasis on *your wife* gave me this surge of pride. Felt like I could beat on my chest or knock down a whole building. Or call up any guy she had dated before and tell them to suck it and then immediately hang up.

I coughed, forcing the vibrations in my throat first so I didn't scratch my words out. "We can get an annulment."

"Yeah, yeah. An annulment before I brunch with your *entire* family in..." She looked at the time on her phone. "Thirty minutes?" She whispered it like they were already in the room with us. I fought the pull of my lips for her sake.

"Breathe, Stevie." I only pulled out the middle-name card on rare occasions. This felt like a good one.

She pointed a menacing finger at me, as if to silently say *don't you dare use that against me right now*, and I raised my hands in a shield.

"We can both take the rings off for now. Go downstairs and eat like nothing happened. I'll talk to an attorney when we get back to Philly."

I made sure to keep my tone even and calm for her. Not that it was necessarily hard. It was my job to stay calm under pressure, and waking up to find out I had somehow married this woman was not the worst pressure I had been under, that was for sure.

Rachel looked from me back to the oval-shaped diamond taking over her finger and looked almost disheartened. Her throat bobbed in a heavy swallow, and she let her eyes lift back up to mine. She was practically a big, blue-eyed puppy, looking as though I was taking its bone away.

Relief flooded me. She *did* like the ring for sure, then. I assumed she would when I purchased it, but her freak-out earlier had me second-guessing everything.

Despite wanting to smile, I groaned and avoided her stare. She wanted to keep the ring on. Of course she did. She'd always loved jewelry. A shock to me, since I hadn't expected her to be such a pink-bowed, always-wearing-heels, nails-never-*not*-done kind of girl when I met her, but that was exactly Rachel. A mind full of wit and music wrapped up in the prettiest packaging.

Unapologetically high maintenance, with no interest in changing that for anyone. As she should be.

For our first Christmas as friends, she forced me to do a gift swap. I didn't understand at the time how much of a holiday nerd she was, so I had no complaints when she said we had to draw names and couldn't tell each other who we had. I didn't have the heart to tell her we were the only two playing, so I kept quiet. She seemed really pleased about that. I got her earrings, remembering her mentioning in a text once about her losing a pair in an Uber. The ones I got her weren't super nice or anything, but she went on about them for an absurd amount of time and still wore them to this day.

So it shouldn't have shocked me to see Rachel looking at her ring as if she was being forced to say her hardest goodbye. I squinted down at her.

She huffed. "It's just so pretty."

I let myself admire the rock on her finger. Clear stone on a gold band against her tanned skin. It did look good on her. I fought the smile that threatened to break out of me.

Rachel lifted her left hand, letting the ring sparkle in the light once more. She shrugged, slowly dropping her hand back to her lap. "They won't even notice. Luke and Layla were too clueless to see they were in love with each other for three years, and Nathan and Calla are always busy staring at each other's butts, so they're not an issue. Crew will probably be at the buffet the whole time, and your mom and dad...let's say a prayer they won't notice."

Mom would notice. Chances were that she already knew through some kind of telepathic motherhood instincts, but I knew that was bound to scare her more, so I stayed quiet.

"You could...just leave it here," I suggested once more, but I immediately winced as her eyes cut daggers at me.

She flashed the diamond my way, as if I hadn't studied it before. "And risk someone stealing it? This ring is worth more than me."

"Nothing could be worth more than you."

Silence fell between us after I said it. The bench, the entire room, was suddenly too small for both of us.

This time she was the one to cut the silence by clearing her throat, looking from me to the ring. "Let's go downstairs and take it a moment at a time. You go first, though. It's more realistic for me to be fashionably late than you."

I rose from the bench and reached for my tennis shoes, where I'd left them perfectly lined up by the door. My fingers itched to align the heels that were haphazardly thrown about, but I was working on suppressing that side of me. Pushing down the part that needed control, needed power. If I was going to somehow get her to stick around, then I would have to.

My fingers were reaching for the doorknob when her voice stopped me.

"How are you so calm right now?" she asked with this hint of awe. As if the thought of her wearing my ring on her finger was something I should have been disgusted at.

The best answer I could muster without tipping my cards too much was "When have I ever been known to freak out?"

CHAPTER SIX
Adam / Then

Currently playing: Too Sweet by Hozier

***

This is ridiculous. You look like a stalker.

Granted, I wasn't far from being one at this point.

Flashes of my night with a random blonde had been spiking in my head all week. The way her hair splayed out on my pillowcase, the clean orange scent on my sheets every time I went to bed. How Crew mentioned wanting to get new headphones, and I knew that the music-loving girl who so bravely ordered whiskey straight would have the perfect recommendations. The way she'd held long talks about different types of records for half the night. How she made it sound like she was already in a committed relationship with music itself and there was scarcely room for anything, or *anyone*, else.

The best part was that she understood immediately that I didn't know how to hold a conversation. Maybe that wasn't the *best* part. But it was really nice. No need to explain that I wasn't trying to be a rude guy, but that I was a listener, not a talker. After the day she'd had, she needed a listener. I just happened to be in the right place at the right time.

All I wanted was her name. That was the only reason I was here. I couldn't rest until the question was answered. I'd meant to get it before we got too preoccupied, but we'd gotten caught up in the moment, and it had slipped.

I wasn't sure what I was thinking the other night, offering a drink to her like that. I liked my peace. I liked quiet, simple solitude. The click of her heels and the tiny skirt, mixed with her ordering straight whiskey, gave me a tip that she was anything *but* simple. But she sat there, muttering about not being cool enough to shoot whiskey. And between the pout in her pink-painted lips and the way her eyelashes curled when she squeezed her eyes shut in a whole body–shaking cringe at the taste of alcohol, I felt bad.

It was kind of ironic how the one time I didn't order the same beer I got at Froggy's every week was the time she was there. Like God was playing puppets with us, manipulating me into ordering something she would like before I even knew she was there. Going from that to holding her warm, soft skin in my hands felt like a dream I was going to wake up from any minute now.

"Just get it over with," I muttered to myself, pulling my hood down in an attempt to not look like such a creep. The scar across my eyebrow probably didn't help any.

It was usually the first thing someone saw when they looked at me, the tight faint-pink line that looked almost like a lightning bolt above my eye. But she didn't. Her eyes first went to my tattoos. She shamelessly stared at them as if she was considering tracing them with her finger. I wouldn't have stopped her if she did. It was rare I talked to a woman willingly. It was even more rare that I allowed an entire night of conversing that led to bringing her back to my apartment. The only time that happened was on the odd occasion when I was stationed out of the country and there was a sure-fire guarantee that I would never see the girl again.

I certainly would never connect with someone local at the bar I visited once a week. But yet there I was this morning, researching every record store in Philadelphia, trying to find out which one was rumored to be closing soon so I could...what? Apologize? Ask for more? Tell her that I hadn't stopped thinking about the small freckles on her shoulders since I first saw them? I didn't know. I hadn't thought that far. Correction: I hadn't thought anything. At all.

Taking a deep breath, I reminded myself that I'd survived hell in training. I had gone five days with only ten hours of sleep, enduring every pain you can imagine and hallucinations. I was top of my class at that. *A natural leader* they'd said as I graduated. I saved men from plane crashes and war fights for a living. Anxiety wasn't something I knew.

And yet I sat here outside a stupid record store, sweating my balls off because I was too freaked out to figure out the name of a woman I'd spent a single night with.

I shook my shoulders out and nodded to myself. I wet my lips and ran a hand through my hair before forcing myself to take the few small steps to the door and inside.

A bell chimed quietly above me as my boots stomped across the black-and-white checkered floors. Band posters hung on each of the walls, a few recognizable to me but not many. It was warm, a dash of pastels here and there, with woven light fixtures like the ones my sister-in-law had begged me to put in her new house. It smelled of cinnamon and oranges, almost nostalgic. A steady thrumming played over the speakers around the room, a man singing about learning to fly.

A sweet, almost angelic voice with a hint of firmness called out. "Hi! Welcome. Let me know if there's anything I can find for you."

It was her. There was no doubt. I took a step farther into the store, craning my neck to follow the sound of her voice. Her back was to me, and she was bent over, sorting through what looked like a mountain of files. My eyes trailed up from her platformed boots to the short denim skirt that had a white T-shirt tucked into it.

Her blond ponytail swayed as she bobbed her head along with the music playing above. My lips tipped slightly. I was willing to bet she was in charge of picking which songs to play in the store.

Realization dawned on me as I watched how she innocently had no idea I was standing on the other side of the counter. This was creepy. I was being creepy. What woman would want some scarred man walking into her workplace after extensive research just so he could know her name?

I was quiet, sure. I liked being alone, and I wasn't exactly social, but I wasn't a creepy guy. Or I never had been before. My brain began ticking off things about me that it had apparently decided were very *not-creep-like*, such as, the other day, I carried a stack of laundry to my bedroom, and I tripped over my coffee table. And I had a stuffed dinosaur in my closet from my seven-year-old nephews, who insisted I take it with me to "keep any monsters away."

None of those things helped. This still felt weird.

Part of me wondered if I could slowly back out of the store before she realized I was here. My left foot descended after my right as she began turning around.

Seeing her face in broad daylight felt like a punch to the gut. In dim lighting, with only a few lamps on and neon flashing lights at the bar, I knew she was pretty. I knew she was far out of my league. Far prettier than anyone I had seen in a long time. Maybe ever. But now, watching as she stared down at a few files in her hand with a small book on top, flipping through them as she hummed, I knew this was a mistake. She was far, far more beautiful than I'd allowed myself to remember.

She smiled to herself, her rosy cheeks lifting and her pencil tapping against the corner of her mouth like she was considering something. Like she was excited about it. Faster than sound, her eyes met mine, and realization struck across her face, her mouth opening and her chin dipping.

Shit, too late.

The papers in her hand and the thin book, along with her pencil, crashed to the floor.

Her voice dropped, raspier this time. "Oh...I—it's you..."

It's you. Was that a good thing? She didn't seem entirely turned off by me being here. More so confused. Her head tilted to the side and her eyes widened.

My knees bent as I knelt down to pick up her assorted papers, and…a sudoku book. Along with a tiny mini golf pencil. Huh.

She cleared her throat, watching as I tried to organize the papers in a neat stack for her. "Funny. I've seen your house, and I know what color couches you have, but I don't even know your name."

I laid her stack on the counter, lifting my gaze back to her, forcing down the natural part of myself that said to stay silent and nod along.

"Adam. My name is Adam."

Now tell me yours so I can rush out of here and never come back.

At my name, she took a deep breath, like she was inhaling the words. Memorizing them? Her initial shock had eased into a soft smile, and I was grateful to see not a hint of regret in her eyes.

She nodded her head at me. "I'm Rachel."

There. That was it. All I needed. Time to be on my way and back to my cold apartment.

Except I had this dying urge to ask more. *How long have you worked here? Do you have plans for if they decide to close? When is your birthday?* None of the answers to those truly mattered, considering I wasn't going to see her again. But it was like I had to fight my own brain to convince myself to leave.

"So…" she dragged on, rocking back and forth on her feet with her hands clasped behind her back.

Oh. Yeah, I probably should have explained why I was even here.

I rubbed the back of my neck, taking notice of the heat forming there. "I was just walking and thought I would look for…a, uh, record."

That was the only reason people came to record stores, wasn't it? Although I did see a book section off in the corner, so I could have said that too. I was flustered, too concerned about what she thought of me now that we were in broad daylight, where I couldn't hide behind a smug smile and a few beers.

Rachel's eyebrows drew closer, her face tightening as she pursed her lips. She was seeing right through me, and there was nothing I could do. It wasn't like I could come out and say *sorry to seem like a stalker, but I've hardly slept at all in the last week because I keep thinking of your laugh and the really grotesque jokes that come out of such a pretty mouth.*

"What *kind* of record?" she challenged.

Kind? There were kinds?

"I…don't know."

She snorted and gave me a soft smile, apparently not going to call me out on my crap. "How about we go look at some soft and easy classic rock? Not anything too heavy. More of a…foot-tapping kind of smooth rock?"

She stepped out from her post and walked across the checkered floors to the rock section of the store. It was impossible to ignore that the place clearly needed work. The vinyl floors were pulling up in some spots. Walls needed paint too. And although it was well-staged, there were undeniable structural issues underneath my boots as I followed her. The floor rose and fell under my feet, and I immediately began wondering what kind of foundation this was on. Seemed like this place was on a slab, and if so, there shouldn't have been a need for wavy floors. Unless they had previous water damage somewhere.

Was that why they wanted to sell soon? Too many renovations to take on? I had an incredible urge to ask, but my time here felt borrowed, and at the end of the day, I'd come in here for her name only.

Rachel hummed along to the next song as the music switched over, her tongue clicking and feet tapping. She reached the rock section and settled in place before turning my way, taking me in from head to toe and nodding to herself. As if it was some kind of evaluation.

"I'm thinking...early Eagles. Maybe some Billy Joel?" Her fingers flipped through the vinyls organized in front of her while she muttered a *hmm,* then a *nah,* a *nope, maybe,* and *wait a second.* Eventually, she pulled out a black-and-white album with a man sitting on a striped bed and a mask sitting next to him.

She looked me up and down once more with a smirk, clearly satisfied with her decision. "*The Stranger* fits you very well."

I wasn't really a music person. Didn't complain if it was on, but I certainly couldn't piece together what kind of artists fit me best at the moment. I was more of an audiobook or plain silence in the car kind of guy. Any other time I could have been listening to music, I just... didn't. Maybe I needed to now, though.

There was hardly anything for me to say without giving away my complete ignorance over the genre, so I simply nodded and stuck both hands in my pockets.

She nodded back and began to turn around and head back to the register. She looked over her shoulder, curling a finger her way. "Come with me."

As if there were anywhere else I could go. My legs followed her before my brain could catch up. It felt like I blinked and was on the opposite side of the register from her, as if I had floated there.

I watched as she flipped the record over, typing the numbers from the barcode into an older-looking system. Her lips rested in this soft smile, and I wondered if she always looked this happy, or if my presence had any slight effect. Her long, painted nails tapped away as she rang me up, and it dawned on me. Records were...valuable, right? I had heard of other people collecting them for money. Was I looking to spend fifty dollars or five hundred here?

It didn't matter, really. I was good enough at saving money that it was almost concerning how little I spent on what some people considered *fun* items. Each check I received went to bills, groceries, savings, and donating. In that order. No need for anything extra. Before now, anyway.

Rachel slammed her hand into the side of the register, clenching her jaw and rolling her eyes. "Come on, you piece of—" She pushed the device once more, brows furrowed, until a small light at the top turned green.

"Ah, there we go. She just needs to be manhandled a bit."

I cleared my throat at the word *manhandled* and quickly handed over my card.

She took it from me, her fingers grazing mine and reminding me of how sweet it had been to hold her hand.

Tapping my hands against my pants, I watched as she wrapped the record up for me. I wasn't ready to leave, despite my earlier hesitation, and it felt like I had to grasp for any reason to see her for a little longer.

"What got you into records?" I asked, hearing the rasp from my voice but unable to control it.

She smiled to herself, looking up at me as she finished wrapping. "I always thought it was so neat how they work. How much better the quality is since it's not passing through a phone speaker like what we have now." She paused as she tucked a corner of the gift wrap down and stuck a piece of tape to it. "Plus my dad and I used to collect them. He has early onset dementia now and can't do it as much, so this is kind of keeping the memories alive in both of us."

I briefly remember a couple of comments the other night about her father. He was prior service, a SEAL. She'd mentioned his slipped memory once, but I hadn't considered it was anything as far as dementia.

This girl was real. Authentic, genuine, whatever else you wanted to call it. She held such substance. Way too much for someone I had planned on having a single night with and tossing out the next day. No wonder I couldn't easily forget her. She was cemented in my brain.

I recalled her other discussions about music. How she said it was an escape. How she felt like every moment needed a soundtrack, and that she was really good at picking them out. My eyes dropped to the record she'd placed in the bag. *The Stranger.* Huh. I was going to have to listen to it tonight, to see a glimpse of how she truly thought of me.

I wasn't good with words. Never had been. Always liked to communicate in actions. People could speak all day long, but who knew if any of it was authentic? Actions said more, spoke volumes louder. Maybe that's how she felt with music. Maybe this was her way of conversing without having to say the hard things.

"So you are pretty familiar with it, then?" I blurted.

Her brow cocked. "With what?"

I pointed to the gift bag holding my record. She twisted her lips, feigning confusion, as if pulling me to say every thought out loud.

"Music. Records. That stuff."

"That stuff," she echoed with a tiny snort and a scrunch of her nose. "Yeah, you could say that."

I nodded along as if I understood. I needed to go, but I had so much more to ask. More to find out and piece together. But she handed the bag to me, smiling my way with these bright, kind baby-blue eyes, and I felt a rush of heat wash over me.

My fingers reached for the paper straps, strategically avoiding where she held it so as not to make our hands brush against each other once more.

I looked back at the door and lifted my thumb behind me, as if to say I needed to leave. She nodded, not fighting it either.

"I'll, uh, see you around, yeah?" she questioned with this warmth in her tone that I couldn't quite decipher.

Nodding my head, I turned to the door and began walking away, initially hoping to avoid any answer to that.

Would we? See each other around, that is? Probably not. It was a big city, full of different areas of downtown, and I hardly ever left my house right outside the town. I was deployed for half the year, and the other half, I stuck to myself, other than the weekly dinners with my family. So chances of me getting another shot at this were slim to none.

I stopped in my tracks, clearing my throat and looking over my shoulder at her. Her eyes hadn't left mine, and there was so much wonderment in them that I knew if I didn't get this out now, I never would.

"I was going to let you know...the other night." I cleared my throat at the mention of it. "It's a rare occasion for me. I mean I don't...do *that* a lot on purpose. I don't really have time for a relationship, so I was—"

"I know," she cut in with a smile.

"What?"

"I know you don't do it a lot."

Oh. My face turned hot. I hadn't had any complaints from women in my bed before. But then again, it wasn't like I asked for them to fill out a survey afterward or anything. But she'd seemed *enthusiastic* at the moment. To say the least. Plus, the way she waited till the last minute to leave, how she took every minute after so slowly, putting on each item of clothing, lacing her heels back up sloth-like.

She shook her head, correcting herself. "That came out wrong. I meant I know because I don't either...hardly ever. I recently dropped out of college to take care of some family things, so I also don't have time. It's okay. I'll still see you around."

I coughed up a choke. "College? How old are you?"

"Twenty-two."

A heavy weight settled in my stomach. I shouldn't have felt guilty. There was no need. She was an adult who could make her own decisions. But it felt deceitful on my end. I mean, she was eight years younger than me. We were in two completely different stages in life. She was young and bright, with a future and dreams ahead of her. I was getting ready to settle into what I assumed was going to be the rest of my life. Work, sleep, see family occasionally, repeat. Twenty-two. What had I been thinking?

"Why?" She tilted her head. "How old are you?"

Part of me wanted to lie. Just to make this easier. To not see her look at me like I was a disgusting old man. Which I wasn't, but still. "Thirty."

All right, in hindsight, thirty wasn't that bad. I was still young-ish. I kept up with my health, mostly due to my job. I worked out every day and did my best to stay in shape. I certainly didn't feel thirty physically. In fact, I was stronger now than I had been at twenty-two. But mentally, I was an old man, ready to yell at kids for crossing my lawn. My brothers always said I should have had gray hair at the age of fifteen.

Instead of disgust or shock showing on her face, she simply tilted her head to the side with a slow grin. "Huh. You're very…" Her eyes dropped down my chest and back up. "*Spry* for your age."

The tension in my body released, my brows relaxing and my chin dropping. I was taking that compliment with me, going to replay it all night.

I pushed my tongue to my cheek, trying my hardest not to smile. "Uh, thanks."

She opened her mouth to speak again, and with that smirk, I wondered what kind of comment she was prepared to make. But the door behind me chimed.

"Hey, girl. I brought you leftovers. Luke didn't want any—"

I turned my head to the familiar voice at the door. Layla Wright stood there, her brows furrowed at me and her lips pursed. Layla was a family friend, I guess you could say. She was going to be family eventually, anyway. As soon as my brother Luke got his head cleared and realized they were both desperately in love with each other.

"Adam? What are you doing here?"

I stared at her for a moment, silently praying for God to give me some kind of reason why I, someone without a record player, would possibly be in a record store.

"I, um—"

"He thought it was the tattoo place next door. Somehow, I convinced him to get a Billy Joel vinyl, though." Rachel winked my way and instead of adding to the conversation, I just nodded along.

"Do you two know each other?" Rachel asked Layla. I looked back and forth between them. Layla and I weren't close by any means, but she was a nice girl, and eventually, she was going to have my brother's last name, so although we weren't what I would call *friends*, our circles overlapped.

Layla answered for me, thankfully. "Adam is Luke's brother." She looked over at me. "Rachel's my roommate."

Rachel and I caught eyes at the same time. We would be seeing each other around, then. I didn't know whether I loved or hated that.

CHAPTER SEVEN

Rachel / Now

Currently playing: You've Got A Friend by James Taylor

***

My fingers gripped the hotel doorknob as I slowly let the door shut behind me. I looked back and forth down the wallpapered hallway before taking a step out and checking one more time. The *Pink Panther* theme song would have been perfect at that moment if I had been smart enough to grab my headphones from my room the night before.

Although I supposed I had been a bit distracted, and my head wasn't in the mindset for next-day activities. Thankfully Adam had thought a few steps ahead of me, and apparently, before he had taken a shower this morning, he'd slipped into my room and grabbed a pair of denim shorts and my ratty ELO T-shirt. It was the comfiest article of clothing I owned, so the holes could be forgiven.

Things would have been incredibly more difficult to explain if I were wearing a white dress and heels to a family and friend brunch with my *husband's* family.

My stomach sank at the thought. Oh gosh, I had in-laws now. Though if I were to do a whole fantasy football–style draft for a mother-in-law, Mama B would be my first pick. None of that mattered, though. She was never going to find out, and this would all be over within a week. We would sign those annulment papers, celebrate *without alcohol*, and laugh about it later on down the road.

Despite my reassurance, I was still dreading this whole brunch. Layla and Calla could both read me like a book by now. I was awful at hiding my feelings in the first place—these eyebrows can't lie—but it was even harder between the two of my three closest friends. Thank the good lord Marigold was off on her honeymoon and not joining us, or she would call it out instantly. She had this freaky mom instinct that allowed her to see into your brain. I hoped I got that one day too. It really psyched people out.

I hummed along to the soundtrack in my head as I made my way to the elevator. It would be fine. I would be fine. This was a little speed bump in life. No one knew, and Adam was an excellent secret keeper—mostly because he never talked. And I would go in fake-it-till-I-make-it style. It would all be fi—

A door slammed behind me. "What do you think you're doing?"

Uh-oh. I knew that hiss and the demanding voice behind it.

Breathe in, Rachel. She has no idea.

I turned on my heel, forcing a smile. "Calla! My dear friend. I am…walking down the hall." I looked at her shoulder, focusing my attention on the strap of her tank top to avoid her gaze.

"Yeah, like you work for the FBI," she whisper-yelled and looked behind her. "Come on," she hissed. Then she pulled me into the elevator as she feverishly pressed the *close door* button.

The moment the doors shut, I found myself being pulled by the hand. My left hand. Calla held my new ring to her face, and her eyes widened in shock. "Why do you still have that ring on?"

I gasped, pulling my hand back lightning fast and hiding it under my crossed arms. "What ring?"

She pointed to it. "The gigantic boulder sitting on your left ring finger after you and my idiot brother got married last night."

Wincing, I uncrossed my arms and lifted the ring to my own eyes. It really was beautiful; simple but elegant. A princess-cut diamond with a thin gold band holding it up. Timeless, classic, and heavy. It sucked that I'd have to eventually give it up.

My shoulders slumped. "You knew?"

Calla rolled her eyes. "Of course I knew. You texted the group chat with all the girls saying *wifey for lifey.* Then you sent a picture of you flashing us your ring finger. And then another picture of your hand grabbing Adam's bicep."

Mouth falling open, I considered it for a moment and then shrugged. Because, well, yeah, that sounded about right.

She sighed. "So what are you two going to do about it?"

Adam was casual about this, so I could be too. We were adults. Grown people who could hire lawyers and handle things professionally. Or at least he was. I could just follow him.

"Get an annulment when we get back to Philly. No biggie. What happens in Vegas stays in Vegas and whatnot, right?"

She nodded along, and her face seemed to settle at that. "How did this even happen? You guys don't ever talk."

I wasn't sure why Adam and I had kept our friendship under wraps so much. It was our little secret. The late-night texts and hangouts when no one else was around. I liked that he allowed me to be myself unapologetically. He liked that I never forced him to talk more than he wanted. Freedom, that's what it felt like. We enjoyed keeping it to ourselves, though. It would have felt...wrong, I guess, to tell others. Like if everyone else knew we were this close, it would ruin the rhythm we'd built.

Clearing my throat, I answered. "Too much alcohol, and his tattoos under those rolled-up sleeves."

She winced and faked a gag. I hadn't ever mentioned to her how hot her brother was, even if he was my closest friend. But there was no way she didn't know. Didn't she have girlfriends in high school who wanted to hang out just to stare at him?

I could see the moment a lightbulb flashed in her eyes. "This is exactly like that romance book I read where they stayed married so they could get extra money from the government each month and she could get really good health insurance."

"Wait." I straightened my back. "People do that?"

Calla nodded. "All the time. Celebrities do too."

I fell silent for a moment. That was crazy. Seriously insane. Right? I mean, to get married and just stay married for money and health benefits? Absurd.

It was quiet for another minute.

"And it works?" I asked.

She shrugged. "Probably not, but anything can happen in a romance book."

Yes. In a romance book. Not in a real-life scenario. Because no one would do that.

The elevator slowed to a stop, and a ding chimed over us. I was preparing myself to walk out into the lobby when I saw we were only on floor three. The doors opened, and on the other side stood Crew, Calla's youngest sibling, in a baby-blue Hawaiian shirt with koi fish printed on it.

Calla stared at him, confused. "You're not even staying on this floor. What are you doing here?"

He solemnly shrugged. "I made friends with a group of old ladies at the six-thirty yoga class. They convinced me to play mahjong up here. Just lost thirty bucks and my favorite hat."

Crew stepped in, and I instinctively hid my left hand behind my back.

"What's new with you guys?"

Calla and I exchanged looks. I gave her a silent plea, and she gave a subtle nod back.

"Nothing," we said in sync, and I was incredibly grateful when he didn't question it.

We all rode the elevator down to the lobby, and I couldn't help but consider what Calla had said before. My thoughts trailed to the stress waiting for me back home: Dad's assisted living bills stacking up and his lack of healthcare.

I bit my lip and looked back to my ring behind my back, considering.

CHAPTER EIGHT

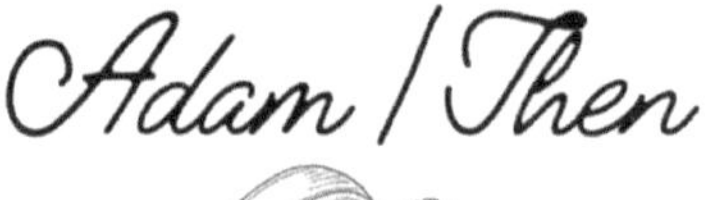

Currently playing: Starfish and Coffee by Prince

Unknown number: Hiya, sailor.

Who is this?

Unknown number: guess.

no.

Unknown number: I should have known you were a stick-in-the-mud. Layla said you were grumpy, but I chose not to believe it, considering how much fun we had the other night.

Rachel?

Unknown number: That's me :)

How did you get my number?

Rachel: Layla's phone doesn't have a lock. She said you were who knows where saving lives. Thought you might like some company.

This is company?

Rachel: You tell me, sailor.

You know I'm in the Air Force, right? I'm not a sailor of any kind.

Rachel: Potato, potahto. Pot, kettle.

No. Not at all.

Rachel: You're still a sailor in my mind when I picture you steering ships and jumping out of them to save drowning people from sharks.

That is not even close to what I do. At all, actually. It's kind of concerning you would think that.

Rachel: So, what's your night like tonight?

Thrilling. Lying in bed since all the guys wanted to go out.

Rachel: And you didn't?

I don't really like going out.

Rachel: But you were out the other night with me.

Coincidence.

Rachel: Ooh, so I am special, then?

Lucky you.

Rachel: Careful now, grandpa. One might think you were flirting.

I'm not.

Rachel: Mmm, we'll see.

What are you doing tonight?

Rachel: Currently working on a sourdough starter with George Michael.

Boyfriend?

Rachel: I wish you could hear the laugh I just let out.

Rachel: No, George Michael is not my boyfriend, sadly.

So why is he making bread with you at ten at night?

Rachel: Oh, this is so sad. You're old enough to know better by now, Adam.

I looked him up. I get it now. You didn't have to say it like that.

Rachel: And miss this whole conversation? No, that was beautiful.

No.

Rachel: So now that you have my number, we can be friends, right?

No.

Rachel: You have a terribly wicked sense of humor. So you can give me your elderly advice now, right?

That's about all I can give you.

Rachel: Not true. You gave a lot more than that the other night.

Who even are you?

Rachel: Rachel. Did we not already go over this? Geez, the old-man brain is kicking in early, huh?

Good night.

Rachel: Just remember to turn on your CPAP.

CHAPTER NINE
Adam / Now

Currently playing: Float On by Modest Mouse

***

I was mid-stride, on my way to the tiny café in the hotel lobby, when a familiar manicured hand reached out to grab my wrist. I had the strength to not stop in place, but when it came to the blonde a few inches shorter and a heck of a lot more nimble than me, I'd given a lot of that strength up years ago.

I turned around to see Rachel biting her lip and looking up at me with these round, apologetic eyes. She pulled her hand back and wiped both of them across her denim shorts. Then she settled them in a grasp at her waist. The unease on her face alone was enough to make my heart race, but the undeniable tremble in her fingers set me on the edge.

Craning my neck, I looked to see if anyone was following behind her.

"What's wrong? Did someone do something?"

She shook her head. "I need to talk with you."

My stomach sank. She wanted to get the marriage annulled before we left. Wanted to pretend it hadn't happened and scratch off our talk from last week. I couldn't blame her. In fact, I had been waiting for that to happen. Didn't necessarily make it any easier, though.

I took a glance back at the café and to the empty space down the hall, then pulled her with me there to keep my nosy family from seeing.

When we settled, her eyes had what looked like fear in them. I couldn't hold back as both my hands gripped her shoulders and I dipped to force her to look at me. "What's wrong?"

Rachel took a deep breath and raised both hands. "Hear me out."

Without hesitation, I nodded.

She pointed an accusatory finger at me. "Do not yell at me."

"I've never once done that."

"Mmm. Are you sure?"

"Why would I ever yell at you?"

"Sometimes you do it with your eyebrows."

I rolled my eyes. "Please get this over with."

She sighed deeply. "Okay, okay." She puffed out her chest, lifting up her head to me. "I think...we should stay married."

I shrugged. "Okay."

Rachel raised her hands in defense. "Hear me out. I know it's crazy, but we—wait." She pulled back. "Did you just say okay?"

"I did."

"Adam, you can't—" she sputtered. "This isn't like us agreeing to split a lunch or something. I'm talking marriage. I would be your wife. *W-I-F-E.* Wifey for lifey would become a real, daily term."

"I'm familiar with the concept. Though I would rather not call you wifey. Now or ever."

She scoffed. "You haven't even heard my reasoning. Why would you just say yes?"

It all felt simple to me. If she wanted to stay married, who was I to argue?

"You're the only person I'd ever want to marry. Why would I argue?"

Her eyes went wide, and now I was beginning to wonder if we were on the same page at all. "Adam. You cannot be this irrational. You are a grown adult. Think here for a moment. This is not something you can just say okay to. I need you to be the brutey, grumpy troll you are right now."

"I did think about it. Right before I asked you to marry me." And possibly before then too, but that was irrelevant right now.

"Stop being so literal here." She furrowed her brows like an angry chipmunk.

"If you wanted me to be against it, why did you even ask?"

She took a deep breath. "I do not want to sound like a gold digger—"

"Great start to our marriage," I mumbled.

"*But* Calla may or may not have mentioned that military members who are married get extra benefits."

I nodded. I would be lying if I said I hadn't considered that in the shower this morning. Her dad needed help, and so did she. Rachel loved to pretend like she was fine. She loved to pass everything off with an *it is what it is* excuse. Meanwhile you could visibly watch the pain grow in her eyes. I'd watched her break down before over the bills piling up. How she couldn't get her dad on Medicare yet due to his younger age and because his early onset dementia wasn't enough to qualify him for the resources they needed. How, since he'd passed all of his health evaluations with flying colors, his slipping memory didn't allow them a lower cost in healthcare. It was all a load of horseshit. And she'd had to carry it by herself for years. She'd quit school to take care of him, worked a mediocre paying job, and spent every minute of her life saving others.

If I could lighten that load by legally being her husband, I was willing to do just that.

"We do."

"So I could maybe get on your health insurance. And since I am in charge of Dad's medical bills, maybe he would be connected. Or at the least maybe get him a couple benefits that the VA couldn't on his end."

"He would."

Her rambles went on without a breath between them. "So it would really, really help me out. I know that sounds extremely selfish, but you know how hard it's been on both of us. I feel like this would be an opportunity for me to set us straight so I won't have to spend so much on healthcare visits and—"

"Rachel. Stop." I reached for her hand, wrapping my fingers around hers and letting my thumb rest on her ring. "How many times have I offered to help?"

She sniffled, and my heart cracked. "A million."

"And you would never take it. You practically cussed me out every time I even tried. I'm not offended, and you shouldn't be either. Plus, there are benefits for me too."

"Like what?"

Her eyes looked up innocently at mine, and I wondered if I should spill it all here. Tell her every bit of truth from day one and leave nothing behind. Say screw it to some family brunch and tell her everything I had spent years working hard to keep to myself.

But no. This wasn't the time or the place. She deserved it, yes. Deserved to know everything. But not in some rushed ramble after we had already made drunken mistakes the night before. We needed to get settled. Needed to get home and breathe. Then I would share it all. Every piece of me.

Therefore, my answer was simple. "I would receive extra compensation each month."

She eyed me, scrunching up her face. "Aren't you basically rich?"

My lips curled. "No, I'm just good at saving. But I have an investment with too many monthly expenses that I need to pay down. This would help." It wasn't a lie, but it wasn't entirely the truth either. It was enough to get by on till we got home.

She paused. "So you are *also* a gold digger?"

"No."

"Face it, Adam, we're basically the seven dwarfs, except there are only two of us."

"I...no."

She smiled, most of her skepticism wiped off her face by now. "But still, you're sure about this? I feel like you should be pushing back at least some."

I should be. I should be asking questions. I ought to have at least some hesitation regarding marriage. But for this part, I could easily tell her the truth.

"I wouldn't have asked you to marry me if I didn't want to."

A faint blush creeped up her cheeks. "Fair enough. You're not freaking out about this as much as I need you to."

How could I explain this without sending her running? Without making it sound like I was over my head in all of this? I didn't mind being married to her because there was no one else I could ever be married to.

My eyes shifted from her ring to the floor. "It's not exactly a secret that I don't love..."

"People?" she cut in. "Human interaction? Accepting the fact that sometimes you have to talk to others in order to live?"

"Yes. But it's..." I paused, searching for the right word and coming up short. "It's different with you. It's not like I was going to get married anytime soon. I'm getting too old to try the whole Tinder thing."

She waved a hand. "That's arguable. You could always try meeting a nice lady at Dad's assisted living home."

"Listen, smart-ass. I'm saying that if that's what you want, then I'm fine with it. You could use the help with your dad, and I could use the extra money and the excuse to help me avoid being deployed too far and traveling so much. It's fine."

A lot of my coworkers were married, and although they were held to the same standards, it helped when push came to shove that I was the only single guy in our unit. If someone's wife was having a baby, or their kid was suddenly not doing well, they would send me out first. I'd never cared before, but now I felt an urge to be grounded. Well, as much as they would let me.

Rachel sighed and looked down at her ring, twisting it around her finger. Then her face relaxed, like it had some kind of magical power to put her at ease. That alone also relaxed my shoulders. I grabbed her soft, dainty hand and pressed my thumb against her finger, just above the ring.

We'd be fine, because we'd be together. And that was enough.

CHAPTER TEN

Rachel / Then

Currently playing: Come on Eileen by Dexys Midnight Runners

***

My best friend was officially a published author. And an exceptional one at that.

Setting up her book signing at the record store hadn't been easy. I'd spent the entire week convincing Arthur, the owner, to let me host it there for her. He felt like it would bring in a different crowd, but I reminded him of two things:

One: We had an entire book section to the side of the store.

Two: I was a mastermind at shining up a turd- as my Dad would say.

It still took rounds of convincing, but I eventually got him there when I assured him that we should receive extra sales from it. I was pretty sure he was getting desperate for traction at that point, and me mentioning potential sales was too tempting for him not to reach.

Therefore, I spent the last week or so making Sip 'n' Spin (now heavy on the spin because our coffee machine hadn't been working for the last couple of months) the perfect hangout for a book signing. Good thing too, because this big town had shown up for Layla. Calla and Crew helped by setting up balloon arches and signs while I spent the morning trying to keep Layla from panicking and ensuring she didn't leave our apartment looking like a grandma bundled in her many cardigans.

I'd managed to get her into a pair of black tights and my form-fitting brown leather skirt with a black T-shirt tucked in. She was the perfect picture of sexy but classy. I felt like a proud pageant mom, ready to show off her kid everywhere and take all the credit.

It was a good night. I was dreading the end of it, and yet it was already flying by. Mostly because my hands had been kept busy all afternoon, refilling refreshments, straightening anything out of place, and keeping the never-ending line to my best friend going.

But despite my busy hands, my mind kept going back to seeing Adam leaned against a wall in the far corner of the store. Tattooed, broody, insane-to-look-at Adam, who I could not kick out of my brain tonight. I'd wondered, in the back of my mind, whether Luke's family had planned to be here, specifically if Adam would be here. But it was Layla's night, and she deserved my focus for as long as I could give it. Even so, I was still going to check out her almost brother-in-law from afar.

As I straightened a sign that was beginning to slip from its nail, Calla set a hand on my back. "Why don't you get something to eat and let me handle things?"

My eyes trailed to the plate of appetizers that Crew had made, and my stomach growled, a deep ache pulling at me.

"You can rest. It's almost over, and you've done an amazing job."

I turned to Layla, who was sitting behind a table with Luke right behind her, smiling as she signed book after book.

"Okay. Yeah, I think I will." I gave her an appreciative smile and grabbed a small plate, stacking it high and making my way straight to the grump.

Adam looked over at me, and I swore, for a millisecond, I saw the man smile.

Plopping my full plate on the tall table next to his empty one, I leaned in. "Nice to see you, grandpa sailor."

"I am not a sailor," he grumbled.

I leaned back, tilting my head to take him in. "I don't know, your whole vibe screams sea shanty to me. Sailor fits. What other nickname could I give you?"

"Not that one."

A snort of a laugh left me, and I popped a jalapeño bite into my mouth. "Fine, fine. Just not much to work with on Adam. Got a middle name?"

"Ezekiel."

"Hmm. What does that mean?"

He hesitated. "God will strengthen."

I leaned back, tilting my head to take him in. Wide chest, large forearms, strong grip, remembering how light I felt in his arms. How I had never met someone so utterly masculine before. "Strengthen, he did."

His eyes lightened up a little. "And yours?"

"Stevie." I smiled. "Dad picked it because of Queen Stevie Nicks, of course."

Adam nodded. "Ahh. Steve."

"Not Steve. Stevie."

"Whatever you say." He shrugged casually, but I didn't miss for a second how his mouth twitched in amusement.

I wondered what I would have to do to get the guy to smile. A real one, showing all those pearly whites. Someone had to, so why not me? I was generally good at working a crowd. And I was pretty good at this casual flirting and the back-and-forth we had going. He was lucky I was a girl who could read physical reactions. Otherwise, I might assume he really was an a-hole and not a teddy bear inside.

"No, not whatever I say," I laughed and boldly took a sip from his champagne flute in hopes he wouldn't deny me. "I refuse to be called Steve."

"It fits you."

I laughed. "You are such a—"

Bzz. My obnoxious vibrating phone on the table between the two of us caught our attention. Shoot, it was Dad. I'd completely forgotten it was a Friday night.

My fingers itched to answer, hand reaching out. Sure, we were mid-conversation and I was prepared to spit verbal fire at this guy, but Dad came first. He always had and always would. There were no exceptions. If I didn't put him first, who would?

"Hey, sorry I didn't realize the time," I rushed out before he could speak.

"I wanted to make sure you were okay, is all." The nostalgic raspiness of his voice settled over me like warm honey. "You don't have to come. I know you're busy."

My heart beat fell back into a regular rhythm at the clearness in his voice. Today was a good day.

In all the craziness of Layla's event, I hadn't considered that it was dance night at the community center in Dad's complex. I'd never missed it. Not once. And let me tell you, learning a tango with a double ear infection is awful. "No, no. I'll be there. Tell Joann to wait until I'm there before she plays any CCR."

"You know she won't." He laughed, and it felt like a hug, his arms holding me tight like when I was little and he would dance around the room with me on his toes.

"Okay, see you soon." I smiled as I hung up and reached for my keys.

"CCR?" Adam asked with a quirk in his brow.

"Oh, they're—" He didn't know anything about music, right? He had said so that one night. "Never mind. It's line dance night at my dad's assisted living complex. I always go. That way, he has a partner."

He nodded his head and took a sip of his drink, his lips placed just where mine had been. "Have fun."

I guess that was his version of goodbye. But I wasn't quite ready for that. I hadn't seen him all night, and it was still early. I mean...

"You could come with me," I offered with a smile.

His hands reached into his pockets. "I don't dance."

I squinted at him in evaluation. "I don't know...you've got some J-Lo hips in there somewhere."

Adam snorted sarcastically before shaking his head and crossing his arms.

Well, I'd tried. I wasn't one to beg, and as I said before, Dad came first. If Adam was the type of man to be offended or off put by that, then it was best to know now.

I twirled the band on my keys around my wrist, catching them in my palm. "Your loss. Could've made you a really great dance partner…" I dragged out. Then I turned on my heel, hoping for some resistance on his end.

But Adam didn't resist. He watched as I walked to the front door. Blowing a kiss to Layla and waving a hand at Calla, I wrapped my arms around my torso and stepped outside, then walked briskly to my car.

I'd meant what I said to Adam the last time I saw him. I didn't have time to date or do anything more than that. Didn't mean I didn't want him to try a little. It was a shame. I did like him a lot. But the dad test was a tried-and-true trial to see someone's intentions with me. If they weren't comfortable coming to see my father with me, then chances were we couldn't be friends. And we certainly couldn't be more.

That was okay. It was a good thing, really. Easier to let that settle in now rather than down the road when my expectations were unrealistic. I was just going to have to ogle Adam from across the room at every Wells family event from here on out. At Luke and Layla's wedding, we would make awkward eye contact with an uncomfortable wave. I would leave early because of "a bad stomachache," and that would become the new normal.

"Rachel!" A raspy shout from behind me stopped my hand from opening the car door.

Adam jogged down the busy street, weaving around tourists, with a hand in the air, signaling for me to wait up. My heart leaped out of my chest, my pulse racing and heat rising under my skin as he approached.

He rubbed the back of his neck and then crossed his arms. "I, uh. I'll go."

My entire face lifted, a smile slowly pulling up and my eyebrows rising. Adam Wells was going dancing with me. I felt the undeniable urge to go find my journal from sixth grade and write an entry in it. *Dear diary, a strong, tattooed pirate is whisking me away for a night of ballroom dancing with the highly elite at the Graceful Care Community Center. Suck it, Nancy from homeroom.*

Adam, seeing my pleased expression, dropped his eyebrows. "I'm not dancing."

Hmm, we would see about that.

CHAPTER ELEVEN

Rachel / Now

Currently playing: Sir Duke by Stevie Wonder

***

Forcing Adam to walk into the café first, I waited outside the entrance, mentally singing "Big Me" by Foo fighters.

It was just over two minutes. I knew because I had been singing it for years as my *brushing my teeth* song. Two minutes seemed like a perfect amount of non-suspicious time for my entrance to the table. It wasn't so late that I was being rude, but it meant I didn't have to walk in with Adam.

My hands shook as I reached the last chorus and ran them through my hair. It took a lot for me to get anxious. I was a more confident person than most, and if this had been anything simpler, I could have passed it up as a laughable thing. But this was real. It was semipermanent. Or at least permanent until I had saved up enough and felt comfortable signing off on the papers. So maybe two years?

And really, in the grand scheme of life, what was two years? Just a blink. It would come and go, and we'd look back on it with fond memories. Like a best friend marriage pact that had come to fruition. Except this was on a whim. And we were using it as an excuse to bring in extra income. That part, I didn't feel too bad about, considering we'd gotten married and *then* come up with the idea of reaping the benefits from it. So it wasn't technically illegal. At least in my head, anyway.

Reaching the end of the song, I took a deep breath and forced my legs to move inside the area. My eyes searched the room, snagging on a table in the far corner full of Wells family faces.

With my thumb, I turned my ring around, leaving the diamond on the underside of my finger. I'd keep it under the table 90 percent of the time, and when the time was right, Adam and I would figure out how to break the news to everyone. Simple.

"Good morning." I sighed and took the only open seat. Adam was on my left, and Nathan sat on my right.

They all replied with their own greetings, and the casual, relaxed tone of it all helped my shoulders drop a little. It was stupid of me to freak out. These were my people. More than they knew at the moment, but still. They had treated me with nothing but kindness and acceptance from the moment I met each of them. Why would I expect anything different now?

Calla and Layla both made eyes at me as I sat down. Layla lowered her brows at me and then obnoxiously widened her eyes at Adam sitting next to me. Yes, I'd married my best friend's brother-in-law without a word to her until after the ceremony was over, and now I was sitting across from her, pretending as though it had never happened. I could already hear her nagging in my ear like the sound of Howler. *Rachel! How dare you marry my brother-in-law without calling me?*

I gave a sympathetic smile, my cheeks pulling tight and my eyes full of sorrow. I really hadn't meant to leave her out, and if I could go back in time, I would have gladly done things differently. But I only had that vision now, and there was nothing I could do about it.

Small talk erupted around the table, discussions of Marigold and Liam's reception, and the boys talking about how excited they were to have their parents under the same roof again. Nathan and Calla went on about their perfect jobs. It all felt entirely normal, and I was entirely grateful for normal at the moment.

Once we all settled with food on our plates, the discussions died down.

While everyone was occupied, I felt a light touch above my knee. Out of the corner of my eye, Adam kept eating as though nothing had changed. His fingers rubbed back and forth with a comforting firmness. Ease washed over me even further. I almost felt ridiculous for beginning to freak out earlier.

His pointer finger gave a delicate tap.

Are you okay? it said.

I rubbed my thumb over the back of his hand. *Perfectly fine*, I replied.

Crew suddenly slammed his fork down on the table, jolting the rest of us at the table. His eyebrows furrowed and his mouth twisted. "Is no one going to talk about it?"

Mama B tilted her head to the side. "Talk about what, dear?"

Crew all but stood, leaning over the table and pointing at Adam and then at me.

Oh lord. Warmth rose into my cheeks in a blush. No, a blush was subtle. This was a bright, red-hot heat that made me look like a traffic sign.

"Adam and Rachel. Clearly, they got married last night, and we're sitting here eating Mickey Mouse–shaped chocolate-chip waffles as if nothing has happened."

Adam cleared his throat. "You're the only one eating that."

"Not the point."

Nathan chimed in. "Did you make that yourself at the waffle bar?"

Crew groaned. "Still not the point."

I raised my left hand, turning around the mountain on my finger. Okay, it wasn't that big. Or maybe it was. I didn't exactly know ring etiquette, but this one felt larger than most. Flashing the ring to his family, I sighed. "It's true."

Layla and Calla let out synchronized fake gasps, hands reaching up to clutch strings of pearls that weren't there. Bless them.

My eyes stayed on Adam's parents as I waited for shock to sink in. It never did. Mama B's face stayed the same, except her eyes softened toward me. Jerry gave an affirming nod to Adam, which he returned.

Luke turned his gaze from Layla over to Adam. "How did that happen?"

Adam shrugged, not looking up from his bacon and taking a bite as though nothing had happened. "Been thinking about it for a while."

I knew it wasn't the truth deep down. The logical side of my brain kept that in check. But it didn't stop my gut from doing full-on somersaults. This giant, tattooed, motorcycle-riding bear saying he had been thinking of putting a ring on it "for a while" was not going to just casually fly out of my brain. Despite our friendship over the years, I couldn't simply turn off a magic switch and ignore Adam's undeniable attractiveness. Hearing him affirm me and not chalk it up to a mistake warmed my heart.

Mama B spoke up at that. "Ah, love *can* come from all corners, can't it?"

"What's the plan now?" Nathan questioned.

"Taking it a day at a time. We just got married. We want to figure it all out as we go," Adam answered, still not looking anyone in the eye.

"Do you guys know what you're going to do from here?" Luke asked.

"How come the guy who stays in his Batman cave got married before *I* did?" Crew interrupted before Adam could answer.

We each continued eating as his family hit us with a barrage of questions and Adam handled each one with Olympic grace. I took a deep breath in relief, squeezing Adam's hand beside me. We would pull this off. Not because of anything I could do, but because of him.

CHAPTER TWELVE

Rachel / Then

Currently playing: I don't feel like dancing by the Scissor Sisters

***

Adam Wells rode in my car, his giant shoulders taking up all the space. The longer we drove down the road, the more I could peek at the floral tattoo crawling up his forearm into dangerous bicep territory.

He was a friend. A nice one at that. Someone to talk to who had no preconceived notions about me, considering he didn't know much of who I was. An outside perspective that was about to get an inside view.

Our text conversations over the last month or so while he'd been gone had gotten deeper the more we talked. And by deeper, I simply meant that Adam was no longer replying to everything I sent with one-word answers.

But still, a friend was all he was, and it was all I had availability for. It didn't mean I couldn't enjoy the way his aroma filled my tiny car.

Eagerness pooled in my chest at the thought of him meeting my dad. It was rare for him to have visitors other than me. He always got excited when I said I was bringing someone along. Usually, it just meant Layla. Though one time Calla came with me when she heard they were having a plant propagation class. Either way, I was looking forward to seeing his face light up at someone new.

After hopping out of the car, I directed Adam to the front entrance of the community center portion of Dad's complex. It was the middle area, with a large gym, a movie room, and multiple areas for classes. His section of the multiple duplexes was only about three buildings down, so he spent half of his time here and the other half at his home.

The decision to get him in an assisted living area was hard enough on its own, but finding a place where I felt comfortable leaving him that also allowed him to feel like I wasn't watching his every move was challenging. It took almost nine months, but when I'd settled on this place, it had felt right. It was a tough transition, but he had been here now for three years and had made a good bit of friends. He was definitely one of the youngest guys here at only fifty-two, but with his memory slipping more as time went on, it was necessary. I knew he got frustrated that there were people here whose job it was to check in on him. It made him feel invalid, but he never blamed me for it. He never acted as though I was selfish in my decision to not care for him by myself, and I appreciated that more than he would know.

Almost reaching the front door, I stopped in my tracks and turned to Adam. He was trailing so closely behind me that he bumped into my chest, causing me to almost fall back before his hands gripped my arms. I placed my palms on his wide chest and looked up, forcing myself to see past his strong jawline.

"I should warn you before we go in there."

He curled an eyebrow.

"Dad might think he has met you before. If you remind him of someone he went to school with or maybe an old coworker when he was young, he will get confused. Also, don't be surprised if you tell him your name and he forgets it by the end of the night. Please don't get offended. He is the nicest man in the world and would never hurt a fly—"

"Rachel," Adam's hands roamed up and down my arms in a soothing caress. "It's okay. My grandmother had dementia when I was little. I don't remember much, but I know the feeling of it all. I chose to be here."

He had, hadn't he? He'd chosen to leave a fun party with his family to come to an assisted living dance class with a woman he'd randomly become friends with. My heart warmed at that, and a sense of ease seeped through my body, allowing me to rest. He was right. It was okay.

I opened the door, and Adam followed behind me. At the front desk sat Betty. She usually worked the night shift here since she'd been hired last year. I always made a conscious effort to check in on her. Every now and then I would find her staring into the distance like she was going to fall asleep standing up.

"Hi, Betty," I announced, and she jolted up in response.

"My darling, Rachel. I was worried you wouldn't make it tonight. You know Jack has been all excited."

I smiled. Of course he was. "I wouldn't miss it for the world." I turned and held a hand out, gesturing to Adam behind me. "This is my friend Adam. He *loves* dancing."

Adam's neck turned a light pink as Betty smiled at him. It was really cute.

"Well, you're going to love tonight. I heard the instructors have a whole new routine planned."

Oh, this was going to be great.

After catching up with Betty and learning all about her son's newest wrestling obsession, we slipped down the hall to classroom D. Approaching the room, you could hear the loud bass of Earth, Wind, and Fire's "Let's Groove" playing through the surround sound mixed with the sound of feet tapping. Adam had no idea what he was in for.

I opened the door to see about ten or so couples dancing in a circle. One man in particular in the middle, the one wearing a flannel I'd bought for him last Christmas, was so focused on the dancing that he didn't realize everyone around him was smiling and clapping his way. That would be my dad.

My heart leaped at his smile as his feet tapped to the beat and his hands clapped in the air. He'd always been such a dork. One year, he got me a karaoke machine for Christmas. It required a CD, and the only one he'd bought was *Best of the '80s*. It featured a good mix, including Michael Jackson and Bruce Springsteen. I was convinced he'd mostly bought it for himself, but I loved it still. Each birthday and Christmas after that, we got a new

CD for the machine. I put on a show for my family, requiring them each to "purchase" a ticket, a.k.a. colored paper with my name on it. He watched me lip sync to Alanis Morissette and even drew a pretend lighter and waved it slowly in the air for me. Mom and my sister absolutely hated it. I snorted at the memory.

I reached for a nearby chair that was leaning against the wall and unfolded it before setting my keys and water bottle on it. Adam scooted closer to me as I waved to a few familiar faces around the room.

I looked over my shoulder, finding him inches away from me, looking at everyone warily, like a toddler hiding behind his mom's leg in a grocery store. It was almost comical how much he hated a crowd.

The song died down, and everyone clapped. The instructor with leg warmers and an old headset lifted his microphone and told everyone to take a break.

Dad turned to face us, his smile growing even bigger as he raced across the dance space over to us. "There's my girl!" he shouted, yanking me into a hug as if I hadn't seen him the day before.

My eyes instantly fell to his shirt, checking for any missed buttons or signs that he had a hard time getting dressed this morning. There weren't any. I wrapped my arms around his torso and gave a tight squeeze, cherishing the fact that he was having a good day. Bad days, the ones where he couldn't remember why he was here or where his family was, were few and far between. But they hurt. They left scars and marks in my brain that I feared would never heal. Which was why I liked to never take moments like this for granted. I never knew when it would be the last.

"I brought a friend with me if you want to meet him." I gestured to Adam behind me, who nodded hello.

Dad eyed him warily, his focus going from his tattoos to the scruff on his jaw. He turned to me and spoke close to my ear. "He has tattoos."

I chuckled to myself. "So do you."

He looked down at the few inked spots on his arms and huffed. "How am I supposed to threaten him after he watched me salsa?"

"If it helps, I don't think anything threatens the guy. Besides, he's just a friend."

"Hmm." He squinted and moved around me to get a better look.

Adam held a hand out, not the least bit threatened. "Adam Wells."

"Jack." Dad shook his hand, eyes stuck to Adam's arm, taking in the airplane with a symbol I didn't recognize behind it. "Air Force?"

I guess that was a universal thing? I wondered how many more of his tattoos related to something in his past and how long it would take me to find out.

"Yes, sir." He nodded.

"You're still active."

"I am."

"Hmm."

They stared at each other, some kind of silent back-and-forth happening between them. Maybe being in the military just ensured that you learned how to communicate telepathically.

Adam was taller by almost a foot, but my dad was strong. He never let a day go by where he didn't work out in some kind of way. He used to say it was so he could keep up with my mom's looks. A sad waste, considering she was currently somewhere in California, probably trying to seduce some poor man who owns a yacht into taking her on it and feeding her succulent grapes while she fans herself. Now I figured he did it because, though his mind was slipping, he wouldn't allow his body to as well.

After an unusually long staring contest, my dad nodded, and a slow smile yanked his lips up. "How do you know my Rachel?"

Adam and I made eye contact, blood rushing to both of our faces and our eyes widening. It would be in his best interest if we didn't mention *how* we'd met or what followed after.

"Layla is my brother's fiancée."

I waited for Dad to ask me who that was, but today must have been even better than I thought, because he nodded. "She's a nice girl."

Adam nodded back, and they went back to their silent stare off. This was...odd.

The beat over the speakers picked up, and I instantly recognized it as Four Tops "I Can't Help Myself." When I looked over at Dad, he smirked at me, raising his brows, and I laughed.

"I know, I know." I reached for his hand to get in a free spot on the floor.

Dad turned to Adam, who had his arms crossed and was looking out at the floor like it was going to kill him to get anywhere near it. Looking over his shoulder, Dad asked, "You coming?"

He looked from the floor to us, making eye contact with me and widening his eyes in a look that screamed *help!* I winked back at him. *Sorry,* the look said. *You're on your own.*

Adam cleared his throat. "I'll, uh, watch."

I chuckled. We would see about that.

"Put your hips into it, son!"

"I, uh. I'm not really a *hips into it* kind of guy, sir."

I spun on my heel, turning away from where my dad was doing a samba, to face Adam. "Don't listen to him, Dad. He totally is." I winked with a laugh.

Adam groaned and followed my steps as I did a grapevine. He cursed when he almost stepped on Margaret's shoe. She eyed him, and I wondered if she was going to threaten to pepper spray him again. It had happened four times since Adam joined us.

After fifteen minutes of sitting in the corner, several people from the group began pulling Adam into the circle. Probably from being hip-bumped back and forth like he was in a game of monkey-in-the-middle with some geriatric women that made him give up and join us.

"I'm only doing this so they will leave me alone," he grumbled. I turned to see half the woman in the room now behind Adam, ogling as he made some attempts to follow the steps.

"Sure, you are." I laughed and reached for his hand, letting our fingers slip together. The smallest hint of a smile tugged at his lips as I turned myself under his hand in a twirl.

The tempo picked up for the last round, and I moved next to Adam. I smiled over at him as he watched my dad's feet move effortlessly. Dad had done each dance so many times by now he didn't even have to think about it. It was pure muscle memory. I would be willing to bet money he even practiced the first couple of months at his house, making sure he knew it all perfectly before the next class.

As the song ended, everyone clapped, and we all attempted to catch our breath. It always managed to shock me how much work it took to keep up. No wonder some of the ladies were taking breaks. Between that and the way Adam's pants clung to his behind, I could understand.

I sighed, taking a seat next to Adam, grateful when he handed me a new water bottle.

"Phew. It really tires you out, huh?"

Dad blew out a breath and stood in front of us, wiping the sweat off with his shirt.

Nodding, I took a sip of my drink and leaned back in my chair. Another song started up, but the three of us decided to sit it out. Not that Adam needed much convincing.

Dad chuckled at some of the other couples, one in particular being extra in their matching orange sweat suits.

"It's more fun with a partner." He smiled. "Your mom always loved to dance."

Cold sweat broke out at my neck, my fingers becoming clammy against my water bottle. It wasn't the first time he had asked, and it certainly wasn't going to be the last. But still, the mention of her was always enough to cause my anxiety to rise. Most of his flare-ups were caused by my mother being brought into conversation. I had to handle it with grace each time, or it could ruin his entire week.

"She sure does." I forced a smile, holding back any disparity. Adam's gaze felt like a warm, comforting caress over my jawline to my cheekbone, but it wasn't enough to calm my racing heart.

"Where is she tonight? Couldn't make it?" Dad asked with this innocent look that tore me in two. He had no idea. His heart was so pure. He had completely lost a piece of his life that was dark and cold, and it was up to me to keep it that way.

I had found it was best to just...play along. But the best thing was never the easiest. It felt like I was lying to the one person who meant the most to me. Like I was casually letting him believe his whole life was only what he'd made it up to be, keeping the dirty secrets all mine to hold. They got heavier each day.

I cleared my throat and straightened my back, attempting an easy tone. "Nope, she couldn't today. Just me for now."

Dad laughed, and relief flooded me. If there were no more questions tonight, then I could slip out of here. He sat down next to Adam and elbowed him jokingly. "Suppose that's good enough."

On that note, we needed to leave.

I said quick goodbyes to the familiar faces around me, being sure to give extra-long hugs to the ones I knew didn't receive visitors. Then I made my way back to Dad. I wrapped my arms around his neck and squeezed tight. "Had fun tonight."

"Ah, me too, kiddo. Always a blast with you." He looked over at Adam, who was holding both his water bottle and mine, with my light jacket slung over his arm. Dad pulled me in once more and whispered in my ear. "Bring him back again, yeah?"

I nodded with a smile. I think I would.

CHAPTER THIRTEEN
Adam / Now

Currently playing: Goodbye Yellow Brick Road by Elton John

***

Rachel's knee was bouncing feverishly next to mine, shaking our seats as she looked out the window.

It was a four-hour flight, and if she kept wringing her hands and making the plane ricochet back and forth, I was going to go insane. She looked down at her phone, refreshing her text messages, and locked it—before repeating the process again.

She'd done the same thing the entire way here, anxiously waiting for something to pop up that she didn't want to see.

I leaned toward her seat, spreading my legs enough so our knees touched. "You're worried about Jack."

Her pout deepened with her nod as she looked up at me. She didn't bother asking me how I knew. At this point, I knew her well enough to read her like a book, and she knew that. It was part of my job. To pay incredible attention to my surroundings.

She didn't bother beating around the bush with me, because there was no point. It was like how she understood me, whether I felt like talking or not. Every furrowed brow, every rumble in my chest, she translated. Anything I didn't say, she already knew.

Rachel sighed. "It's just, if something happens or they have a question or anything at all, they can't reach me for four hours. I can't help but be a little nervous. Plus, he started taking that medicine for his acid reflux last week, and what if he all of a sudden gets an allergic reaction? It could be fatal. He could—"

I nodded along to her rambling, letting her fire off every potentially dangerous scenario that could happen in a span of four hours.

My eyes caught on her cheeks. They were void of any makeup. Fresh freckles danced across her nose, all the way to her ear. Usually, they were so covered up you'd never even know they were there. They were so light you'd have to pay close attention to even notice, but when you did, it was like you couldn't look away.

She must've really been nervous, because I could count on one hand the number of times I had seen Rachel without make-up. She always said if she wasn't 100 percent put together, then she was either deathly ill or taken over by aliens. She wore heels more than tennis shoes, and was rarely ever caught without her face perfectly done. I liked that she dropped her walls around me. It took at least a year, but when she did open the door to let me in with her hair in a loose braid and her face void of anything extra, my heart stuttered. Even in her ridiculous pajamas and the Snuggie draped over her, she still made my body react in ways no one else could. My cheeks lit in a flame at the sight of her, and I was *not* a blushing man. It felt like her way of saying *here I am. I'll allow you to see this part because I trust you.*

Watching her ramble along about possible allergies he could develop over the course of a plane ride and flailing her arms around dramatically, I took a mental picture of her. The pale skin and pink cheeks. Full lips that were naturally rosy and eyelashes that curled upward. I wasn't going to say she looked better or worse with or without makeup. I liked looking at her regardless. But there was something so appealing about having her guard down like this. With no flirty wit or winged eyeliner to block her true feelings. I liked her that way. It felt like there were fewer walls between us.

She continued her runaway list of potential mishaps, her voice raising louder. "And God knows that if they try to call my sister, she'll have no clue what to do. She doesn't even know which building he's in. It would take her at least six hours to get there anyway. She may not even have the same number. I mean, what do they do if she doesn't answer? They better not call my mother. I would light a flame up someone's—"

I cleared my throat as an old lady diagonal from us gave us a death glare.

Rachel took in a deep breath and turned her head to the window with a sniffle. She hated crying, hated it more than anyone I had ever known. It made her feel angry and defeated.

Desperate to stop any tears from rolling down her cheek, I mumbled out, "So you wanna move in with me or what?"

She jerked her head back to me, the tiniest tear stuck in the corner of her eye, hanging on the edge. "What?" she whispered back.

"We're married. You should probably move in," I reaffirmed.

The switch from her disheartened state to the sputtering that came out of her mouth as her eyes grew wide was cute. "I—you. We. Move in—" she scoffed. "We don't even really, well. I mean, we do. We did, anyway. I don't think—"

"If we're going to be married, it's best if we live in the same house. It would be suspicious otherwise, right?"

Her head dipped back and forth, like her brain was doing a mental game of table tennis as she weighed the pros and cons. "Yeah. I guess so."

"You'd save on bills there too—"

She shook her head and lifted a hand to my lips to shush me. "No, no, no. I might be desperate enough to take the government's money, but I will not be taking yours. We are splitting everything right down the middle."

We wouldn't. I would make sure of that. The point of this deal was for her to save money for her dad's care. The difference between her rent and my mortgage would eat all of that up.

"We will settle on something. You can...pay the water bill."

She pointed a finger at me, her nail inches from my eyeball. "Stop that. I don't want the tiny bills. You said yourself that you needed the money too. You have to have some kind of debt you're struggling with too."

I cracked my knuckles one by one.

The difference was my debt was unexplainable to her. She would find out soon. I was sure of it. I needed the right time. A four-hour plane ride where we were stuck together didn't seem like the ideal setting.

"It's not unmanageable. It would just be nice to tackle it head-on." That was the best I could come up with for the time being.

During take-off, we argued back and forth, haggling over every small bill, until I finally got her to agree on a seventy-five/twenty-five split. She wasn't happy about it, and neither was I, so it worked well enough.

As the plane steadied its course, Rachel pulled out her earbuds, and her shoulders relaxed. She leaned into the seat with a small grin on her lips. Like she'd been reunited with her best friend. Other than me. On the way here, one flight attendant had said she was going to have to confiscate her AirPods if she didn't take them out for the safety presentation. I thought Rachel was going to come apart at the seams.

Connecting her AirPods to her phone, she handed me the left one, and I smirked. I was working slowly on music education. I still had a way to go, but I wanted to understand her in these songs. Understand a deeper meaning of who she was, how she felt.

As I placed the device in my ear, I leaned back in my chair, ignoring the kicking against it by some kid behind us. A slow thrumming played over us, and I looked down to see her phone lighting up in her lap, showing Elton John's "Goodbye Yellow Brick Road."

A few moments later, her head dropped to my shoulder and her breathing steadied into a slow rhythm that matched the music's tempo. I planted a small kiss on the top of her head as I felt her drifting to sleep against me, her hand with my ring on it lying right next to mine.

CHAPTER FOURTEEN

Adam / Then

Currently Playing: I Say A Little Prayer by Aretha Franklin

***

Rachel: Have you listened to my playlist yet?

I have not.

Rachel: Rude.

Hard to find time at work.

Rachel: Between the shark attacks and helicopter rides over the sunset, right?

Rachel: I feel like you're in a…U2 mood currently.

What does that even mean?

Rachel: Moody, heartfelt, thinking.

You don't know me that well.

Rachel: Or I know you very well.

How does U2 match with Stevie Wonder?

Rachel: Oh, so you did listen?

Are you going to keep doing this?

Rachel: Doing what?

Talking.

Rachel: Planned on it…why? Is it bothering you?

Rachel: I'll take your silence as a no. Good to know.

Rachel: If you could be any animal, what would you be?

What does that matter?

Rachel: Well, for the sake of us becoming friends, I feel like it's important.

Rachel: I think I would be a deer, or maybe one of those capybaras. What about you?

Rachel: It's been an hour. Are you on some kind of secret mission or something?

Nope. At the main air station, waiting on the rest of the guys to come back.

Rachel: Do you ever do secret missions?

Do you ever stop talking?

Rachel: Ohh, love the sass. I usually stop talking as soon as someone answers me.

Doesn't seem like it.

Rachel: I think you would be a really good panther.

Rachel: Or a hippo.

I am not a hippo.

Rachel: Don't be offended. They have three times the jaw strength of a lion.

Adam: Okay...

Rachel: And somehow they're still freakishly cute. Just like you.

I don't think anyone uses the word "cute" to describe me.

Rachel: I just did :)

CHAPTER FIFTEEN

Rachel / Now

Currently Playing: Happy Together by The Turtles

***

A wave—no, a *mountain* of relief—washed over me once we landed.

Being able to call Dad and physically hear his voice saying he was doing good, and also going into grave detail about how his grocery delivery person gave him low sodium chips instead of "the good stuff," was an enormous weight off my chest. I smiled along with his recap of the day. He went on about how he worked out more today than usual so his back was sore all the way. Then he gave me details of how he was hoping to order a Philly sandwich for dinner.

The whole way through leaving the airport, through baggage claim, and to the car, I kept him in my earbuds, and Adam didn't say a word. As soon as I mouthed, "he's okay," he simply nodded back with the hint of a reassuring smile. No rolling his eyes and saying "I told you so," or "see? No need to worry." Because Adam knew that wasn't what I needed to hear.

Truth be told, I didn't need to *hear* anything. I needed Adam's physical reassurance and support, and he always provided it. Even as I tried to carry my own bags out to thc Ubcr, he insisted I focus on the phone with Dad. By insisted, I mean he would grunt and push my hand away any time I reached for the handle on my luggage.

We figured our best bet was for me to go home and grab some essentials before heading to Adam's house. Once we got to my apartment, I reached for my keys in my bag on his shoulder before coming to a halt. My fingers tapped against my key chain—a little orange bird that said *come back again*. Adam had shipped it to me when he was deployed to Florida.

A blush crept up my cheeks. Adam was going to see my apartment in the very, very disturbing state it was in. It wasn't exactly anything new. He understood I was kind of a hot mess when it came to keeping things organized. But we were technically married now, and he was Mr. No Shoe Should Be Out of its Straightened Place by the Door. I knew for a fact the man ironed his bedsheets. I also once saw him using a miniature vacuum to clean his normal vacuum. The so-called debt he did have was probably a stock investment in Lysol or Mr. Clean.

Besides, who even knew what lay behind this door? I was having what some might call a *mental breakdown* before our flight to Vegas, so I couldn't be 100 percent certain that there wasn't some pretty gross stuff waiting for us in my apartment. My mind immediately went to the memory of my preflight self rifling through my closet in search of the perfect shoes for my bridesmaid dress. There were at least three bras lying on my living room floor, and I honestly couldn't say whether there were dishes in the sink. We'd only been gone for two days, but still.

Up until this point, Adam had seen almost every raw piece of me. He knew me inside and out. However, the few times he'd come to my apartment—since we mostly hung out at his house or with his family—I would run around at the last minute to get the place looking somewhat tidy. Despite our years of friendship, and now thirty-two hours of marriage, I had managed to hold some form of mystique. So he had no idea that I was his worst nightmare when it came to roommates.

I cleared my throat and fumbled with my keys. "I, uh, think you should stay here."

He eyed the door behind me as if something was going to pop out of it and looked back at me. "Why?"

"I think it's best" was all I could manage. It was a whole lot better than *Well, I don't know how to say this, but your wife is a pig and you live your life like you get paid to clean.*

Between my wide-eyed stare full of silent pleading and the way my arms were now spread across the doorway like a *caution: do not enter* sign, he gave me mercy. Adam raised his hands in defense, and in a low baritone, said, "I'll just be here."

He backed up to the hallway wall and leaned against it with his arms crossed. I stared for a moment too long—mostly at those biceps straining against the seams of his short-sleeve tee—before he dipped his chin at me as if to say *go on*.

I sighed in relief and turned to unlock my door, opening it just wide enough to squeeze through to keep his gaze away from the zoo inside my apartment.

Once the door closed, I breathed in a deep sigh and looked down at my ring, twisting it back and forth. I was an entirely different person last time I was here. I was a single, very much still frustrated woman who was struggling between strangling her best friend or kissing him on the spot. And now I stood there with a ring on my finger and an agreement to remain married to said best friend.

I shook my shoulders in a shiver. This was going to take some getting used to.

My apartment wasn't as bad as I thought. Yes, there were clothes all over the place and my eyes did immediately catch on a bright blue bra sitting in the middle of my living room, but there were no dishes in the sink, so that was a plus.

I stepped over the path of clothing to my room and grabbed a duffel bag. Between what I'd taken to Vegas and this, I figured I would have enough to last me a week.

Looking over my room, across the mounds of rifled-through clean clothes and the stacks of makeup and skincare cases on my vanity, I took a deep breath. "All right, Rach. Just the necessities. You got this."

I did not have it. I didn't have anything. Except the overwhelming feeling that I had too much stuff in a too tiny apartment and I was being forced to pick my most necessary items when everything felt essential.

Record player, check.

A stack of my most listened-to vinyls, check.

Two bags of skincare products, check.

Three bags of makeup, check.

My fairy wings from last year's Halloween party, also check.

I stared at the bin of tiny pink bows that I liked to tie onto all my favorite things, considering whether I would need them at some point in the next week. I tilted my head. The rational side of me said no, but the other side—the one that had convinced me fairy wings were a great idea—said what if I got to Adam's apartment and there was a need for them? I picked one up and twirled it with my fingers, rattling the ideas in my head back and forth. Finally, I groaned and flopped back on my pile of underwear and socks. This was ridiculous.

The sound of my front door should have shocked me into sitting up and trying to hide the mess I'd made in this room, but instead, I accepted my impending doom.

Slow, dragging footsteps led to my room, and I couldn't help but notice that even the way he entered the room was hot.

Adam pushed lightly on my door with his knuckle. It slowly swayed open, and he leaned against the doorframe. His arms crossed over his chest, his forearm tattoos winking a hello at me.

I stared up at the ceiling, waiting for his comments. Waiting to hear *this place is a pigsty. How could you be so unorganized? I would never live like this.*

But he didn't say a word. He simply huffed the smallest bit of amusement and then walked over to me, crouching down and lying next to me. He stared up at the ceiling fan with me, unknowingly using my stack of clean folded socks as a pillow.

"What are we doing?" he asked in a husky voice.

"Feeling overwhelmed. Wallowing in self-pity," I mumbled.

Adam slowly sat up, looking down at me. "Let's get up. I'll help."

I sighed, considering it for a moment. Lying here for the rest of the day sounded nice, though. Getting up meant facing responsibilities and organizing.

"I can't. I'm lying on all of my bras."

"Nothing I haven't seen before." He reached a hand down to clasp mine. "Let's go, honey."

He used a fraction of his strength to pull me up to my feet. I was too lightheaded and focused on the word *honey* coming out of his mouth to bother fighting it. Adam's hands held the backs of my arms, keeping me steady as I gently swayed to regain my balance.

I tried to ignore the flames in my body at the way he called me honey. Was he a pet name kind of guy when it came to his girlfriends? Or should I say *wives*? Well, wife. There was only one of me, I hoped.

He hadn't had a girlfriend since we'd become friends, unless he kept that part of his life off limits for me. Wouldn't be a total shocker. Sometimes we would be sitting there watching a movie and he'd casually mention that he went skydiving a year ago and didn't tell anyone. Just to see if he could do it still. Either way, I always pictured him as more of a dark, mysterious, *my wife* kind of guy. Not a *honey* guy. It dripped off his tongue like warm vanilla sugar. Comforting like a soft, heated blanket that I wanted to lie in all day.

"Did you hear me?" he asked, shaking me out of my vision. A vision of him as one of those hunky heroes on the covers of Calla's historical romance books. A guy with his shirt ripped and holding a fair maiden—a.k.a., me—with his hair blowing in the wind and his muscles rippling.

I cleared my throat. "Uh, yes. What was that?"

His eyebrows dipped. "What are you struggling with?"

I looked around the room at my fully packed duffel bag next to my fairy wings and a stack of vinyls. Wincing, I looked up at him. "All of it?"

"Explain."

I sighed. "I have too much stuff. And I want to take it all with me."

Adam shrugged, looking down at the excessive amount of clothing I'd piled on the bed. "I have an empty house you can fill up."

"You don't mean that," I said, looking from my mess to his eyes, knowing his perfectly made-up house did not deserve my chaos.

He simply dipped his chin at me. "I do."

"What about Christmas?" I asked, despite knowing it was only June. "I like big Christmas trees."

"I'll get you the biggest one." He shrugged as if he didn't just say the sexiest thing someone like me could hear.

I lifted my brow. "What if it's too big for the house?"

"I'll get a bigger house."

Oh, good lord. I don't know if my heart was going to survive this temporary marriage/roommate thing. Not when he kept talking like that.

"All right," I lifted my shoulders and stuck out my chest. "But you asked for it."

We were on number four, where he would hold a piece of clothing, and I would respond with yes or no. Most of them were yeses, and where I expected Adam to chime in and tell me I was excessive or that I had no need for all of this, he instead nodded and helped me fill up three bags' worth of "essentials."

Once I felt settled enough to head to his house, he stood and grabbed two of the bags, letting me pick up the smaller items until our hands were full.

"Feel better?" he asked in that deep baritone. I breathed in, glancing around my now less-cluttered room, and smiled. "Much."

He nodded and turned to head to my living room. I began to follow but stopped when my eyes snagged on something. "Oh, wait!"

I walked a few steps, hearing Adam come up behind me, and attempted to kneel down to get my fairy wings.

A fair share of grunts came out of me as I leaned down to try and pick them up with my very full hands. Adam tapped my shoulder with one of the boxes in his hands.

"Okay, we have to draw a line somewhere."

He was right, but I couldn't just leave them here. "But they were custom made from a small Etsy shop." And cost me way too much for a single occasion.

He rolled his eyes. "In what scenario do you need that at my house?"

"If we get invited to a last-minute costume party. Or if Miles or Dallas lose a tooth and want me to pretend to be the tooth fairy."

"They're almost eleven."

Oh. Was that too old for the tooth fairy? I wasn't great at the whole kid thing.

"Either way, we should bring them." I nodded, my mind made up.

He groaned and bent down to pick them up. Then he placed them on top of the things piled in my arms.

I shook my head. "Nuh-uh, bud. I can't carry all of this. You have to take them."

Adam let out a low growl. The sound made my stomach flip, but not enough to make me sway. "I am not carrying fairy wings through your apartment complex and out to your car."

A snort came out of me. "Of course you're not going to carry them."

He nodded and attempted to hand them to me once more, but I deflected and moved my boxes away from his reach. "You're going to wear them."

Dropping all of his bags, he raised his voice ever so slightly. "Like hell I am."

I sighed, clicking my tongue and shaking my head. "Adam, *honey*." I threw that in to really sweeten the deal. "I have a backpack on. I can't wear them myself."

"Then I will wear the backpack." He grunted out the words like they pained him.

"Oh." I tilted my chin and gave him an understanding look. "I see. You're afraid you aren't masculine enough to wear them. It's okay. I can wear them and you can still look like the big, bad wolf."

Adam stopped dead in his tracks in my doorway. "No, no." He turned on his heel. "That is not it."

I gave him a sympathetic pout and nod combo. "*Sure* it's not."

Tongue in cheek, eyes rolling, Adam set his stuff—well, my stuff—down and stuck one of this giant man hands my way. "Give me the damn thing."

My smirk lifted further as I delicately placed the wings in his hand. He slipped them over his shoulders, resting the iridescent art over his back. They was incredibly small on him. The wings looked more like a toddler's Halloween costume when attached to his broad back.

He bent down, picked up the rest of my packed bags, and stood straight with his head held high before walking to my living room.

I snorted. Male egos were so fragile. But I had to admit that it was annoying how easily the guy could pull off anything.

We'd barely made it out the front door when one more thing clicked. "Hold on—"

"I am not wearing anything else you pull out of there," Adam interrupted in a disgruntled tone.

I rolled my eyes before stepping into the kitchen. "I know, I know. I have to get Myrtle."

"Who is *Myrtle*?" His eyebrows lowered in confusion.

"My little friend." I shrugged.

Adam's jaw scraped the floor, his face twisting in pure shock. He closed his eyes and shook his head, like he was attempting to process what I'd just said. "Your...little friend."

"Yes, that is what I said. She has to be fed almost daily."

"Do you have a cat or something?" he asked. His words were incredibly slow, like he needed to dumb the question down for me.

An amused huff of air left my nose. "No, she's not a cat. Although her food is pretty pricey and she can get very fussy when not fed correctly."

I reached up and pulled a mason jar from a shelf in my fridge, along with a bag of unbleached rye flour and Myrtle's favorite set of bowls.

Blowing out a breath, I turned back to the entrance. "Okay, I'm ready."

Adam blocked the doorway before I could move past him. His big shoulders and tall frame took up the entire exit as the straps of my wings pulled tight against his T-shirt, giving me a very clear view of his chest. I'd seen it before, of course, but sometimes it was nice to be reminded of how perfect it was.

"What is that?" He dipped a chin to my jar and set of bowls.

I looked to my full hands and back up to him, realization settling in. "Oh. Did I not introduce you two?"

"Introduce...Rachel, that is a mason jar."

"No. This is *Myrtle*, my sourdough starter. She and I have been in a committed relationship for four years now." I dipped my head to the almost full jar in question. "Myrtle, this is Adam. My husband for as long as he can manage to not kick us out."

Adam clicked his tongue and shook his head before turning around to walk out the door.

I widened my eyes and gasped. "Are you not going to say anything? She thrives when given words of affirmation."

"*She* is essentially a jar of water and flour."

"Who has feelings the same as everyone else, Adam. If you're going to be married to me for the foreseeable future, I should hope you would accept my child as well."

"Your chi—you know what? Fine." He turned his head over his shoulder and eyed Myrtle, in all of her healthy, bubbly glory. "Hello," he grumbled, clearly unsatisfied.

"Was that so hard?" I mused.

Adam didn't answer. He simply opened the door to the hallway and stepped out, propping it open with his foot for me.

He flexed in his stuck position. He was an absolute sight. All muscled legs he worked incredibly hard for and a ripped back that was still sporting the most delicate wings on as he held my bright yellow luggage. He was something deserving of a magazine spread. Or maybe a column in a BuzzFeed article.

"Myrtle, your daddy is looking mighty fine," I whispered to her.

"What?" Adam asked loudly from the hall.

"Nothing."

CHAPTER SIXTEEN

Adam / Then

Currently Playing: I Still Haven't Found What I'm Looking For by U2

***

Listening to my dad and Crew fight over who should have won the trophy in *Master Chef* season six was not how I planned to spend my Saturday night.

But I never really made plans most nights anyway. I spent the majority of my time working, and when I was home, I found my hands itching to get busy.

It was what jump-started my collection of "impossible puzzles." It began as a joke. Liam got me a fully white puzzle a couple of years ago for Christmas. I liked a challenge. I liked to push myself to my wits' end and see how far I could stretch. It took me almost a week, but I did it. Then I found more: clear puzzles; all-black puzzles; and rainbow, but the colors faded and bled into each other. Each one was more difficult than the last, yet somehow addictive.

But instead of sitting at my table, listening to that ridiculous playlist Rachel had made for me while I considered each piece and sipped on a black coffee, I was here. Here wasn't bad, necessarily. I loved my family. They got on my nerves a lot, but I did like to see them. Just in moderation. It was the same way I liked everything else. Other than Rachel.

But the loud nights with multiple conversations going on—Calla boasting about almost being done with school, my mom talking about baking, and Liam nonstop messing with Marigold—added up. My ears would start to burn, and my feet would be desperate to push me to the door so I could breathe again.

It was the same every time. I would convince myself it was all in my head and force myself as long as I could. I'd try to make it to dessert, to enjoy time with the few people who cared about me. But without fail, by the end of dinner, I'd be over the conversation, overstimulated, and desperate to get back to my quiet apartment.

The back door opened with a creak, then Layla and Luke walked in hand in hand. My hands wrapped around my glass when I heard a soft but confident voice. "Hey guys."

My chin jerked up and my eyes widened at the sight of Rachel, who was dressed in a bright yellow sundress, standing in my mom's kitchen. The water lodged in my throat. My face went hot and my chest got tight. I coughed up a choke, beating on my chest. I dipped my head down so no one would see how red my face was turning.

It wasn't like we hadn't been around my family together before. She had been at the book signing, and we'd been at

Romfuzzled on the same night. But I'd always been able to plan for it, work around it, mentally prepare myself for whatever she was going to come out with or the possibility that she'd show up in one of those tiny denim skirts again.

I cleared my throat, glancing up and discovering that everyone else's casual pre-dinner conversations hadn't stopped. Because why would it? It wasn't like they knew anything about Rachel and me or what had happened between us.

My mom's arms wrapped around Rachel's back and pulled her into a tight hug. I could make out the words "it smells amazing in here" coming from Rachel as she embraced by mom, but my mind was stuck somewhere else. Stuck on that short yellow dress with white polka dots on it and the tall wedges she'd paired with it.

Funny how I had never been attracted to women like her before. I always wanted to be the quietest in the room, the one who pulled in the least attention. Women like Rachel—beautiful, bright, always done up—were always going to attract all the eyes around them. Being with someone like that would deprive me of my solitude.

I knew that, deep down. But watching her smile light up each room, knowing that she had a dark background and still carried a smile so big? I was enamored. I had tried to ignore her. I had tried to pretend my heart rate didn't kick up like I was mid-run when I caught sight of her at the bar the first night. And then again at the record store. I should have left it alone after that. I knew her name, and I knew she was all too close to my family for us to ever be anything. But then she invited me to see her dad, to see this little sneak peek behind the scenes of what goes on in her daily life, and I couldn't resist. I loved a good puzzle.

Dad and Crew carried on their conversation, arguing over the top two contestants of their favorite show. I stood silently, passing by them and sneaking out of the back door. I needed air and space. I choked around her, mentally and physically.

I took a seat on the white Adirondack chair off to the side, facing the lights strung across the backyard. Each time I came here, it seemed like there was something new. Started with the potted flowers, then the hot tub, and then the extension on the deck. My dad had been renovating the place in the same way Liam was doing to his own house, nonstop keeping their hands busy. Guess that was a trait all of us Wellses possessed.

A brief moment passed before the back door opened. I didn't have to guess who it was, because the summer night wind carried her scent to me. Tangerines and clean laundry. It was how my bed had smelled for days and how my shirt had smelled after she danced with me.

I took a deep breath through my nose, focusing my vision on the ripple of water in the pool caused by the pump. Watching the tiny waves slowly bounce from one wall to the other.

Her tall sandals tapped against the wooden deck as she made her way to the chair next to me. She slowly dropped into it and shifted her dress to cover her legs.

"Your mom told me to get you for dinner." She said it almost like a whisper.

I hummed, somewhat amused. Of course she did. Mom met a girl one time, mentally paired her with one of her sons, and heard wedding bells instantly. It wasn't a surprise that she would handpick Rachel to come get me rather than any person from my family inside.

Part of me felt guilty sitting here, knowing I hadn't told Rachel I was back in town. To be fair, I'd only gotten back the night before. I was going to eventually say something. We had been texting for the last month. Not always consistently, but she knew I was thinking of her, and I knew the same for her.

She shifted in her seat, her long legs facing my direction, causing me to shift as well. "Nice to know you're back in town."

She didn't sound angry or upset, and not exactly surprised either. Just neutral, which somehow made this feel even more uncomfortable. I glanced up at her. She wasn't necessarily smiling, but she looked amused, pleased with herself. Her eyes narrowed at me softly, her pink lips lifting in the corners ever so slightly.

I cleared my throat. "Got back yesterday."

It wasn't like I needed to apologize. We weren't even friends. Why would I text her that I was back in town? It would have felt weird and clingy. So why did the word *sorry* sit on the edge of my tongue, desperately trying to make its way out?

Rachel hummed, looking from me out to the backyard. The golden glow of strung lights danced across her face. I liked that she never pushed me to talk. If anything, she probably liked that I was quiet so she could fill the room with her own conversation. Somehow it made me want to say things. Made me want to expand on more than my average less-than-five-word sentences.

"Are you upset?" I asked, forcing my hands into my pockets so as not to wring them in my lap.

She snorted an amused laugh, and my blood pressure immediately skyrocketed. This was why I didn't do anything more.

Complicated feelings that I didn't know how to pick up on left me feeling like my brain was overwhelmed, my head too heavy on my shoulders. Why couldn't people always say exactly how they felt? No more of this wondering bullshit. I wanted real, authentic, raw truth.

Rachel must have picked up on my confusion because her smile lowered into a softer one. "No, Adam. I'm not upset. Although in the future, it would be nice to get an update when you're in town. Who knows? Maybe I had a surprise for you."

"Did you?"

"No." She smiled at me. "But I would have."

That made me snort. I didn't need some kind of gift for doing my job. You wouldn't bring a surprise to people working at the DMV, so why do it for me?

"Don't do that," I mumbled.

Her head cocked to the side as she lifted her hand, bringing one of her braids down to twirl it between her fingers. "Why? We're friends, right?"

"No." My response was sharp. But the last thing I wanted to be was *friends* with this woman in front of me. I didn't have friends. I most certainly didn't sleep with them and let them run through my head for weeks after.

"Are you sure?" She squinted at me. "I *feel* like we're friends."

I dropped my eyes to her white fingernails twirling her braid, my thoughts racing with the need to pick up that hand and hold it. To pull her to me and remind her of how I kissed her, how she felt underneath me. How pretty she was, how it felt like holding a tulip. Like I was scared to move one way or the other, worried it would break in my fingers.

I croaked out, "We're not."

"You met my dad. Not even all my bestest friends have done that."

Crap. That only made this worse. I didn't have time for more. Neither did she. She'd made it as clear as I had. As far as visiting her dad, I wasn't sure what I'd expected, but a young and healthy vet threatening to hunt me down if I ever hurt his daughter wasn't exactly it. I liked the guy. He was brutally honest, but he held that same light that Rachel carried around with her. I hated for him to get the wrong idea and go assuming that she and I would ever be anything.

"Well, I don't really do friends."

She sighed with a shrug and stood from her chair. "Seems to me like you don't do *just* friends."

Turning on her heel, she clicked back inside as if she hadn't just thrown a bomb at my chest.

I tried to leave. Multiple times. But each time my eyes and feet pointed toward the door, I felt this pull like I had to stay. Like a tiny thread was tying my shoes to the chair I sat in. I could easily break it. I simply couldn't make myself do it. I wasn't exactly wanting to stay and listen to family conversation as my mom forced us each to have at least one slice of cake. Luke and Layla were in their own world. A world, I assumed, where they could both use telepathy, because there was definitely some kind of unspoken conversation happening there. Beside them, Rachel happily listened to my dad, leaning in toward him as he discussed his old love of model trains.

I waited for a signal. For her to turn and give me "help me out over here" eyes. But she didn't. Instead, she asked him questions, leaned close to hear him better, laughed at his poor jokes, and agreed when he offered to bring them out next time she came to dinner.

I couldn't help but wonder if she was so content here because she didn't have this herself. The bits and pieces I'd picked up on from her told me the only true family she had was her dad. And if that was the case, when was the last time she'd even had a family dinner? When had someone forced her to eat home-cooked meals and chocolate cake made from scratch? My mind began imagining her and her dad at Christmastime alone, exchanging gifts and eating dinner in his retirement home. My chest ached at the thought. No, I didn't want to be friends with her, but I didn't want her alone. In fact, when I imagined next Christmas, I pictured her at this exact spot. In some kind of fancy holiday dress with her hair perfectly done. I would probably have to dress nice too, to stand next to her, but that was all right.

When dessert was finished up, Crew excused himself so he could go back to his food truck and help his employees out for the rush hour. Marigold and the boys slipped out since it was a school night, which meant Liam was right behind them. Calla yawned and claimed she needed to get back to her dorm since she had an early class. All of them trickled out one by one.

I always missed this part. Usually, I shoveled enough food into my mouth to satisfy my mom and then made sure I gave my siblings each their respective time. That was all there was to do. No sense in staying. So why couldn't I get myself out of this chair and out of the door?

Instead, I watched as Luke and Layla discussed his new bar, going on about upcoming renovations and ideas for new drinks.

Rachel would chime in here or there, but she mostly sat in silence for once, taking slow bites of her cake as if she wanted this night to last a little longer.

"Adam, dear, could you help with the dishes?"

My mother's voice chimed from the kitchen, forcing me to stand and leave the table. Luke and Layla continued their conversation. Rachel looked up from my dad to give me a reassuring smile before paying attention to him again.

The dishes were 90 percent done, but my mom stuck me on drying duty as she hummed to herself and rinsed out the last few glasses.

"You stayed later tonight," she said, as if it was a simple observation and not like she was trying to pry into my brain.

I hummed low. "Nothing better to do."

Which, technically, was true. I had an all-blue puzzle back home that was halfway finished, and I probably would have worked out in my basement some, but that was it. Being here was better than either of those things at the moment, so I'd stayed. As if I had a choice.

"Right, of course." She nodded and picked up another glass. Silence fell between us other than the distant talking between the four of them at the table and the soapy water sloshing between tiny dessert plates. I took extra time drying them, working my hands through the smaller glasses as I focused in on Rachel's soft voice pouring in from the dining room.

Layla asked about her dad in some way. Not sure what exactly, but her response had my ears perking up.

"He's good. Struggled a bit earlier this week. They adjusted his medicine slightly for his blood pressure, and I think it messed with his levels a bit, so he got slightly confused about a few things. Nothing too bad, though. I was planning on seeing him tonight, but he said he didn't sleep well, so I figured rest would be better than me bothering him."

I could hear the smallest hint of a smile as she spoke, like she was reassuring Layla and herself both. She hadn't mentioned any of this in her never-ending texts. Majority of it was saying what music she was listening to that day. I recalled a lot of Tom Petty and some Bob Dylan. What did those say about her mood? If I listened to them tonight, would it give me another piece of her?

"Were you listening to anything I just said?" My mother twisted a towel and whipped my exposed bicep.

I straightened at the sting, lifting my disassociated gaze to her. "Sorry. Was thinking."

Her eyes squinted into slits. "*Sure.* I asked if you knew how long you would be in town for."

It was a question I never knew the answer to. I typically gave guesses, because truthfully, they could call me now, and I would take off. I loved my family, truly, but nothing tied me here. My parents were busy together, covered up with their extreme hobbies. Luke and Layla were in that obsessive phase before marriage and still kind of annoying to be around. Calla was in college, and although I loved seeing her, after I helped her move in one time, she swore girls in her dorm didn't stop asking about me for weeks. That gave me the creeps, and I officially decided to never go back. Liam was busy with his house and his two sons, plus constantly bothering Marigold. Crew had his booming food truck business to attend to. So that left me.

If work called in, I would answer simply because it kept me busy. Busy meant no time for thinking about pretty blondes who had been unknowingly taking up space in my brain.

"Not sure. About a month if I had to guess."

I set the last glass in the cabinet and closed it, turning back to my mom, looking down at her. She nodded with a smile up at me. "Good."

Moments later, Luke, Layla, and Rachel all padded through the kitchen, carrying their keys and looking ready to leave. She'd ridden with them. Of course she was going to leave with them. Logically, that made the most sense. But I had an overwhelming urge to offer to drive her. To watch her walk into her apartment and hear that door lock, knowing she was safe for the night. That wasn't my job to take care of, though. It's just...if I wasn't going to, was anybody?

"We're going to head out. Luke's got an early morning tomorrow," Layla explained before giving my mom and I both a quick side hug.

I dipped my chin in goodbye at my brother and turned my eyes toward Rachel. In that sweet dress, heels that brought her to my height, and her hands clasped in front of her waist, she swayed side to side like she was waiting for something. From me? Oh no. Was I supposed to hug her? What was the protocol here? I mean, I had kissed the woman no less than fifty times in a single night, and yet I was about to break out into a sweat thinking of a purely platonic side hug.

Sensing my panic, Rachel moved past me to give my mother a quick hug. Then she turned to me and placed a gentle hand on my bicep, giving it the lightest squeeze. Her smile reassured me. It was a slow one, but it was genuine.

"Night, Adam." She whispered it low, like a little secret between us. I glanced over at my family: Mom handing Layla a recipe ripped out of her notebook. Luke pretty much staring at his fiancée.

I turned my gaze back to Rachel, leaning into her gentle grip on my arm. "Night." My voice turned to gravel, forcing me to push it out.

Her smile grew ever so slightly at that before she pulled her hand back, leaving goose bumps in her absence.

As they walked out of the back door, I placed my own hand where she'd had hers, gripping the heat there.

"What a nice girl," Dad said as he entered the room, lifting his reading glasses to his head.

Mom nodded with a smirk. "A lovely girl." Her voice dripped with hidden meaning that I knew all too well. The woman always tried to be some kind of matchmaker, trying to look in our eyes and sense our future. It was the reason she refused to take down Liam and Marigold's wedding pictures. She was so sure they were going to end up together again.

"I see what you're doing." I reached for my keys to keep my hands busy and away from the phantom hold that had Rachel left on my arm.

Mom hummed before tossing her hand towel over her shoulder and leaning into my dad's side. "I see what you're *not* doing."

CHAPTER SEVENTEEN

Rachel / Now

Currently Playing: Home by Edward Sharpe and The Magnetic Zeros

***

Adam so kindly let me stuff his SUV full of my things, and I do mean *full,* to the absolute brim.

Any pushback I expected from him had yet to hit, if it ever was going to. He encouraged each bag that we filled the back seat with, and I tried with all my might to hold back any laughter as he struggled incredibly hard to pull off my very fragile fairy wings. He placed them on top of a bag and then moved the bag to see if they would fall. When they didn't sit as firmly as he liked, he ended up moving them to the center console between us, keeping his elbow propped up during the entire drive, in case they were to slip.

I once said he was a panther. I knew better now. The man was a teddy bear, all soft and doughy goo on the inside.

Myrtle sat in my lap, taking in the view of downtown Philadelphia as we made our way out of town, where Adam's house was on the outskirts. She never really got out of the cabinet much. I was sure she was bound to be extra bubbly tomorrow morning when it came time for me to make discard bagels.

Adam also let me be in charge of the auxiliary. He was used to it by now and didn't flinch when I reached for his charger to pull up Apple CarPlay. Today felt good. Productive and positive, filled with hope and a pinch of anxiousness. But the good kind. Therefore, Steely Dan's "Reeling in the Years" felt the most appropriate for the mood.

My foot tapped along on the side of the door, and I hummed the lyrics to myself as we reached the end of downtown. Adam's shoulders visibly dropped as he leaned back in his seat, slumping slightly. He always seemed more comfortable outside of the city than in. I was pretty sure it was the buildings. He once claimed he liked to see his surroundings better outside the city. Something from the military, if I had to guess, since Dad was the same way.

"Are you scared about me moving in?" I asked, breaking the quiet between us.

Adam lifted a brow in question before turning back to the road.

My lips turned into a grin. "It's okay if you are. It's a lot. I'm a lot, and you like your quiet space. It's okay if it's too much."

"You're not too much. You're just right." He turned on his signal, looking over his shoulder before switching lanes.

Heat trailed up my spine at that. *You're just right.* No, it wasn't some glowing declaration of who I was, like I'd foolishly dreamed about as a girl. Wasn't some long, drawn-out poem about how I was funny or smart or kind—I was, at most, average on each of those scales. But it felt good all the same.

Butterflies coursed through me at the thought of how quickly he said it, as if he hadn't had to think about it. As quiet as Adam was, when he spoke, whatever he said, he meant. You never had to wonder about the authenticity of what he said. The man was brutally honest, sometimes in harsh ways like when I'd asked what he thought of my somewhat "quirky" scarf last winter and he responded with "burn it."

I turned both air vents toward me, desperate to cool my flushed cheeks. "All right, Goldilocks. Whatever you say."

When we pulled into his driveway both of us grabbed a single bag as we made it to his front door. He fished out his keys, balancing my luggage in one hand before opening the door.

Whatever you pictured as a single man's bachelor pad—posters of half-naked women, dirty socks on the living room floor, perhaps some random woman's bobby pins in the guest bathroom—wipe it from your mind completely. Adam Wells's house, to no surprise, looked like an Airbnb that needed to be featured in a *Home and Garden* magazine. Shoes perfectly straightened at the door, a simple gray sectional in the living room, white walls, large TV mounted on the wall, wooden kitchen cabinets, curtains. The man had curtains. I didn't even own a dishwasher.

I had been here before, several times. But it felt like I was seeing it through new eyes this time. *Wifey* eyes. Before, I'd never paid too much attention to my surroundings because it didn't occur to me that I should. I never noticed the man had dish towels hung up perfectly in the kitchen or that he owned stone bathmats and towel warmers. Who would have thought that, this whole time, grumpy, broody Adam liked his towels to be warmed?

"You can...look around. I'll go grab more stuff," he announced as he stepped outside again.

He knew me so well. I would have protested, but curiosity got the best of me. I was too busy being hypnotized by perfectly clean floors and not a hint of dust in the room. Where were his dirty socks? Probably laid perfectly in a laundry basket next to his label maker and his abundance of cleaning supplies, right behind his mini vacuum.

I peered around the kitchen and down a long hallway leading to two rooms. My feet padded down the hall as I quickly peeked into each open doorway.

One was an office with forest green walls and a cleared-off mahogany desk. There were no pictures or shelves, simplicity. Very Adam. I turned to the other room, a guest room with a dark-blue accent wall. The remaining three were painted white. A queen-size mattress in the middle, an oak nightstand on either side of it. My room, I would presume.

Unless...was I supposed to sleep in his room? I mean, sure, we were married, but that didn't require us to share a bed, right? I felt like a good majority of married couples slept separately nowadays. This had to be fine.

I turned around, my boots clicking against the stained concrete floors. Poor guy had seen my apartment, and he'd probably had an entire heart attack behind that cool, collected scowl. He didn't have a single thing misplaced. Even the bed had fluffed pillows and a throw blanket that looked extra snuggly.

With a bite to my lip, I glanced out toward the hallway, checking to make sure it was clear before running straight for the bed. I lay on top, sinking into the white comforter, the mattress bending underneath my weight and cradling me like a mom holding her newborn. Marriage or not, this guy was going to be stuck with me until I could afford a Purple mattress. This was glorious.

The front door creaked, followed by heavy footsteps and some deep groaning. I sat straight up, reaching my hands out to fluff the creases I'd made. I took my shoes off, keeping a mental note to straighten them at the door later so I didn't seem like a total mooch.

Back in the living room, Adam carried half of the carload in his arms—boxes on top of bags and my backpack on his back. He set down each luggage piece with grace, looking entirely adorable in his very gray house with my very yellow baggage.

I watched, making a show of the beads of sweat at his brow, as Adam single-handedly carried my things in with no complaints. All I was missing was popcorn and a remote so I could slow him down and rewatch him over and over again. On the next trip, he lifted his shirt up to wipe his forehead, and I knew immediately this must have been the guy Bonnie Tyler was singing about when she said she needed a hero. Here he was, in his living room, carrying a box full of heavy record player equipment as if it were nothing. I could see why she'd need a guy like this. I could get used to it. But she couldn't have him. This one had my ring on his finger, so suck it, Bonnie.

During the last round, I gave the guy pity and grabbed a couple of the smaller boxes. Just enough to keep me from feeling entirely lazy. But not before I pulled my phone from my back pocket, discreetly lifting it to snap a quick picture of a sweaty Adam holding a box full of my "necessities." I immediately went to text my best friend.

Layla, you should see the show being put on in front of me right now.

Layla: Since that is technically my brother-in-law, I shouldn't say anything but…smash.

I wonder how much money I would make if I set up a live stream right now.

But I also want to keep it to myself.

Layla: It or him?

Both?

Layla: Careful now, you sound jealous.

Is it bad that I am? I think this ring is getting to me. I'm feeling very wife-like watching him carry all my things in.

Layla: Oh my gosh. This is exactly like LOTR.

Can you not?

Adam cleared his throat, pulling me back into the present. With everything moved in, spread across his spotless floor, he looked up at me, nodded toward the room, and tilted his head. *Do you like it?* I could practically hear it in that deep gravel.

I looked down the hall and back with a smile. I loved it. He had to know I did. The guy didn't expect me as a guest, much less his wife, and yet he had the perfect room set up for this scenario.

"You've been holding out on me. I didn't know you were this much of a caretaker. You have folded towels in the guest bathroom at the ready?" I threw a thumb over my shoulder.

His lips tipped up in amusement. "I like to take care of things that are mine."

"Does that include me now?" I leaned in with clasped hands and batting eyelashes like the doting wife I was.

His eyes dropped to my lips and back to my eyes. "Do you want it to?"

Oh, great heavens. Yes. No. Adam was not allowed to flirt with me. Not while I was in this state. *I* was the flirter. He was the flirtee. That was how this always worked. But if he started acting like this, carrying in all my things, acting as though I *was* his, wearing my stupid fairy wings, what chance did I have of keeping myself intact?

My brain began to shut down, random words like *mine* and *want to* rolling in my brain like a tumbleweed in an otherwise very empty space. I wouldn't have been surprised if my tongue lolled out of my mouth and my back bent over as I stared at the poor man in utter confusion.

"Too much?" he asked, a hint of vulnerability in there that made me feel a little bad about practically panting over him moments before.

I shook my head before placing a rogue tendril of hair behind my ear. "Not too much. Just not expected."

He nodded along, as if to say he understood. "Do you want all of this in your room?"

It was a lot to squeeze in a medium-size space, but I felt more comfortable forcing it all into the guest room than taking over his entire house.

I nodded. "Yeah, that would be great. I'll help."

Adam grabbed two boxes as I picked up my record player, glancing around us. He padded down the hallway, and I smiled. Maybe this would work out.

"Myrtle said she likes it here. Just so you know," I called down the hall toward him.

"Good," he deadpanned. "I was worried."

CHAPTER EIGHTEEN

Rachel / Then

Currently Playing: You Really Got a Hold On Me by Percy Sledge

***

There was nothing that a bacon cheese scone and Elton John couldn't fix.

Specifically, 'Tiny Dancer.' It fit in perfectly with the rain dripping outside the store's floor-to-ceiling windows and the fact that my boss was still considering shutting the place down.

Arthur and his wife, Cheryl, had owned Sip 'n' Spin for as long as I could remember. When I was eight years old, Dad pulled me into the store and showed me the prettiest covers, going into grave detail about how the grooves in each vinyl caused vibrations, like how our throats do. How music was a real, physical, tangible thing. Not just Bluetooth and speakers or something you can pull up on a touch screen. But how it started here, how each record held its own story. A past, a memory.

He told me that each microscopic groove, left or right, was imperative to music. They each held a purpose, they added value to the entire experience. He bent down to my level and said I was the exact same way. I, as small and young as I was, held incredible value to this giant floating rock in space.

Life hadn't been the same since.

Now, that same store was looking at possibly closing down this year. And I was supposed to idly sit by and watch it happen without a word? No. I was a groove. I was small but mighty, not some insignificant employee who kept her mouth shut, and Arthur knew it.

"Rachel, honey. I know it's hard."

"Hard? Crocheting is hard, making dinner without burning something is hard. This?" I waved my hands at the front of the store. "This is impossible. You can't let this go." My voice was wavering, but I forced down any inkling of tears that were building up in my eyes. I wasn't going to pathetically cry over this. Not in front of him, anyway. I was going down with a fight.

Arthur sighed, took a spare cloth, and wiped his brow as he sat in the old white leather chair behind him. "This was always Cheryl's thing. I loved it because she did. But she's gone, and I need to rest. I need stability, this place"—he waved his hand around the store—"doesn't give that."

But that was the thing, wasn't it? Sip 'n' Spin was anything but standard. It wasn't some new, cool place that people came into because of flashing neon signs or because of its trending accent walls. And sure, there were a few leaks, maybe some asbestos in the walls, but that was all part of the beauty of it.

It could use updates, absolutely, but if they sold it to some investor, I could guarantee they would slap white paint everywhere and turn it into a trendy coffee shop with new light fixtures. Maybe they'd have one stack of records in the far back used for photo ops.

And unless some new owner was willing to keep the girl who was belovedly attached to a physical building and was going to scream if they dared to take down our original *Abbey Road* art and throw up some kind of *Live, Laugh, Love* sign in its wake, then I was jobless.

Or unless I could convince Art that there was enormous value here. That with the right updates and some expert social media coverage, this place could be packed full every day like it had been during Layla's book signing.

Lightbulbs began to flash in my mind at the thought of renovating it. No, not renovating. Rebranding. Keeping the good, getting rid of the bad, and tying it up in this pretty bow that wouldn't kick out the authenticity of what this place was and what it meant to people like me.

I leaned against the clear counter in front of Arthur, both of my hands pressed into the glass, and a smile broke out on my face. "What if we could make it like how Cheryl did?"

Art made a point of looking around the store with a grimace. "It's hardly been touched since Cheryl did it."

I shook my head, fully prepared to figure out how to make him see. "No, I mean what if we could make it *feel* the way Cheryl made it feel?"

He didn't scowl at me or brush me off, but he didn't show any satisfaction at the idea either.

I continued. "Remember what it was like at its peak? People lining down the street to come in? How everyone felt like this place was so classic but yet still keeping up with the times? I mean we could do that."

Art grumbled with his wrinkled hand waving around. "Bah. I don't have the budget for something like that. I redid the place once, and I don't want to do it again."

My fingers tapped on the glass as I reached my tiptoes. "No, no. No redoing or ripping out floors. Nothing like that. I'm talking about changing logos, rearranging storage. Maybe moving this to the far wall where the coffee stuff is." I turned to the front of the store, pointing around like this was *The Sims* and I was rearranging my virtual bedroom. "Bring the bookshelves closer and maybe find a cool accent chair here. Oh and—"

"Listen, doll. I appreciate what you're trying to do. I know you and your dad loved this place like it was your own. But I don't have the time or energy for this—"

"But I do!" I butt in, lifting my hands to my chest. "I could do it. You could give me a budget, and I could pull numbers, and oh! Charts. I'll make charts and pull pictures from Pinterest and make some mood boards."

"Mood what?" He squinted.

I rounded the corner of the checkout area over to our chairs, taking a seat in mine and leaning toward him. "Oh Art, come on. It could be incredible. And then you wouldn't have to sell, and I could keep my job."

He took his glasses off with a sigh, pinching the bridge of his nose in annoyance before looking up at me. "I'm not saying no—"

I bit my lip in a smile and shook my body from side to side.

"But I'm not saying yes."

Who was he kidding? Of course he was saying yes. And why wouldn't he? Art knew I adored this place, and I refused to let it go.

I stood up and clasped my hands. "Thank you, thank you. You're going to love it, old fart."

"I've told you a hundred times to stop calling me that."

Ignoring him, I squealed with excitement and reached for my keys. We'd closed down about an hour before, when Arthur had sat me down and said he was prepared to list the place by the end of the year. That timeline meant I had almost ten months to get to work on convincing him, and I knew exactly how I could do it.

Running out of the back door and through the gravel parking lot, I reached for my phone and immediately texted Calla, considering she was the marketing guru of the Wells family.

On a scale of one to ten, how difficult would it be to have you help me rebrand the record store?

Her response came in a moment later.

Calla: ARE WE WORKING ON SIP 'N' SPIN??

Calla: A 3. Possibly a 2 if we can get Philly cheesesteaks on the job.

A smile broke out on my face as I tapped my feet in excitement. I knew she would be excited, since she was in the middle of getting her marketing degree. Calla was known to sign up for any projects involving branding or social media.

I climbed into my car, getting out of the light drizzle tapping against the door. Settling into the driver's seat, I began to reply, but I was interrupted when my phone rang.

Adam.

Crap. I forgot to tell him I was running late.

We'd begun a sort of tradition. Well, I had, mostly. It consisted of me calling him every time I worked nights. He'd gone on some rant weeks ago about how many women go missing every year and the number of unsolved cases involving people who work late at night in big cities. My solution was to call him as I walked to my car and drove home. He refused to hang up until I got into my apartment. But that being said, it usually led to us talking for far longer than we meant to. Sometimes I would wake up in the middle of the night on my couch, clutching and drooling on my phone.

"Hey," I answered.

"You didn't call," Adam rasped out with panting breaths, like he was running.

"Sorry, my boss and I were talking for a while and, well, it's kind of a long story."

I couldn't see him, of course, but I could feel him nodding across the line.

"Is he going to sell?"

That question was hard to answer. Convincing Arthur not to sell wasn't going to be easy. It was borderline impossible, but it would be worth it. It wasn't that I wanted the poor guy to work forever. I really wanted to show him the possibilities this place had. If he kept me as manager and truly let me take charge of rebranding and setting up this place so it practically ran itself by just implementing a few new systems, he wouldn't have to work another day in his life. And he would keep his wife's most valued treasure.

"I…don't know." A tiny piece of hope flickered at the thought of a yes. That hope was tiny but mighty, like I was. It was enough to push me through and inspire me to do the next right thing. That was all there was to do.

I lifted my shoulders. "But it's possible. I'm going to work on an entire new branding shift. Calla is going to help, and between the two of us, I feel like we could convince him."

The silence from Adam didn't feel like his usual quiet nature. It felt daunting, like he was holding back. Each beat of stillness made me more uneasy about my plan until I broke the tension.

"Is that not a good idea?"

"No," he supplied without hesitation. "It's a great idea."

"But?" I added, knowing there had to be a contradiction in there somewhere.

"But what happens if you spend all this time and energy, and he still says no?"

Truthfully, I hadn't let myself get that far. It was more of a coping mechanism. A *we'll cross that bridge when we get there* mindset to save me from dying out like a flickering flame. Right now, that was what I was in control of. That was all I could process, so that was what I was sticking to.

"Then…I'll have done my best. But I can't do that if I don't try my all."

Adam cleared his throat, his breathing picking up again. "Sounds like a plan."

I started my car and peeled out of the parking lot. "Are you running right now or something?"

"Yes," he firmly replied with this puff of air behind it.

"Is someone chasing you?"

"No."

"Then why are you running?" I sneered.

"It's relaxing. Calms your mind."

I wondered what kind of things ran through a mind like Adam's. Other than the basic necessities in life. Did he dream? Think of future goals in work, family, maybe even marriage? Did he think of his siblings, his parents? Maybe even me?

"I prefer a sudoku for things like that."

I turned on my right signal, heading toward the area of town where my apartment was.

"I remember that." His throat cleared again. "The time I came to the record store."

A smile painted over my lips. That was a cute little memory. Stuttering Adam, back when I didn't even know his name, much less his relation to my best friend and former roommate. A slither of hope had rested in me at the thought of him asking me out. But disappointment settled in the second I saw him and Layla talking. Luke's brother. Off limits as anything casual. And casual was all I could ever do. But still, I figured he would be a nice guy to look at. Great kisser. I never pictured an actual friendship blossoming out of it.

"Yes, you gave me a heart attack and made me drop it."

A sarcastic snort came from my phone speaker, widening my smile. "Why did you have it with you at work?"

I shrugged. "I make sure to do two a day. One in the morning and one at night. Keeps your brain young."

I would be lying if I didn't admit it was partially because I was terrified of ending up like my dad. Something that was probably not going to happen, considering his doctors traced it back to his military days, taking too many hits at such a young age. But it felt like a comfort to tell myself it was somewhat avoidable either way.

"Hmm."

A comfortable, familiar silence fell between us. The kind of silence that settled in when I kept him on the phone while running errands or eating dinner. Where neither of us was speaking, but neither had to, either. It was enough to just be living our lives with each other in the background.

As I pulled into the parking garage connected to my complex and parked, I settled into my seat and leaned back. "So, now that we're besties—"

"No."

"Amigos, then. Does this mean you'll look over what Calla and I come up with before I present it to Arthur?"

He fell quiet for a moment, his breathing leveling out and his fast-paced jog seeming to slow into a gentle walk.

"Of course," he confirmed with his deep, slow, molasses-like voice that gave me goose bumps all over.

Adam didn't say much, but when he did, he had all the right words. Even if it was a flat out no.

CHAPTER NINETEEN

Rachel / Now

Currently Playing: Open Your Eyes by Snow Patrol

***

I loved Adam's house in the morning.

It was great last night, especially when I asked where Myrtle would have a little cozy warm spot in his kitchen, and he provided me with this perfect little corner cabinet. But this morning was wonderful too.

Waking up to a note on the counter that said *Going on a run. Coffee is ready. Just hit button* was super cute. As if the man thought I didn't know how to work a Keurig. Either way, I tucked away his little note as a reminder to leave him one later. *To lock house, key goes in deadbolt and turns.* It would probably tick him off, but I liked doing that to him here and there. It usually made this one vein in his temple pop out. I saw it very rarely, like an old friend saying hello.

My hands reached to pull Myrtle out of her cozy cabinet. Behind her were her favorite flour and a bottle of whiskey that cast a soft golden glow against the glass of her jar.

"Good morning, my dear. You are looking bubbly and full."

I gently set her on the counter and reached for a mixing bowl, which was one of the first things Adam showed me in his kitchen, as if he knew it was the first thing I would be grabbing this morning.

Taking a half cup measurement, I scooped half of the mixture into the bowl and immediately grabbed the unbleached flour stowed next to the whiskey.

Mid-feeding, Adam opened his back door, walking in with a bare, panting chest, his mix of floral and nautical tattoos staring at me. I think the siren/mermaid one sent a wink my way. My whisk-holding hand jolted to a stop as I appreciated the view in front of me.

Tall, tan skin peppered with art like a doughnut covered in the most decadent sprinkles. He must have left in his T-shirt but gotten overheated on his run, because the almost-see-through white material was now hanging across his neck, leaving nothing but bare exposed chest muscles flashing my way. I said a quick prayer. *Thank you, God, for the most recent heat wave coming through our town. I know I complained the other day when my leather seats burned my legs, but I take it all back now.*

"Are you making something?" his voice cut in, but that deep, gravelly tone wasn't enough to yank my gaze from his body. My eyes were stuck on the spattered designs that started around his left pec and reached to the top of his shoulder. A couple of words in cursive here and there, an angel near his belly button, a few others I probably should have known but my brain was doing that thing where it spaced out and everything goes blurry.

"Rachel." He checked in with a hint of concern.

"Yes?" I answered his left pec. "Discard bagels. Maybe some blue...berry." My voice drifted away like a fairy in the wind. I might as well have been on another planet.

Adam took a few steps toward me. I took a couple of steps back, not trusting my hands not to reach out and touch. I had seen the man shirtless, of course—nothing too new there—but those times were...different. This felt like I was allowed to stare unashamedly, and believe me, I did.

My back hit the countertop, the handle of the drawer digging into my behind. I leaned back as Adam stepped one foot closer.

My chest fluttered and my breathing kicked up a notch. Was he going to kiss me?

Once again, been there, done that. But still, that was before I had this ring on my finger. Now, if he kissed me, it would mean a whole lot more than two friends who were clearly attracted to each other. This ring made things dangerous. It would change everything if we weren't careful. Layla was right. This was just like *The Lord of the Rings*.

He had me backed into a corner, literally, with nowhere to go. His eyes smoldered, dipping down to my pink striped pajamas and back up, a dark cascade of brown and green mixed like the coziest forest. Oh gosh, he was definitely going to kiss me.

I thought so until his eyes shifted above my face and to the cabinet above me.

Looking back down at me, he lowered his brows in confusion before he tilted his chin up. "Need a glass," he rumbled off in the distance. Or it felt distant, considering all I could do was stare at his chest tattoos.

I cleared my throat and took a step to the left, letting him into the cabinet. He reached for a glass, a real glass and not one of the 1990s collectible *Winnie the Pooh* glasses that filled my cabinets. He filled up his glass with water and threw it down, his Adam's apple bobbing in the process.

Right. This was his house. His kitchen and his place to roam shirtless. I was sure he didn't want me taking over the place and ogling him like this was some kind of reverse Hooters.

I grabbed my mug, thankful I considered the pink one with white flowers to be an essential because the plain black ceramic mugs in Adam's house didn't fit with my pj's or my aesthetic.

"So I was going to see my dad today." I drank a sip of coffee and took my seat at his island.

Adam nodded, his back turned toward me as he made his own coffee.

"He'll like that. Are you going to tell him about..."

"Us being married? I figured I should. The ring would confuse him, and the workers will find out soon enough, so it's best if he heard it from me. If I handle it right, he should be fine."

Dad liked Adam. Well, more like loved him. He asked about him almost every time I visited and usually several times during my visit if he didn't remember my answers. He also said he would need to join us for Thanksgiving this year. So as far as sons-in-law go, he was far from the worst guy my dad could get. And there was a chance he wouldn't remember.

My dad usually remembered past experiences best. He could recall his military days or even my childhood like they were yesterday. His detailed stories about him and my mom on their honeymoon were bittersweet to sit through. But the more recent memories, within the last seven years or so, were where he got the most confused. If I wasn't careful, I would have to explain Adam being my husband at least ten times.

But then again, this was temporary. Just enough to get us both back on our feet and settled comfortably. A guy like Adam, traveling constantly and busy being what I assumed was Philadelphia's most eligible bachelor, wasn't going to want to be tied down forever. And neither was I. Mostly. The whole drinking coffee shirtless in his kitchen had potential to change that.

Adam paused for a moment, taking a sip of his coffee before leaning his back against the countertop. "Do you want me to come with you?"

I considered it for a moment and tossed the idea of going alone or with Adam back and forth before settling. Even if he didn't stay inside of Dad's house when I told him, it would be nice knowing there was support outside or in the car.

So I straightened my back and smiled. I wrapped my hands around the warm mug and pulled it close to me, its heat spreading through my fingers and into my chest. "That would be amazing, actually. He likes you a lot, so it might help more than hurt."

Adam nodded and drank his coffee with me in comfortable silence, basking in the glow of the morning sun peeking through his windows. My first full day here, and yet I was already dreading its end. Already wanting to plant my roots and watch them grow.

When we pulled into the assisted living community, I unbuckled my seat belt and faced Adam. "Remember, he might get confused and lash out. It's not because he's mad or doesn't—"

"Rachel," Adam interrupted before sticking his hand out to lightly grasp my wrist in the most delicate touch. Funny how a man so large and in control could be so gentle. "You do this every time. I know how this goes. Don't apologize. I like your dad."

That confirmation alone settled my steady heart rate, and the warmth wrapping around my wrist from his calloused hand wasn't hurting either.

I nodded and stepped out of the car, coming around to the driver's side where Adam was. I'd made sure to text Dad earlier that I was visiting and that Adam would be coming too. He responded with *I've got Fleetwood Mac going. Come on in when you get here.* Which made me smile to no end, causing Adam to ask what he said. When I showed him, Adam, let out the tiniest smile and made a comment under his breath about his nickname for me, Stevie.

It had to be a good day today, considering I didn't get any kind of heads-up from his nurse after his morning check-in. Not to mention he answered me clearly and quickly. That would make this process smoother, at least.

Adam reached a hand out, locking our fingers together. I looked up at him. He wasn't smiling or frowning. But he wore this reassuring expression, his eyes making sure I knew it was going to be okay. The tightened squeeze he pulsed through his fingers to mine steadied that reassurance. I nodded. He nodded back.

A silent agreement between partners that no matter what happened, we had each other. And in times like these, I was incredibly grateful for that.

Dad told us to walk right in, but no matter how often he said that, I could never bring myself to actually do it. So I knocked and waited patiently as Dad shouted, "I am not buying another one of those damn cookie dough boxes from your grandson, so keep on moving, Brenda. If he wants to go to space camp so bad, then tell him to build a rocket to get there."

Adam snorted beside me, and I covered my twisted mouth with my hand before elbowing his side. "It's us, Dad!" I shouted back.

Two seconds later, the door was open wide with my father on the other. He was in his typical khakis and Phillies baseball tee, with a splitting grin across his face. "There's my girl."

He reached out to envelop me in a hug, wrapping his arms around my back and pulling me tight. I pulled back and let him and Adam shake hands. They both nodded to each other, my dad smiling up at him before he opened the door wider to let us in.

His place was always so well kept. It reminded me of Adam's. I guess military habits died hard and whatnot, but still. Dad's house was basic. It was one of the smaller units, since the bigger ones were meant for couples or if someone had a family member staying with them. But all he needed was the standard two bedrooms, one bathroom, a small living room and kitchen, and a tiny office space in the corner. It was enough to keep him from feeling cramped, but not so much that he lost track of his things and got easily confused.

Before I'd gotten him settled in here, I'd come in with extra details to make his life easier. Label makers, extra signs, etc. Anything that seemed to cause added confusion in his life, I labeled. From marking where his toiletries go to adding a flippable switch on the dishwasher that said *clean* or *dirty*. I wanted anything that was going to make his life easier and happier.

He was still going to get lost. He was still going to have bad days and lash out. I knew that. But if any part of me could lighten that load when I couldn't physically be here, I did it.

He wasn't lying before about having Fleetwood Mac ready to go. In the far corner on his desk sat his record player, pouring out the *Rumors* album. His personal favorite and mine.

I smiled and sank into his comfortable couch as he handed Adam and me both a glass of lemonade. We thanked him and leaned against the back cushion, our knees inches apart.

"So..." I started. "Did you have a good day yesterday?" I asked as Dad relaxed in his recliner on the other side of the coffee table.

"Yup, yup." He clicked his teeth and tapped his foot to the beat, like he couldn't help himself. "Didn't get much done. Wish I'd gone to Marlo's or something."

I smiled and played along, despite knowing he hadn't been to Marlo's doughnuts in years. Mostly because he didn't have a car to drive and the Uber app was confusing to him on most occasions. But I brought them to him regularly, so I made a mental note to grab him an apple cider doughnut the next time I visited. Layla had brought him one way back when she first met him, and out of all of the things he could hook on to for a memory, it had to be that doughnut.

"They are the best. So, Dad, actually, Adam and I came here to talk to you about something."

Dad's eyebrows raised across from me, his head tilting as he glanced back and forth between us. How was I supposed to explain this? I couldn't openly say *Hey, Daddio, we drank too much and got married, and instead of simply getting an annulment, we decided to reap the rewards and basically steal from our government.*

I sucked in a deep breath as Adam's hand slipped behind me, rubbing slow circles on my back. It was fine. It was going to be fine.

"We decided to get married." An anxious smile played on my face as I lifted my left hand to flash my ring his way.

I watched his reaction in detail, waiting for any hint of emotion. Instead, his eyes traced my ring, like he was physically wrapping his brain around it. The corner of his lips pulled into a slow smirk, his smile line wrinkling and his eyes starting to scrunch at the corners. Then he let out a single, low "ha." He lifted a hand to Adam and shook his pointer finger at him. "You took longer than I thought."

My head swiveled to Adam beside me. A flush was starting at the base of his neck and reaching up to his scruffy chin, then disappearing behind his beard.

I shook my head. "Well, it's a bit sudden, I know—"

Dad scoffed loudly before sipping his own lemonade. "*Sudden*," he mocked. "Yeah, right."

Adam looked over to me and widened his eyes, as if to say he had no idea what he meant, and I leaned back against his hand in encouragement.

Well, he was still confused. But it wasn't the frustrated kind of confused or mad, lashing out kind of confused. So I would take it.

Dad stood from his recliner. "Well, come on. Give me a hug." He reached his arms out, so Adam and I stood.

I walked toward him with open arms, but Dad bypassed me and went straight to Adam, wrapping his arms around him and squeezing tight. "'Bout time, son."

Adam wrapped a single arm around his back, patting him once. He nodded my way with a wink and mumbled a quick "yes, sir." My heart soared at the small interaction. He didn't understand how much playing along meant to me, but maybe one day I'd find a way to do the same for him. I smiled at Adam behind Dad's back and mouthed a thank-you with a wink right back.

Turning to me, my father reached over and hugged me next before lifting my ring to his eyes. The light caught on the oval diamond and danced around my finger as he moved it left to right. "Ah, he did good, huh?" He looked over his shoulder at Adam. "I told him a princess cut was perfect for Little Miss Royalty over here."

My heart dropped ever so slightly. It felt like I was lying straight to his face. We hadn't had some big proposal. Adam hadn't asked my dad for permission beforehand. We didn't even have any of our family at the wedding itself. Nothing about this was traditional or what I'd dreamed up as a little girl, and my dad had no idea. He was in his own world, and even if that world made him happy, it broke my heart to not have him on this planet with me. It was selfish, but I didn't care. I was angry at the universe for taking someone so incredible and throwing them into a pit of confusion.

Sensing the cracks in my heart, Adam spoke up. "It fits her perfectly. You were completely right." He nodded to my dad, quick and short. "I'm glad I listened to you."

This man. Oh, this wonderful man that was better than a best friend. Better than I ever deserved and yet kept coming back again, over and over. He was such a light. Not the normal, flip-of-a-switch bright light that hurt your eyes when you entered the room. But he was this slow dimmer switch. With each day, with each action, he slowly brightened your life, and before you knew it, the whole room around you would be blanketed in a warm glow.

I smiled at him, feeling my body relax, piece by piece, down all the way to my toes. My thumb swirled my ring back and forth around my ring finger, and I bit my lip.

Dad went to sit back down. "Marriage is a beautiful thing. Not good for a man to be alone. God himself said so. He looked at man and said he needed something, so he made woman. And with that comes companionship and trust. It's hard, more days than not, but it will be worth it."

Fortunately, my dad mostly remembered the good days of his marriage. So he couldn't recollect my mother and sister both walking out on us when times got tough. Therefore, of course, to him, marriage was a beautiful thing.

"Keep in mind that love is a choice. One you have to choose daily. Do that and you two will be just fine." He nodded.

I looked over at Adam and smiled. No, we weren't in love. Well, at least not in the way my father was assuming. But I did think there was some form of love between us. It was just foggy on what kind or how it applied. Regardless, I knew that Adam was pivotal to my joy, and that meant I'd keep him around a little longer.

Dad cleared his throat. "Now, all of that being said, I'd like some grandkids here soon, so if you two could hop on that."

"Oh, I. Hmm. Well." I snorted at Adam's stuttering state, the way the pink of his cheeks deepened into red.

This had gone far, far better than I could have imagined.

CHAPTER TWENTY

Adam / Then

Currently playing: Dancing In The Dark By Bruce Springsteen

***

How's the sip 'n' spin stuff going?

Rachel: It's going great! Calla and I spent two hours on it the other night, and I'm feeling pretty good about it.

Rachel: I even have pie charts. Everyone loves pie.

They do. And if he's a smart man, he'll know that this is the best decision.

Rachel: Maybe. We'll see.

Attached* picture of Adam reading a book, forearm tattoos showing and feet propped up on a small ledge, wearing his uniform

Thanks for the book, by the way.

Rachel: Can I sell this pic on only fans or something? I feel like we would make a fortune together.

No.

This book is really….

Rachel: Fun?

Is that what they call it?

Rachel: According to your sister.

Didn't need to know that.

Rachel: I didn't need to know a lot of things that girl tells me, but here we are.

Just because you know doesn't mean I have to.

Rachel: Good book, though, right? How far into it are you?

It's pretty okay. Pirate Alek boarded the princess's ship. Things got…weird.

But I like the notes you put in here.

Rachel: Thought you might like my opinions on each scene. It's kind of like I'm there reading it with you! Like I'm in your pocket, following you around.

It's nice.

Rachel: *You're* nice.

Don't make it weird.

Rachel: Whatever you say, pirate Adam.

What did I just say?

Rachel: Arr, matey.

CHAPTER TWENTY-ONE

Adam / Now

Currently playing: Fast Car by Tracy Chapman

***

Rachel was closing tonight at Sip 'n' Spin tonight, and since I had nothing better to do than follow her like I was a lost puppy, I came to Crew's house. He was my only single sibling and the only one who I knew wouldn't be busy tonight. When I called, he was working on his truck. Something about tightening the rods in his engine. It was perfect timing, because my hands longed for something to do, even if it meant listening to him babble and fidget with the truck. We finished up within an hour, and with nowhere else to go, I followed him inside and accepted the cold craft beer he handed to me.

Over the last three weeks, Rachel and I had fallen into a routine. Since I was at home for now, we spent the majority of our free time together. Each morning, we had coffee together after my run. She would talk about her day's plans, and I'd listen intently. I mostly worked out when she was gone, or I took on projects, helping one of my siblings or working on my house. We shared dinner together every night. Sometimes she would sit down to do one of my puzzles with me—whilst calling me a grandpa—and we always went to bed separately, with a swift good night. If Rachel was the only one scheduled to work at the store, then she would ask me to feed and take care of Myrtle once a day. It kind of creeped me out at first, but now I was slowly becoming attached to the freaky jar of live mush. Don't know how that happened.

I liked our schedule. It made sense for both of us, and it meant seeing her as much as possible.

"So tell me, do you think if Einstein were alive today, he would enjoy street corn?" Crew popped his head out of his fridge, holding another bottle.

It was hard to know what was going to come out of the kid's mouth most days. I learned it was best to just go with it. Since Crew was the baby of the family, despite him now being twenty-two, he'd probably always feel like a kid to me.

"I, um..." What was I supposed to say to that?

"Because here's the thing: the thief across from me—"

"The woman who parks in the public parking lot next to you?"

"Sure, if that's what you want to call it. She's really into chemistry, apparently."

I took a sip of beer, leaning back into his couch. "How do you know?"

"I researched. Anyway, I overheard her make some kind of comment about some Maurice Cootie science lady and how she thinks she would love her food because she was a lady of good taste."

I stayed quiet, waiting for him to elaborate.

"So I thought the only science guy I know is Einstein, and I can't help but think he would enjoy some elote."

I wasn't sure where to go with that. But that was the nice thing about Crew. He carried the conversation himself. It probably wouldn't even matter whether I was here. If something was on his mind, it was already out of his mouth.

"I mean, the guy had class. And he knew what he was talking about. But I can't help but think he was a bit on the wild side with that hair. Hence, elote."

My phone buzzed beside me. A message from Rachel. I looked up to Crew to see him going on about *who cares about chemistry?* and reached for my phone.

Rachel: Don't bring pizza home tonight. I closed shop early and made some pasta and sourdough garlic bread.

Sounds great, I'll see you soon.

Rachel: Oh, we don't have anything to drink other than water, so maybe stop and grab something if you want?

Of course.

"You know?" Crew finished his tangent, and I looked up.

I nodded, despite my confusion over his entire argument about the girl and stood as I pocketed my phone. "Rachel's home. I should go."

Crew leaned back in his seat, his arms resting behind his head. "Ah, the honeymoon phase. Go on. I'll be here basking in my bachelor life."

I looked around at his living room. The discarded clothes and empty beer cans were a clear indication that he was, indeed, a bachelor. "Yup." I nodded before heading straight to my car.

Homemade pasta and garlic bread. I was getting spoiled by this girl.

I had no idea how much I loved sourdough bread until she moved in. She made two loaves a week, but I wish it was four. I'd never been a carb guy. I'd always stuck to a strict diet and didn't deter from it unless Mom was forcing me to eat her coconut cake. But when I came home to my house smelling of flour, honey, and butter, how was I supposed to resist? I was going to end up a hundred pounds heavier by the end of this arrangement, and I wasn't even going to complain.

Even harder to resist was Rachel in my kitchen, wearing a short floral dress that swirled around her thighs and an apron tied around her waist while dancing in circles to "Hey Jude." She'd see me come in and lean against the doorframe, watching, and she'd smile, spinning around faster, as if my presence made her want to dance more. An impossibly bright light in my cold house. A wildflower surrounded by weeds. I never knew how badly I needed that, how I had been stuck in survival mode without her. It made me wonder how many years I'd been stuck in that cycle, head stuck so far in the sand I couldn't even appreciate my surroundings for what they were.

I connected my phone to the console, reaching for the playlist she'd made for me years ago and putting it on shuffle. Maybe it was pathetic to keep listening to it. Probably something my work friends or brothers would scoff at if they knew. But I couldn't seem to give it up. It was the first piece of herself that she'd given me. That meant something, right? Even if it didn't, it had gotten me through some rough nights in the past, and I wasn't ready to give it up yet.

A couple of miles down from the house, I stopped at a corner store for a few drinks. I went to the back and looked at the long line of wines, not knowing anything about how they worked or what they paired with. Rachel was the most high-maintenance woman I'd met. She said so herself. She carried herself like royalty. I would assume that meant she probably knew something about wine and how much of an idiot was I going to look like when I pulled up to the house with some cheap fermented off-brand grape juice.

I did a quick Google search. *What wine goes with pasta?* I looked over the results, which made me even more confused, so I settled on the most expensive one. If she didn't like it, I'd just come back.

Checking out at the front, an older man scanned the wine. Behind him was a box full of premade flower bouquets.

She liked flowers, right? Always wore flower-print dresses. Had them on her phone's wallpaper and whatnot.

My eyes glanced down at the price. ***Assorted flower bouquet - $9.99.***

I'd never bought flowers for a girl before. Never felt the need to. Hadn't gone to prom or anything in high school, and the couple of girlfriends I'd had over the years didn't seem to care for it. Or maybe I was just an ass and didn't know it. It never really crossed my mind to buy them for any girl.

"Is this it for you?" the older man asked with a shaky voice.

I glanced at the flowers once more, feeling every kind of conviction to buy them. Imagining her wrapping her hands around them, dipping her nose in to smell them, and pulling them to her chest with that pretty smile I liked so much. My heart began to thud against my chest.

"One of the bouquets too." I pointed behind the older man. It wasn't like it had to be some kind of romantic gesture. Just a husband buying flowers for his wife.

Consider it a *congrats you made it through three weeks of living with my grumpy ass* present.

"Smart man," the cashier laughed and then coughed into his elbow, reaching for the bouquet behind him filled with pink, orange, and light purple blossoms. "Happy wife, happy life."

I nodded along, giving a grateful smile to the man. For once I did feel like I was living a happy life. A real one, right alongside her.

Walking into my house, my knees nearly gave out. It smelled of comfort itself. Like butter and Italian seasoning and a warm hug. Like when you were a kid, your mom had been cooking all afternoon and you were coming in after a long day of rolling around in dirt.

Rachel had her back turned toward me as she leaned down to take the bread out of the oven. "How was your day?" she asked without looking up.

She wasn't in a dress today. Probably a good thing, considering she was bent over in front of me. But she was in her pajamas with little bows on them, the tiniest tank top straps that bared her shoulder to me. Even her pajamas were cute. Her hair was pulled back into one of those claw things that freaked me out but she seemed to love so I never say anything about them.

I looked down at the flowers in my hand, at the blooms falling out of place. "Uh, good."

Waves of doubt rushed over me. She wasn't making dinner for this to be some kind of date. The bouquet I'd gotten her wasn't even that nice. Some flowers were like a hundred dollars. She wasn't going to want some insignificant dyed daisies that looked like a Mother's Day gift from a child.

What was I thinking?

For a brief moment, I pictured myself throwing the flowers out the window. I'd come back out and throw them into the trash tonight after she went to sleep, and she wouldn't even notice. But I'd gotten them for her...thought she would like them. Thought the pink in them reminded me of those heels she'd worn the other day and how they had been stepping around in my mind all day.

She may not want flowers if she thought this was all platonic. If she assumed I'd only married her because we were in Vegas and drunk and I had nothing better to do.

Throw them out, you idiot. She hadn't seen me yet, or the bouquet in my hand. I had time.

My feet shifted to turn, but then, Rachel spun toward me, her eyes instantly landing on where I'd hidden my left hand behind my back, the stems poking out around me just slightly.

With no hint of emotion on her face for me to read, she pointed to me. "Are those...for me?"

I wanted to say no, but with the hope on her face, the raised brows, and her lips dropping in shock, I couldn't hold it in. My willpower snapped in half as I sighed, my chest deflating. "Yes."

"You"—she pointed at my chest—"bought *me* flowers?"

Was it that hard to believe? It was too much. I was being too much. *Geez, man, three weeks of living together didn't mean anything*. The ring, the wedding, her straightening her shoes at the door for me and me leaving coffee ready for her didn't mean anything. Because we were just friends to her. Married friends, but still friends.

I sputtered. "They were sitting by the register. They were on sale. I'll take them back tomorrow—"

Rachel gasped, striding toward me and ripping the flowers out of my hand before curling them into her chest. "Don't. You. Dare."

She cradled the flowers and looked at them like they were some kind of precious ruby. An artifact meant to be handled with a gentleness that a man like me didn't have. Essentially how I felt having her anywhere near my arms. A glass vase in the arms of a...what did she call me that day? A hippo? The prettiest glass vase in the arms of a hippo.

She shuddered as she sucked a breath in, and I swore I heard the tiniest sniffle coming from her nose. Crap. I was even more terrible with crying women than regular women. What was I supposed to do, say? My eyes darted to the door and back. I could probably run out, and she wouldn't even know.

But then she smiled up at me. This big, beautiful smile that held nothing back and eyes that shined up at me like I was some kind of hero for buying ten-dollar flowers. Like I'd hung the moon for doing the bare minimum.

"No one's bought me flowers before."

My brows furrowed. Who was she going out with before? They were a last-minute decision, cheap and easy, and I thought she'd look pretty holding them—and I was right. Maybe I was as much of an ass as her past boyfriends in life because I never felt the need to buy other women in my life flowers. But watching her now, feverishly searching my kitchen for a vase to put them in, looking at these ridiculously dyed flowers like they were more valuable than her own wedding ring, made my heart do backflips. Made me wonder why I hadn't done this years ago.

"I'll get them all the time, then," I said.

And I would, every event, every birthday, random Tuesday nights like these. No matter what, I was going to keep buying her flowers.

She pulled out an ugly vase, one I'd gotten as a housewarming present from my boss's wife, and happily filled it with water, plopping the flowers in and sighing at them. I set the wine next to the mouthwatering pasta in a baking dish on my stove. Rachel acted like she couldn't cook. She'd warned me that dinners would be disappointing if she was making them, but then she'd whip up these incredible meals that tasted like home. Or maybe my standards were just that low at this point.

She lifted a finger, twirling one daisy back and forth with her nail. Her shoulders drooped as she sighed again and she blinked away her tears.

I set my keys and phone on the counter next to the wine and took a step closer, leaning down. "You okay?"

Her hesitation gave me enough of an answer, but she replied anyway. "Dad had a rough day..."

"What kind of rough day?" I asked.

I'd known, to some extent, the ups and downs her dad had. I didn't think I'd ever fully know how it felt. But I'd seen him at some pretty low points, and I'd watched Rachel's heart crack at them.

"Not terrible, but not great." She sniffled, and I felt like she was going to cry again, so I took another step forward and wrapped my arms lightly around her back. Accepting my hug, she turned toward me and embraced me with her head on my chest. The smell of her shampoo mixed with her perfume made me dip my head down and breathe in through my nose before lightly pressing my lips to her forehead. I hadn't noticed the music before now. I should have known, though. When was she not listening to music?

I didn't recognize the song exactly, but the voice was low and soft and sounded a bit like that 1940s soundtrack she'd played in my car when it rained the other week. If I'd heard that first, I would have known it was a rough day.

"I went to see him after my shift since Betty said he was kind of in an ill mood. When I got there, his shirt was inside out and his pants didn't match and he kept pacing like he wanted to go somewhere but didn't know where." Her eyes lifted to the ceiling as if she was willing it to give her strength to continue. Her voice was shaky when she did. "He just kept calling me my sister's name over and over." She swayed against me. I wasn't sure whether she even realized it or if it had become instinct at this point.

"And maybe I should have accepted it and pretended like I was her, but gah, Adam, it was too hard. So I had to look him in the eye and tell him I was Rachel, not Katherine. He got mad and said he knew that, but then he did it again a few minutes later. He got even more mad when he asked me where Mom was and why I wasn't answering. By the time I left, it seemed like I'd made it all worse."

I didn't answer right away. I didn't tell her it was all going to be okay. I didn't make empty promises like that. Nothing I said could guarantee it was going to be okay. But I could show her I would be here through it all, and that had to mean something, right?

I splayed my hands on her back, rubbing up and down as we swayed gently to the music, almost dancing. I leaned down farther and set my chin on her head before tilting to give the crown of her head the smallest kiss. Her deep breath in after that matched mine.

Rachel lifted her head, her tears leaving a wet spot on my shirt. She looked up at me with these eyes that begged for reassurance that I didn't know how to give.

"When does it get easier? When can I learn to just let go?"

I had seen some pretty awful things in life. Been practically drowned. I had seen death and gore pour out onto streets and had reacted like it was nothing. But holding this strong-willed, confident woman as she cried somehow felt gut wrenching.

Saying the only thing I knew wouldn't change, I responded. "I don't know, honey. But I'll be here until it does."

CHAPTER TWENTY-TWO

Rachel / Then

Currently Playing: Vienna by Billy Joel

***

Arthur wasn't an easy man to convince.

I did an entire slideshow, in very large, bold font so he would be able to clearly read everything. I shared examples of small, inexpensive updates that would change the entire aesthetic of the place and definitely bring in new people. I also showed him how much money Layla had brought in sales from her book signing here and testified that if we could host more events, we would bring in more revenue.

None of it mattered, apparently.

"The fact that you did all of this means so much to me, kid." I could hear the word "no" behind Arthur's resolve. He wasn't going to keep it. I knew that in the deep, deep crevices of my brain, and yet I still pushed myself to keep going and not assume the worst.

His sigh, the shake of his head and the way he lifted his hand to his brows, pinching them together, told me everything I needed to know. My plan wasn't enough to keep it together.

"And I think you could do a really great job with the place." Arthur let out a deep sigh, patting his leg. "But at the end of the day, I can't keep up with it. Someone young, motivated like yourself is what this place needs."

I leaned forward in my chair toward him. "Exactly. I could do it justice. I would never disrespect what you and Cheryl worked so hard to build."

"Never thought you would, kid. You know this place better than I do, but unless you can come up with the funds to buy it or can speak to the next owner and maybe show him everything you showed me, it's not possible."

Except I knew how this was going to go: new owner, whole new building. Renovations all over, with no originality left until this place eventually turned into some cheap coffee shop with a million careless investors backing it. Believe me, if I'd had even a quarter of what the place was worth, the first thing I would have done was make an offer. But the truth was, I was barely making it now. Scraping the barrel to pay assisted living fees, grocery bills for two households, insurance, and a thousand other things. If I could manage to lift one of those expenses off me, then maybe it wouldn't be as heavy. But they were all essential, and I was not about to leave my apartment to live with my dad. I loved the guy, but your girl needed some space.

"I'll wait to list till the end of the year, all right? Give you some time to process and maybe find another place to go as a backup in case this one doesn't work out. I'll do what I can." Arthur stood and gave me a brief side hug before walking out the front door.

So, just like most areas of my life, I watched Sip 'n' Spin crumble away in my mind.

Because that's what it came down to, right? Nothing good in life was permanent. Everything beautiful had an ending.

Dad's diagnosis.

Mom leaving us.

My sister following immediately without even a goodbye.

Layla getting married and moving out. It was great for her, and I wanted nothing but happiness for her, and yet it still left a huge hole in my heart.

Now the one place that truly felt like my home was going to be sold to a stranger.

I stood from my chair and reached for my laptop, shutting it down and letting the bright PowerPoint turn into a black mirrored screen. Grabbing my keys and my tote bag, I locked up the front door, turned out the lights, and headed for the back exit. One of these days would be my last here, and when that day came, I knew it was going to be very, very dark.

Was anything in life permanent? Was any *one* permanent?

My phone rang as the thought crossed my mind. Adam.

I sniffled, knowing if I didn't hold myself together until I got home, I was going to cry in front of him, and it was going to be incredibly uncomfortable.

Climbing into my car, I forced myself to answer.

"Hey." I used the best *I'm totally fine* voice I could muster and straightened my chest up, lifting my chin as if he could see.

"What happened?" he answered, his voice this low baritone that resonated in my chest and sent goose bumps down my spine. "Who upset you?" I could have sworn I heard him grabbing his keys in the background.

For some reason, maybe because I was already on edge from a breakdown, or maybe because Adam had this sense about me, that response made me instantly tear up. My once barely watery eyes turned into flowing waterfalls as I tried to blink away the hurt behind them. I sniffled again before tugging at the sleeve of my sweater and using it almost like a security blanket against my cheek.

Adam paused his raging questions such as *give me names*, and it was almost like you could hear the cogs in his brain moving, realizing what today meant.

"He's not keeping it, is he?" The disappointment in his voice matched what I felt in my bones.

"It's stupid." I sniffled, all snotty and weepy. "It's just a store."

"Not to you."

Gah, this man. It was going to hurt far, far worse when I eventually lost him.

My head drooped as I pulled my knees close to my seat, trying to ignore the dig of the seatbelt into my thighs. Maybe I was overdramatic. I'd always had pretty big feelings when it came to the things I was closest to. I'd seen my sensitivity as a flaw until I realized it was what made me *me*. So maybe to some people, this would be a ridiculous thing to cry over, but Adam was right. This loss didn't feel stupid or dramatic. It dug deep, like a blunt knife in my gut swirling around.

Adam let me cry for a moment before asking, "Can I...help?"

But what could he even do? If anyone was going to convince Art not to sell, it would be me, and I'd fallen flat in an instant. No one we knew was a billionaire who could drop that kind of money spontaneously.

I sniffed. "You can't help. No one can help. All I can do is drown in my misery with Billy Joel and ice cream."

And that was exactly what I planned to do. I had an *in case of emergency* Ben and Jerry's sitting in my freezer calling my name. Time to put a record on and wash away my sorrows on my living room floor with a pint of cookie dough ice cream.

"Are you headed home now?"

"Yeah, but you don't have to—"

"I'll see you in thirty."

A snort left me. My chest was already feeling lighter. "You do have magical hands, Adam, but I don't think that would help right now."

Lies. It would help. Well, temporarily.

I was pretty sure he mumbled something along the lines of "little perv" before speaking clearly. "I just meant to be there like..."

"As a bestie?"

"Please don't say it like that."

I smiled to myself and peeled out of the parking lot. "You'll catch on to it soon, I promise."

By the time I got home, Adam was already there, leaning against my doorway with his broad shoulders taking up a majority of the frame. He wore that gray shirt with his nephews' soccer logo on it that I loved so much. It was cute how he never really said out loud how much he cared for them but showed it in tiny actions like that. Well, between that and him tattooing their names in their baby handwriting across his bicep.

I pulled out my keys and twirled them between my fingers, trying desperately to not look like a part of me was crumbling, but there was no point, really. The way that Adam's shoulders dropped, how he sent me this sympathetic scowl, showed that he knew exactly what I was feeling.

Adam lifted one arm up and jerked his chin at me. Like I was going to pass up on that offer. I took long strides to reach him, then dipped under his arm and cuddled into his chest as he reached for my keys to unlock the door. With his arm around me, we walked into my apartment. His hold on me felt like it was the only thing holding me up, and maybe it was.

"Do you want to explain it all?" he asked when we got settled on the couch, my feet in his lap and an ice cream pint in mine.

"He's going to list it at the end of the year. Arthur said he would try to convince the new owners to keep me on, but chances aren't likely since they'll probably want to bring more modern stores to match the rest of downtown." I took my fancy spoon, one that was pretty small and had floral details on it—I saved it for special occasions—and dug into my pint. "But isn't that the art of that place? The fact that it's not like anywhere else? That you step in there and it's as if you took a trip back in time? It's incredible. I mean, to take that and toss it all away to sell fifteen-dollar cups of coffee makes me sick."

Adam's hand landed on my ankle, his thumb gently rubbing back and forth over my skin, heating me from the outside in. "Have you looked at working at another record store?"

I could. Philly was big. There had to be another place that would hire me with my experience but...

"No." I forced my focus onto the ice cream in my lap. "It has to be that one."

He fell silent for a moment. The only sounds were my spoon scraping the paper container and his thumb still rubbing against my ankle, sometimes giving it a light squeeze.

"Why?"

My heart began racing, my pulse picking up speed under my skin. Telling Adam why I had to work there would leave me bare, raw, open to any hits I might take when he left. Even Layla didn't know, or my dad, technically, since he couldn't remember.

I looked over at Adam. Kind, patient, yet broody Adam, who had never once lied to me. Never tricked me or played me. Never said a word that hurt me. If there was someone I could trust with this information, it would be him.

My arms stretched to set my barely touched ice cream on my coffee table as I walked to my now office. Instantly reaching what I was searching for, I grabbed a bag and walked back to the living room where Adam looked at me, puzzled.

"This is why." I dropped the bag in his lap and took a seat next to him, our legs brushing against one another.

Adam's brows scrunched, the lines in his forehead appearing as his lips twisted. He turned the bag full of broken vinyl back and forth, eyeing it curiously.

"It's David Bowie's *Prettiest Star* album. Pretty rare and an absolute beauty." I sighed at the memory of when I opened it. "Dad got it for me when I was in high school, paid a fortune for it at Sip 'n' Spin. The original owner said he actually had two copies. He gave it to me for Christmas, and I cried for probably a week."

I wanted to laugh when I thought back on how I wore the thing out each day.

"It's not like David Bowie was my favorite artist at the time, it just…it was the principal, you know? That even though he could barely pay the bills, he set aside that money so he could buy that, knowing how important it was to me."

Adam eyed the smashed remnants of the record and twisted the bag to face me. "How did it break?"

"Mom was able to handle the diagnosis at first, she stayed with him while she worked and they got enough disability money from him to make ends meet. But as time moved on, Dad got worse. Paying the same bill twice, ordering things he didn't need but thought he did, falling for random scams. One time he even was fully convinced someone was trying to break in at night and bought a crazy expensive alarm system. Mom got sick of it and eventually gave up. She left just like my sister did. She ran off to California, and Dad became solely my responsibility. She served him papers, and I was forced to witness."

"The day she actually left, we got into a big fight. I told her she was incredibly selfish." I scoffed a laugh. "I think I actually used every cuss word out there. She knew I was right. Knew it was wrong to leave a twenty-year-old in charge of her early onset dementia father, but she couldn't face the truth. She got so mad at me she reached for the first thing she could find." I reached over to tap on the broken record pieces. "And shattered it against the wall. Leaving in dramatic style, as always."

Probably where I got my sense of drama from. She was also probably the reason I stored up treasures and liked to shop anytime I felt a pinch of stress. But if those were the only traits I'd gotten from the evil wench, then I would say I made it out okay.

Adam nodded, his fingers twisting the edges of the Ziploc bag. "So you figured that, by working there, searching all the new inventory, you could..."

"Find the other copy of it. Yeah." I let out a humorless laugh. "Now that I say it out loud, that's ridiculous. After so long, I kind of gave up. I have been through all of the inventory probably five times, and there's no hint of it being there. I fell in love with working there and then...just left that dream to die. Gosh, it really is stupid."

But at the time, it felt right. It felt like the only option for me, considering there was no way I could finish college. And if I was going to work a cashier job, it might as well be somewhere where I could possibly find the twin of my most valued possession.

"It's not." He shook his head. "Not even a little bit. It shows how much you care for the people around you. There is nothing ridiculous or stupid about that."

A tear dropped to my cheek, and I immediately wiped it away. I hadn't even realized I was beginning to tear up. If it was a valuable record, I would have let it go, but it was more so what it meant. My dad worked hard every day so I could have a happy and healthy life. Now it was my turn to do the same for him.

I shrugged, avoiding his gaze. "Doesn't matter anyway. He's going to sell, and I'll have to go work an office job. Or maybe I could go work with you?"

My imagination ran to the thought of following Adam like a lost puppy, doing whatever lifesaving things he did. He'd get *so* annoyed with me. The smallest smile lifted at my lips.

Adam let out a laugh. A real barking laugh that bounced off my apartment walls and left him with this giant smile that I wanted to frame and put on my nightstand. He needed to do that more. I wanted to make him do it more.

"Yeah. Stick you in my pocket all day."

I leaned my head against his shoulder, and he rested a friendly arm around my waist. "You'd always have music playing and snacks to eat."

"Sounds better than my normal days."

My laugh turned into a sigh. "Adam, seriously, what am I gonna do?"

"You're not going to worry about it. You're going to...have faith."

Faith was one of those things I'd never been able to fully understand. Faith meant giving up control, and that wasn't a luxury I could afford.

"How is a girl supposed to have faith when everything around her is falling?"

The only steady thing in my life was sitting next to me, rubbing slow, gentle circles on my hip. And even he would have to go one day. He'd eventually find a girl to wife up. One who didn't like the whole girl best friend thing. I couldn't even blame her. And I would be entirely alone. Again.

His throat rumbled. "That's why it's called faith. It's...peace that makes no sense. Fly-fight-win."

"What does that mean?" I tilted my head up at him, leaving our faces only inches apart. Instincts had my eyes dropping to his lips, the full, very soft lips that I remembered vivid details about and may or may not have had some lucid dreams of.

If he noticed me checking him out, he didn't say anything. "It's pretty much exactly what it sounds like. Adapt and overcome, and before you know it, everything just becomes...easier."

I hummed, the vibrations running through his shoulder. "None of this feels easy."

He nodded, the motion rocking me slightly as his hand raised higher on my back. It was a perfectly friendly caress, but that didn't stop my heart from picking up pace. My libido apparently didn't understand that friends weren't supposed to get their engine revved by other friends. It was out of control.

"I get that. But you have good people around you to help."

That made me smile ever so slightly. I lifted my head from his shoulder, looking into those forest green eyes. "Like you?"

This time, his eyes dropped to my mouth, and for a brief moment, I thought he might just lean in. But he didn't. He simply cleared his throat and pulled back enough to get a full view of my face. "Yeah, like me."

CHAPTER TWENTY-THREE

Rachel / Now

Currently Playing: My Life by Billy Joel

***

It was funny how smells held more memories than most artifacts.

Don't get me wrong, music was what usually took me back. There's nothing like hyper-fixating on a song during an extra special season and then listening to it again a few years later. But what worked the most for me was scent.

I woke up feeling nostalgic. Maybe it was because of Dad's flare up a couple of days ago or being out of my apartment, but something had me dragging out a box of my old things. Well, not just my old things. Some were Dad's too. He didn't have a ton of storage in his complex, and Adam had gone back to my house to grab the rest of my things, reassuring me for the millionth time that he didn't mind me taking over his space.

While I was rummaging through a stack of nearly dilapidated boxes filled with homemade Christmas ornaments and those personalized keychains that I just *had* to have every time we went on vacation somewhere, I ran across an empty bottle of perfume from my high school days. Taking off the cap, I lifted the spout to my nose. Immediately, I got punched in the gut with memories of unnecessary drama, ridiculous crushes, and bad decisions. Mixed with a little fun here and there.

"Phew." I put the cap back on and buried it deep in the box, ready to not see that little guy again for another ten years.

I reached for an envelope next. It was filled with old pictures of Dad and me. Every now and then, there would be one with Mom and Katherine too, but they were rare. I wondered if, even back then, he had a feeling about their loyalty to our family. If so, he never would have admitted it. A laugh sputtered out of me when I ran across one of me wearing plastic heels, giant fake sunglasses, and a banana hat. Dad wore a Santa hat and beard combo, and we each held a microphone, singing karaoke. No wonder Katherine left as soon as she turned eighteen. I was probably the most annoying little sister there ever was.

My smile grew further with each new picture. Dad and me at the zoo. Me on his shoulders with my ice cream melting all over his hair. Me around age five with a mouth covered in marshmallow fluff. A jar and a spoon in my hands and a wide smile on my face. I assumed Dad took that one. Mom would have never thought to take a picture of something she was going to have to clean up after.

I reached for a weathered green envelope labeled *Aunt Trudy* . Having no idea who the woman was, I assumed this was something of Mom's that ended up in Dad's boxes.

As I lifted the envelope, a small leather notebook fell behind it, the box shifting.

My curiosity piqued, I tossed the envelope to the side and reached for the notebook instead. Most of it appeared to be empty. I flipped through the pages back to front until I landed on a single paper with a checklist on it in Dad's handwriting.

Bucket list, it read at the top. One item after another was listed farther down the page. I smiled to myself. He'd always had big goals.

My eyes scanned the list, taking in each one.

- *Make pasta from scratch*
- *Take more pictures*
- *Ride in a helicopter*
- *Run a triathlon*
- *Get a tattoo*
- *Feed a giraffe*
- *Ride a motorcycle*
- *Fall in love*
- ~~*Become a parent*~~
- *Buy a chinchilla*

The only one he had ticked off was *Become a parent*. My stomach churned. He never got to do any of these, really. I mean, I supposed he'd fallen in love with Mom. He had to have somewhere down the line. They were married and they'd had kids. Yet it wasn't marked off, and I couldn't entirely blame him. Even on her best days, my mother was...a lot. Never had patience for loud noises, especially music. Hated toys being anywhere other than in our rooms. Even when I was a teenager, she pretty much walked around with a permanent storm cloud over her. Everything bothered her.

I wasn't entirely clueless as a child. I'd witnessed my father working crazy hours and Mom complaining about them both piling on shifts. Katherine and I took the bus most days, and every now and then, my grandmother would come into town to watch us for a long weekend so Dad could finish up a project on a jobsite. Of course he didn't have time for stuff like this, and since he'd started slipping, he rarely got out of his complex unless I took him somewhere or his old SEAL buddies came to see him.

Guilt whirled its way inside of me, a deep, guttural pain behind my chest. I mean, the guy didn't have to buy a chinchilla, but he could have at least done a couple of these. And yet he sacrificed everything he had for me and my unworthy family. And now he was living this lost life that somehow made him happy. Yet he had no idea how much he was missing out on.

"What's that?"

Adam's rumble from the doorway caused my back to straighten. I hadn't heard him come back from his run.

I twisted my shoulders to look at him. Thankfully he wore a shirt today. Probably figured out it would be best to do so as long as I was here. But his shorts were an inch or two shorter than yesterday's. His strong, thick thighs were on display, and those weren't exactly helping me focus either.

Adam's chin dipped, his eyes focused on the open notebook in my lap.

"Oh. It's Dad's bucket list. I found it in an old box of his stuff."

"Hmm?" He said it more like a question, so I went on.

"Yeah, but the only one checked off on the whole list is *Become a parent*."

He nodded and dipped his head down the hallway. "I got some food. You want to bring it in here and eat?"

I was starving, and since I'd run out of my favorite flour, I hadn't made a sourdough-inspired breakfast this morning. My stomach growled at the thought of whatever Adam had in there. I agreed, walking into his kitchen and taking my seat at the island. He had a dining table, but somehow, we always managed to find our way here to eat instead. I wouldn't have been surprised if he sat at his dinner table every night before I arrived. It seemed very Adam-like.

He pulled out two plates and then set a bag from Marlo's next to it, reaching in to grab an apple cider doughnut. "They didn't have your cinnamon rolls. But Layla likes these, so I figured you might."

I smiled up at him. "Thanks, Adam. That was really sweet."

As I ate, Adam looked over the bucket list I'd found, his eyes scanning each item one at a time and then repeating it again.

He tapped his long fingers against the book, his golden band catching the light and refracting it onto the leather-bound backing. "So he never got to do any of these?"

"Nope. Too busy working and being a dad, I guess."

He nodded. Adam saw how much time and effort his brother Liam put into being a father. Even watching his nephews on occasion was proof enough that parenthood itself was taxing.

"Did you ask him about it?"

"No. I just now found it, and even if I wanted to ask him, it might make him upset. Or make him realize how even though he's happy, he didn't get to do a lot of things he hoped to in life." My shoulders fell at the thought.

Adam looked back down at the list as I polished off the last of my doughnut.

"What if...*we* do them? Like for him?" he suggested.

A chortle left me. "How are we going to find the time to"—I looked over his arm at the paper—"run a freaking triathlon? I barely could even do a 5k."

"I could train you."

He said it like it was the simplest thing in the world. As if we would drop everything going on around us and run off into the sunset like a couple of regular Forrest Gumps.

"Adam, you're gone all the time. I don't really see that happening."

His throat cleared, the base of it turning this warm red as he popped his knuckles. Anxious Adam. It was rare for me to see that side of him. Adam was sure about everything around him.

"I was going to talk to you about that today...I talked to my boss on base and mentioned that my..." He looked above me. "That my father-in-law and wife needed me close, so...I'm here. For the summer at least."

An entire summer of Adam? Full of sourdough bread and flower surprises, apple cider doughnuts and late-night talks?

A smile spread across my lips at the thought. "The whole summer?"

Adam smiled right back, like he could see through me. "Till the first week of September. I will have to go away for a while after, but until then, I'm yours."

I squeezed my legs together. "So we really could do some of these?" I ran my finger down the list again. "Well, I mean, some of these are easy. Take more pictures, make pasta from scratch. I've done that. But I don't see us going on a helicopter ride or feeding giraffes anytime soon."

He shrugged before taking a bite of his food. Something with grilled chicken and egg whites, it looked like. "We could do the easy ones first and just go from there."

I knew this marriage was only platonic, an agreement between friends who cared deeply for one another. That fact didn't stop my heart from racing any less.

"You would really do that for me?"

"You think there is something out there I wouldn't do for you?"

My smile crept up further, and I relaxed, knowing he was right. There was not a single thing Adam wouldn't do for me. I could probably ask the guy for a kidney and he'd jump on the table.

My phone buzzed in my back pocket as I took another bite of doughnut, cinnamon and sugar coating my lips and fingers. I swallowed and wiped my hands on the nearest paper towel before reaching for the device to see who was calling.

It was ridiculous that my first thought every time was that something was wrong with Dad. It was like a looming cloud over my head. The fact that a rhythmic humming caused my heart rate to spike nearly every time was absurd. And inconvenient, considering 90 percent of the time, it was one of my friends or Adam. But still, my heart and reflexes couldn't hold on to reason. They heard that buzzing and instantly thought *He's had a bad day. You'll have to go up there and stop him from swinging on the nurses and cussing everyone out.* It hurt each time, and it almost made me want to put the stupid thing on silent. But if I were to do that, then it would mean not knowing when they needed me, and that felt just as terrifying.

The screen had an unknown number. The area code wasn't local, but I knew a couple of the new employees at the complex had come from out of state, and I wasn't willing to risk anything.

I held up a finger to Adam. "Let me see if this is for Dad."

He dipped his chin in a nod and reached for his own breakfast that looked absolutely glorious. I would, without a doubt, steal a bite of it later when he wasn't looking.

"This is Rachel."

"Ugh, finally." My blood ran cold, goose bumps forming along my arms. "I had to call you from Stephen's number since every time I called, it would go straight to voicemail."

Because I had blocked her. Because she was scum of the earth. A lying traitor that I didn't want near my phone. Because she was my mother.

My body was frozen, mouth dropped down and eyes stuck on the balled-up napkin beside my half-eaten doughnut. Why was she calling? Why, why, why?

"Rachel, honey." Adam's low voice sounded across from me, and I could practically feel his concern wrapping around me like a warm blanket. "Who is it?" he whispered.

"Rachel? Are you still there?" Her shrill voice sent memories waving in my mind, only the ugly ones. The screaming ones. The throwing the record and packing her bags while I begged her on my knees not to leave us. *I'm still young. I have a life to live, and I refuse to live it waiting on someone.* She said it as if she was the nineteen-year-old and not a forty-five-year-old woman who had already lived an entire life putting herself first.

My fingers shook. A ball formed at the base of my throat, and I willed myself not to cry. Not for her. She didn't deserve that satisfaction.

"I'm here," I muttered, finally looking up at Adam, who had his brows creased together and his lips pursed. He pointed to the phone and mouthed, "Speaker."I nodded and followed his instructions before asking her. "Why are you calling me, Mom?" Just calling her that felt wrong.

"Well, like I said, I tried to yesterday—a few times—but your voicemail box must be full, because it didn't let me even leave a message." Again, because she was blocked.

"No, why are you calling me?" I clipped.

"I don't know why you sound so short with me. I'm the one who deserves to be upset here." Out of the corner of my eye, I saw Adam toss his hands up to his hair and pull. "You went and got *married*? Without telling your own mother?"

My own mother. I wanted to scoff at how out of touch she was. It was like she'd left just last week and not so long ago that I'd had nearly eight birthdays come and go without so much as a hello.

"We eloped," I explained, doing everything I could to level my voice. "It was last minute, and it was just us. I didn't think to tell you."

"Are you pregnant?" she spat out.

Adam stood and took a step toward me and held his palms out, flexing his fingers, wanting me to hand him my phone. That would end in an absolute dumpster fire. I shook my head.

"If I am?" I asked, testing. I hated that this woman was my one weakness. The one person I couldn't stand up to and fight.

"Then I would suggest you sort your life out before you become a mother. Who even is this guy? I had to log into Stephen's Facebook to find his account. He is *covered* in tattoos and has a giant scar on his eyebrow. What were you thinking? I thought maybe you had grown up enough to not be so foolish, but I was wrong, wasn't I?"

I couldn't even process that enough to ask who the heck Stephen was. My immediate response was to defend Adam, to tell her that any preconceived notions she had about my best friend—my husband—were wrong. That she wished she was half the person he was. That Adam Wells was loyal, protective, and passionate in a way that she, as a parent, had never once been. But I was frozen. Because that was what she did to me, what she always did to me. My Achilles' heel.

Adam's face slowly turned beet red. He ground down on his teeth and reached for the phone again, but I yanked it away and pressed mute.

"What do you want to say?"

"Tell that old witch to screw herself and never contact you again." I had never heard his voice go that low before, that deep. It was like he was summoning a curse to send to the woman on the other side of the line.

"Rach?" she asked, probably assuming she'd lost signal.

I looked down to the phone, and my fingers began to shake again. "I-I can't. It's too mean."

"Give me the phone, and I'll say it, baby." His voice turned softer, and all the willpower in me left. My phone in hand dropped to his side, and he gladly picked it up.

He unmuted the call, and I had the strong urge to leave the room to avoid the conversation.

"Nah, nah, nah." Adam shook his head at the phone as if she were in the room with us. "You may talk to other people that way, but not my wife. *Never* my wife."

"Are you the father?" She gasped, and I could picture her clutching her pearls, staring at *Stephen's* phone in pure disgust.

Adam scoffed. "I'm no father any more than you are a mother. But I am Rachel's husband, and if you're going to speak to her like that, then you better expect the same right back from me."

A vein in his forehead poked out, and I thought this was it. Adam was going to have a stroke and die right here. He was so full of anger.

"Listen." Mom's voice wavered, and I was almost jealous of how quickly he'd made that happen. "I just wanted to speak to her—"

"No. You listen. If you want a chance to speak to my wife again, then fix your attitude and accept that you abandoned her. You left a nineteen-year-old girl to take care of herself and her father entirely on her own so you could go running off with random men in California—"

"Now hold on—"

"I'm not finished," he growled, and my insides did an entire flip. "You left an amazing man and your even more amazing daughter so you could live your own selfish life. You made your bed, now go lie in it. Next time you call my wife, it better be with an apology for *everything*, or you'll never call her again." He hung up the phone before she could answer and tossed it onto the counter.

I was still frozen in place. My feet felt like they were cemented to his kitchen floor. Adam's hands lifted to his hair and pulled again as he groaned, muttering a couple of low curses to himself. His chest heaved in and out, his face so red and strained that I had the raging urge to take my pinkies and smooth out every crease and tensed muscle.

As if I needed another reason to fall for this man, there he was, defending me with 100 percent of himself, and yet still, I knew he'd held back so much of what he wanted to tell her.

I sniffled, not even realizing that there was a tear already sitting on the high point of my cheekbone. Adam flinched and turned to me. "Stevie, honey. I'm sorry."

I took a step, choosing to ignore that, and walked my way to his side and wrapped my arms around his waist. "Thank you," I mumbled into his shirt.

After a moment, his arms dropped around me, pulling me closer to him. "I told you. There's nothing out there I wouldn't do for you."

I smiled to myself, because yeah, I knew that good and well.

CHAPTER TWENTY-FOUR

Rachel / Then

Currently playing: Wildest Dreams by Taylor swift

***

Layla really was a beautiful bride.

My heart soared for my best friend, watching her dance in slow circles with her now husband. Her hands rested on the back of his neck. Luke bent down to her smaller height to whisper what was probably some incredibly romantic sweet nothings in her ear. Maybe something a little dirty too, considering her cheeks began turning bright red as she avoided all of our gazes.

I took a sip of my champagne before propping my arm on the table and letting out a sigh.

"They really are perfect together, aren't they?" Calla sighed dreamily next to me, her eyes never leaving her brother and sister-in-law.

They were perfect for each other. Years and years of watching the two of them dance around each other trying not to ruin their friendship had led to this moment, and truthfully, it was all worth it. Seeing them sway in slow, rhythmic circles with love light beaming off them. It felt magical.

Adam came back from the small area where the iced drinks were, plopping in the seat next to me with his water bottle.

I had never seen suit Adam before. This was new territory for me. He'd shed his jacket. Now he wore a white button-up with the tie now loosened around his neck, black pants, and shoes that matched the rest of the groomsmen. It wasn't that the suit was anything special. No magic stitching causing him to look so irresistible. But it was the *way* he wore the suit. How he adjusted the cuffs with this deep scowl on his face. The way his neck flexed when he fidgeted with his black tie, down to the way his pants clung just right to his firm thighs without being too tight.

Unfortunately for me, I had gained a little bit of weight since our last dress fitting, so my sage green bridesmaid dress caused me to feel a bit like an overstuffed sausage, spilling out of the top of the low slit neckline. I kept pulling it up to make sure I wasn't giving an unnecessary show to all of Layla's in-laws, but the longer the night went on, the less I could be bothered to be on boob patrol.

Adam...*noticed*. It was clear in the way his eyes dropped low in all of our face-to-face conversations, or when I turned to him and he would turn away entirely. The problem was his unreadable scowl and the way his throat bobbed as he refused to look me in the eye. It was getting more and more difficult for me to hold my feelings for this man back. If he kept that heated gaze on me, I wasn't going to be able to reel myself in. And that scowl was one I couldn't read, not really. Unreadable Adam was unnerving. How was I supposed to know where to go from here as long as he kept every emotion caged in from me?

At the end of Layla's first dance with Luke, she pulled back and faced me, her waterproof mascara slowly starting to become not so waterproof. Black streaks began forming at the base of her lower lash line as she and Luke both cried and laughed in each other's arms. It was family here—and me—so she probably wouldn't have cared so much about the running makeup, but I knew she would want the most perfect pictures, so I turned to Calla.

"I made her an emergency makeup bag upstairs. I'm gonna go grab it." I dipped my chin to the house behind us, and Calla nodded, tossing me a thumbs-up.

Besides, I was feeling incredibly hot under Adam's scowly stare and needed a breather before I was going to just spontaneously combust. Air, that was all I needed. Despite the wedding being hosted outside, my throat felt tight and I was desperate for some air conditioning to cool down the heat burning my insides.

Quietly, I stood and walked to the house, through the back door, and up to the newly updated bonus room where we'd left our supplies.

I dug through the multitude of makeup bags spread across the bathroom we'd used to get ready this morning until I found Layla's. I grabbed the touch-up kit I'd made last minute. Adam might have distracted me with his ridiculous broad shoulders and necktie, but I held a duty as maid of honor to be there for my girl first. Layla needed to come first, especially on her wedding day. And I could be a good enough friend to be there for her and not ogle her new brother-in-law for hours at a time.

Gripping the clear bag filled with travel bottles of all of my best friend's essentials, I exited the bathroom. I briskly turned the corner. Apparently a little too briskly, considering I ran right into Adam. His hands rested on my hips, holding me in place as though he assumed I would fall over like a bowling pin at the collision.

"Rachel." It sounded as if there was a rock sitting in the back of his throat, this rough rasp that said more than his actual words did.

I looked up to his face. His brows were lowered, eyelids heavy, while his thumb caressed my hip in the gentlest of holds. I blinked up at him, my eyelashes fluttering.

"Adam," I said back, keeping my gaze locked on his.

Maybe it was the champagne coursing through me. Maybe it was his hold on my body. Or maybe even the sound of soft music playing from outside that made me lean in. But truthfully, the biggest reason was that whatever part of my brain held patience for him had collapsed, leaving my walls bare, with no security. It was the evening phone calls to make sure I got home safe, the never-ending reassurances toward my dad, the first night we met—all of it like weights stacked on top of one another, standing on my willpower. Standing on the premise that no matter how much I wanted this, I knew it was wrong. Right person, wrong time. I knew that. I wasn't sure if there was ever going to be the right timing because of our situations. If we got together and everyone outside found out, then it somehow...didn't work, it would destroy us both inside. My whole life revolved around my dad's health and my work. I had no business getting into any unknown relationships. But my brain didn't seem to care about any of that tonight.

My heels put us at eye level.

I leaned in as his stare trailed over my lips. "Are you thinking about kissing me?" I asked, my lips lightly grazing his like a lover's caress, not quite a kiss, and not *not* a kiss either. Something so light, I wondered if I'd imagined it entirely.

He nodded at me with this tortured gaze that made me question why we hadn't done this long ago. "Among other things."

It was invitation enough for me. I took a deep breath, my chest expanding to press against his as my fingers dropped the makeup bag to the ground between us. I lifted up, but he was the one to move first and press his lips to mine.

After our last kiss, our last night together, I assumed if we got another chance, it would be the same as before: raw, passionate magnetism that was hurried and delightful, yet lacking...purpose. Something deeper.

Instead, Adam's hands left my hips and reached to grab the back of my neck, his thumbs pressing right into my jaw as he tilted my head up for him. He smelled like leather and cedarwood and every other ridiculous note that was labeled on his everyday cologne, but truthfully, he smelled like my Adam.

My Adam, who'd dropped everything for me multiple times with just a whisper about my bad days. My Adam, who volunteered to sit and talk with my dad because I was working later than usual, knowing he was going to have to repeat himself fifty times in a row and yet not caring. My patient, strong, silent Adam, who had so much to say behind those shut lips.

His thumbs rubbed up and down my hairline with this delicious pressure. Firm, warm hands that felt like safety. I had been on a tightrope—holding, balancing for so long, and now that I'd fallen off, he was right there to catch me in those calloused hands.

"You torture me. Every day," he murmured before lowering his lips to mine in this soft, slow press that drove shivers up my spine and into my arms. "This mouth. That heart. You're so pretty, Rachel."

My hands took a minute to react before resting on his lower back, nails dragging into his shirt in desperate need of more. But that wasn't what he was giving. He wasn't trying for a hurried make-out session in a hallway. He was giving me this slow, open-mouthed kiss that said he wasn't going anywhere. It spoke volumes, this unhurried grip on my neck, the way his lips would press and kiss and pull just right before he would back up and tilt his head, then do it again.

Everything around me faded into this black-and-white dull noise. My only focus being Adam's gentle and patient mouth against mine, dragging this euphoria higher and higher.

Other things, he'd said. I was very, very interested in what other things he had in mind.

His thoughts must have been tied with mine, because his gentle grip on the back of my neck quickly fell to my hips, gripping me with this tight hold, as though I was sand between his fingers, ready to slip away. I pressed my lips to him, tasting his mint and vanilla with a mix of my champagne in this decadent potion, as my hands lifted to his arms, testing and gripping against the sleeves of his shirt.

He was light and warmth and everything good in this world wrapped up in this lovely package that I wasn't allowed to have and yet was peeking at anyway.

"I'm getting to it, Calla. Would you calm down?" A voice from downstairs halted my hands on his biceps.

"Adam," I murmured.

He groaned against me, the grip on my hips only tightening as he buried his face in my neck, kissing and gently biting on my collarbone.

There were footsteps. Coming up the stairs. Just a couple feet from us. Someone was going up those stairs fast. I knew that, but...

"Adam." I hurried, pulling back slightly and silently praying whoever was coming up those steps was going to turn around.

"No," he snarled against me with one more squeeze on my hip. Then he dropped his hands into fists by his sides before taking a step back from me. Both of our chests heaved, my lipstick smeared, and his shirt a disheveled mess, wrinkling at the opened collar. His brows furrowed in this deep scowl that was similar to that of a toddler who had been robbed of his favorite toy. I would normally have laughed at the look, but something about the darkness in his eyes as he bit his lips made all humor rush out of me.

Crew stopped at a halt at the top of the stairs.

"Oh, hey guys." He squatted down to the makeup bag I'd dropped a couple of feet away. "Is this for Layla? Calla is screaming at me to bring it down there."

I nodded, keeping my eyes locked on Adam. "Yeah, I was just"—I coughed a bit—"heading down there with it."

Crew looked at the bag and back at Adam, who was still staring at some space between my lips and this ridiculously tight dress.

"Adam, you good?" he asked with this touch of innocence that only Crew could have toward this thick tension in the hallway.

Adam dipped his chin in a yes, but he still hadn't looked over to his younger brother.

"*Oh*...did you guys have the shrimp? I told Luke it was going to make someone sick. I think there's some Imodium downstairs if you need it."

Just as briskly as he came in, Crew padded off down the stairs with the touch-up bag in hand, leaving only the two of us.

We could kiss again. Probably end up in the spare room a few feet from us. But where would that leave us? Going from where we were—comfortable, content, and carefree—to entirely unknown territory that we both knew we couldn't head toward. Wrong timing. That was all this was. I couldn't have anything serious right now. I was making every attempt possible to keep the store open and juggling my dad's mental health along with my own. Adam was off traveling the world for work, leaving for months at a time and coming back as though he hadn't missed a day with me. It wasn't right for either of us.

Adam's stare left mine, now hyper-focused on the floorboards between us. My fingers reached to adjust my dress. "We, um, shouldn't..." I trailed off, thankful to see him nod in agreement before I could finish my sentence.

It was stupid to be disappointed in my own decision. Ridiculous that I couldn't jump us back in time to the last night we had together. But at that point, what good could it do for either of us other than give us simple temporary bliss? He deserved better than that, and I did too.

I turned on my heel, lifting a hand to my hair in an attempt to smooth the frayed edges of my updo. Layla's wedding. My *best friend's* wedding reception. That was where I needed to be. Not making out with her brother-in-law upstairs.

"Do me a favor?" The rumble of his question stopped me at the stairwell.

I looked over my shoulder at him, just as disheveled as when my lips had left his. "Yeah?"

"Don't wear that dress again."

CHAPTER TWENTY-FIVE

Adam / Now

Currently playing: Time Of The Season by The Zombies

***

Pasta-making was too sensual.

I underestimated how much so when Rachel had texted me earlier with a picture of my countertop covered in flour, eggs, and some giant machine that looked like a medieval torture device. She claimed she'd borrowed it from Crew's house. Said that it was supposed to help speed up the process. Not fast enough, apparently, because I had been watching her fingers pull and flex into the dough for ten minutes now, and each movement stirred me up.

She started with this giant bowl of flour, then dumped it onto the counter and made a big hole in the middle. I kept my mouth shut, despite the fact that every inch of my instinct pressured me to grab a rag and wipe the entire thing into the trash. But she was smiling, the kind of smile that made her eyes crinkle at the corners, so I figured I would stand back and watch.

"You could help, you know." She looked at me across the island with that wolfish smirk.

I smiled back, and for the first time in a really long time, I felt it to my core. Rachel in my kitchen, in my T-shirt—that she'd put on without even asking, like she knew it was enough to drive me crazy so she didn't bother questioning it. This feeling belonged solely to her. And where I had spent years avoiding it, I was going to rest in it today.

With what seemed like twenty eggs in her flour bowl, she grabbed a fork and began whisking the two together, occasionally looking up to watch the YouTube video she had playing on her phone propped against the bag of flour. The more she mixed the ingredients, the tighter the ball of dough got.

Her arms shook as she kept folding it, layer by layer, that vein in her temple popping out the longer she had to do it. She grunted, standing on the tips of her toes to push the dough over again and again.

I walked to the other side and stood next to her, my shoulder bumping into hers. "Let me."

"Yeah, put some of those man muscles to work." She happily walked away, taking a seat at the barstool closest to me.

I began folding the dough the same way the Italian guy on her phone had, pressing down, bringing it over, and pulling it back over, repeating the process again and again. The dough formed into a tight ball, the consistency similar to the yellow ball in the video.

I picked it up and set it down with a satisfying smack to the flour-dusted countertop, looking over at Rachel to see her staring directly at my arms, eyes widened in this distant gaze and mouth hanging open. A child looking through a candy store window from outside.

I wasn't complaining. God knew how many times she'd caught me staring at her in those ridiculously tiny skirts that I was convinced she bought solely to get under my skin.

"You're drooling, honey." I smiled at her, incredibly grateful I wasn't the only one caught up in this.

"The pasta..." She trailed off like she was in a daze. "It looks really good."

My head tilted down to the pasta as I laughed, a deep rumble settling in my chest and spreading out. Both of my fingers gripped the end of the counter, and I sniffed, scrunching my nose up.

She smiled up at me, her dissociated gaze now focused entirely on me. "You laughed."

"I laugh." I shrugged before reaching for my water bottle so I could have something to do with my hands.

"I think I could count on one hand the number of times you have actually laughed around me."

"I laugh. It's usually *at* you when you're gone so that I don't hurt your feelings."

She snorted a gasp and reached down to the extra flour dusted on my counters before flicking it my way, white powder exploding on my black shirt.

Her snort turned into fits of laughter as she backed up with two hands facing me in defense. "I didn't. I—" she gasped, "Don't even think about it."

It was too late. My hands were digging through the leftover flour and reaching for her. Before she could get out of my vicinity, I reached a hand out to grab her shirt—my shirt—and tugged her into me, my hands gripping her shoulders, her waist. Fingers digging into her ribs and twisting in a way that made her laugh every time. Her cackle filled my kitchen and resonated in my chest, bouncing off the walls and settling inside me. The white powder covered her shirt, some sprinkled across her cheeks and dusted in her hair.

I snorted. How this woman managed to look impossibly beautiful in every scenario was infuriating. She followed my gaze and looked down at her covered shirt before dragging a slow pull of her finger down the valley of her chest, collecting enough flour on her finger to reach up and plant it on my nose.

My chest shook as I laughed, digging my hands into the bag of flour beside us and flicking it at her face, a whirlwind of white brushing across us both.

Her laughter poured out into my kitchen, this bright light bouncing off the walls and beaming into my chest, squeezing it tight. My smile grew wider, the tips of our noses only inches apart. The scent of flour and her perfume waved over me. Her long eyelashes fluttered at me, and my heart beat against my chest.

She's so pretty. Pretty like the sun setting when you're out on the ocean. Pretty like the sight of my driveway after a long work trip. She was like this compass, constantly pointing me toward her. Never wavering, never faulty, always to her. Every piece of her felt like home.

My eyes trailed to her lips, pink and plush and so incredibly soft against mine in the few instances where I'd had the privilege to kiss her. I didn't remember every detail of the night in Vegas, but I remembered her lips. Her kisses, her smiles, her laugh that resonated in my head like a never-ending birdsong. Music might be her muse, but she was mine.

"You look good in white."

Rachel smiled up at me with this surprised smile. "Is that why you married me that night? Just to see me in white?"

I shook my head. *If only she knew.* "No, honey. That wasn't why."

Her smile slowly flattened, eyes shifting between mine as if she could find a more solid answer there. I didn't have one. Not that I could voice anyway. I would one day. I ...had to sort things out first. Find a way to explain.

She lifted a shaky hesitant hand to my neck, her nails lightly dragging against the base. Warmth flooded me, my neck no doubt turning a deep red under her touch.

"Are you thinking about kissing me?" she whispered.

The question took me right back to the last time I kissed her. At that wedding. The wedding where she wore the dress I wanted to burn if I could get it off her. The wedding where, all night, she gave me this dreamy, far-off look that said everything she was thinking and how her thoughts matched mine exactly.

I flexed my jaw and nodded slowly. She was already leaning farther toward me with her chin tilted my way. "Among other things."

She smirked back at me in remembrance, and it only made my lips pull up more.

Friends. That was what we were supposed to be. But friends didn't kiss each other the way we did. Friends didn't stay up late at night fabricating scenarios about each other that ended with her in my arms every time. They certainly didn't marry in Vegas on a whim, much less feel the way I did for her.

Nothing about the heat surging through my body as her lips pressed against mine felt *friendly*. It was light, so incredibly light, that if I weren't hyperaware of her body, then I would have assumed it was nothing more than a peck. But she melted under me, my hands on her lower back as she rested fully against me. Her shoulders dropped, her jaw loosened, and she relaxed entirely in my hands.

I kissed her back, pursing my lips against hers as we slid into this perfect rhythm of pushing and pulling.

Music. We were making music together.

"Is this," she said against me, "a good idea?"

I nodded, our noses rubbing against one another. "It's the best idea."

Because suddenly I wasn't worried about ruining our friendship over one kiss. I wasn't worried that she was dissipating from my fingers. I could relax in this kiss because we weren't going to be just friends anymore. Never again did I want to be just friends with Rachel Clarke.

CHAPTER TWENTY-SIX

Rachel | Then

Currently playing: *Magic Carpet Ride by Steppen-wolf*

I'm going to get a motorcycle.

Rachel: That's a shame. All your beau-tiful Greek God skin is about to go to waste.

Come with me.

Rachel: Tempting, but I like to keep my body parts intact.

I would never let anything happen to you.

Rachel: For some reason, I actually be-lieve that. You can pick me up, but only because I want to talk you out of this as much as I can.

Unfortunately, Adam wasn't kidding about his poor decisions. He really was going to get a motorcycle.

I spent the entire ride to the dealership pulling up statistics on my phone and reading them aloud. Only with each pie chart and graph, he would shrug and say something like "I'm not as reckless as those guys."

My hands waved around. "It doesn't matter how great a driver—or rider, I guess—you are. It's other people I don't trust."

We fought back and forth before he parked, letting out a deep exhale and looking over at me from the driver's seat. "I'm buying one. I'd love for you to get on board with it."

I held my eyes to his for a moment, checking for any signs there that said he would consider driving out of this parking lot without a life-taking fun wheel, but there were none. His gaze held mine, and my heart picked up speed until I broke the contact to look around the lot.

We hadn't spoken about the kiss from last week. Not really, anyway. After I went back outside, Layla came rushing to me.

"Are you okay?" she'd said. "Crew said you were sick up there. Oh my gosh, you look flushed. Have you not been drinking enough water?" She gripped both sides of my face and pulled me to her.

It was her wedding day, an evening where she should be whisked away by her husband in a night of bliss and love, and yet she'd found me and fussed over me while, two minutes prior, I'd been upstairs kissing her new brother-in-law. The wave of guilt over me had gnawed at my heart like a dog with a bone, and I swore to keep all eyes focused on her for the rest of the evening, never once leaving her to have to get up to refill her drink or stock up on Crew's fish tacos.

After a while, I noticed people filtering out. Adam was long gone, leaving only me with the couple. And Liam, of course, considering it was his house.

Liam and I had stuck around in silence, picking up the empty cups and scattered trash, collecting folding chairs and tables and essentially putting his back yard back to its normal state. He'd stewed the entire time. Something told me he was hung up on his ex-wife. Meanwhile I stayed quiet, only thinking of Adam.

The next day he'd texted me.

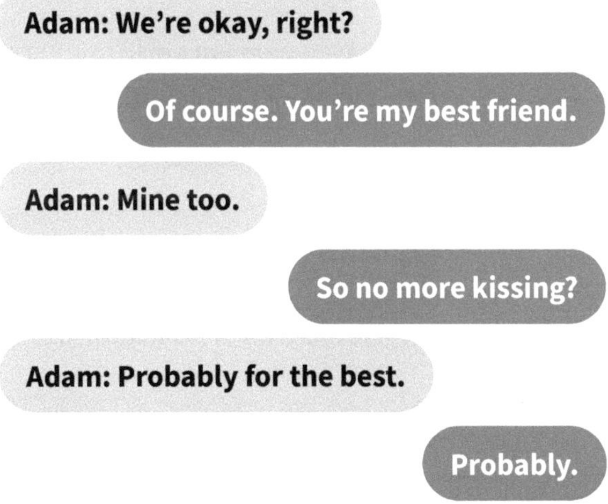

So we went back to normal after that. Or an augmented version of normal. I'd kissed him before, of course. But that had been over a year and a half ago, and since then, we'd gotten so close that if things didn't go back to normal, I wasn't sure what I would do. Adam was the only stable thing in my life at the moment, and ruining that by kissing him was something I wasn't prepared to take on.

I hadn't seen him since the wedding, so when he randomly messaged about the bike, I was happy to go to see him.

"*So*," I dragged the word out, looking around the lot surrounding us full of motorcycles. "Where should we start?"

The young bike salesmen in their khakis and black polos stood near the dealership's door, circling like sharks, with their eyes on us. Adam reached into his back pocket, unfolding a piece of paper with information for the exact model he wanted.

"Yamaha R6. Preferably blacked out." He looked down at the creases in this paper before folding it back up and sticking it in his pocket.

I snorted. "Oh wow. Did you print out a map to get here too? What else is back there, a picture of your glory days and a receipt from your senior coffee?"

"Stop."

"You gonna go home and fall asleep in your recliner watching *Antique Roadshow* after this?"

"You're such a pain." He rolled his eyes and turned off his car before stepping out.

One of the sharks, a younger one, made his way straight to us, his little legs swiftly taking off like a bird at the beach looking for a stray Dorito.

"Good afternoon. Is there anything I could help you two with?" He smiled at us, and I did my best to not zero in on the tiniest spinach leaf between his teeth.

"Yamaha R6?" Adam dipped his brow as if that was a fully sentenced question and not a bunch of letters strung together with a question mark at the end.

My lips lifted as I watched the blond sales guy sputter. This was a common occurrence. When we'd go out to eat, Adam would order like he was new to Earth's customs and hadn't been taught that you needed more than a few basic words to socialize. I used to get onto him, tell him it was rude not to ask how someone was doing when they asked you first. He shrugged and said *I don't care how they're doing.* Which was an odd contrast, considering every time we left a restaurant, he would deep clean the table and seats, stacking our plates and cups so it was easier on our waiter.

"Uh, y-yes, sir. They're over here." The man directed us to the back left of the lot.

I snorted and whispered to Adam. "You're scaring him."

He grimaced at me, his eyebrows squished together and his head tilted. "I just answered his question."

My chest vibrated as I shook my head and smiled to myself. "Okay, big guy."

The poor salesman really did try his best to give Adam a sense of direction and advice toward the bike itself, but what he didn't know was that if Adam Wells was interested in something, chances were he'd been up until three a.m. researching. There wasn't a single thing Adam did without considering all sides.

Eventually the khaki-clad kid—Kole, I found out—gave up on winning Adam over and settled for simply handing us both a helmet and a set of keys to take the bike on a test drive.

Of course, knowing Adam, the helmet wasn't enough, and he insisted they bring out some kind of riding gear. When they came out with only one set of riding pants and a jacket, he quickly pointed to me and said, "For her too."

After we waited a while, someone came out with a smaller version of what Adam had. We each slipped on the pants over our clothes, and although they were baggy, I was comforted knowing I was safer now if something were to happen. Adam zipped up his jacket before turning to make sure mine was on right. He tightened the Kevlar-type material before looking me over once more. We didn't have the proper shoes, but apparently, they didn't have any inside. Adam insisted we would buy some for me soon, which meant he was going to buy this bike whether I tried to talk him out of it or not.

Once Adam checked my gear—three times—he nodded and walked me over to the bike he had in mind.

It was odd to find a motorcycle cute, but if I were to say one was quite adorable, it would be this one. Completely blacked out, just like Adam wanted, headlights tilted like little eyes looking at you. I was going to call it Toothless, but I wasn't going to tell Adam that. He'd already told me once that my obsession with *How To Train Your Dragon* was a little much.

Adam slipped his helmet over his head, dark black encasing his face and leaving only piercing green eyes and a smattering of freckles for me to see. Calla's thing for masked men? I was beginning to get it. It was all making sense now.

He held the smaller helmet out to me. I eyed it and then the bike. I knew he had done this a hundred times before. Nothing new on his end. He told me before about his buddies from when he'd first joined the military that had a couple of bikes. That they'd taken him on rides and he'd immediately gone to get his license in case he decided to get one. He never had before. I immediately warned him of the dangers, but somehow, that part only made him more excited. Either way, riding a motorcycle hadn't ever been on my bucket list.

My lips twisted, and I sucked in a breath.

Adam's head tilted toward me, and he lowered his voice. "Do you think I would ever let something happen to you?"

I considered it for a brief moment. Adam letting me get hurt? The same Adam who refused to let me spend the night alone when my power was flickering?

"No. I'm always safe with you." I smiled at him, and he shook a helmet my way.

He comfortably took his seat on the bike, wrapping his hands around the throttle, squeezing and shifting to test it out. I hesitated to hop on until he turned to me, jerking his head back and patting the empty space behind him.

I'm safe with him.

I hiked a leg, lifting it to one side before trying to settle into the seat. It felt kind of like I was riding a horse, which I had never done, but I guess it's what I pictured this felt like.

Adam looked back at me before double-checking to make sure my helmet was on. Then he gave me a quick tap on the thigh. I leaned into his back, wrapping my arms around his body and sinking into the heat of his jacket. My cheek tightened as I smiled against him.

His fingers wrapped around the throttle and pulled as the engine roared to life underneath us. My heart rate spiked, even though I knew Adam wouldn't allow me to be hurt. Adrenaline rushed through my veins, and I squeezed my arms around his abdomen, pulling him close. The closer he was, the safer I would be. That went for all things.

"You good, Stevie?" He had to yell so I could hear him. His tone was joking, but still. I knew if I told him I wanted to get off right now, he would absolutely let me.

I nodded against him and unwrapped one arm to hold up a thumb. His right hand left the throttle to tap my thumb before forcing my hand back to his waist.

His left leg moved in some way and his hand pulled the throttle again as we slowly inched forward and took off through the parking lot. My hair whipped around the helmet from the wind, and I suddenly wished I'd brought a hair tie so I wouldn't have an entire bird's nest on my head later.

Looking both ways, Adam turned out to the highway and began heading down the road. Adrenaline pumped through me as he sped up, and I clung to him harder. More than ever, it was apparent that I had my whole life sitting in Adam's palms right now. And no matter how thrilling this was, I knew I was always going to be safe with him.

CHAPTER TWENTY-SEVEN

Rachel / Now

Currently Playing: More Than a Woman by The Bee Gees

***

"Adam." I huffed out a heavy breath. "I can't keep...going."

"You've got it, honey. You can handle it."

"It's...too...much."

"You know what you're doing."

I halted my sprint halfway up the hill, my thighs burning with a deep fire and my chest heaving. Adam paused alongside me, chest certainly *not* heaving. Our eyes locked, and amusement flashed across his face. My lips curled.

"I just heard it." I huffed a laugh but then winced because my breath was not a commodity to be wasted on crude fifteen-year-old-boy jokes.

At what point did you get the so-called 'runners high'? This was my fifth day of running with Adam. Each day, he tacked on an extra turn down the road, or he would make me walk up and down his driveway until we hit the goal that he tracked on his fitness watch. Five days, and I felt like my legs belonged in a bowl of blue raspberry Jell-O rather than attached to my body. If I was going to be any type of high, it was going to be from the sheer amount of extra strength ibuprofen I would be popping like candy tonight.

If it was only the exhaustion in my legs, that would be one thing. If it was just the deep ache in muscles that caused me to let out the most pathetic whimpers when I got out of bed in the morning, then I could probably manage to finish this thing.

But it was the breathing that did me in. Fighting to simply fill my body with its required level of oxygen while *not* getting so lightheaded I'd tell my friend/husband that short shorts were made for legs like his was where I drew the line.

Adam said it was a mental game, more so than physical. He said it was your mind telling your body that you can't push any further, and when you do, you suddenly become aware that you are capable of more than binge watching three days' worth of your favorite sitcom in only five hours. His words, not mine.

"Let's talk about something." He continued his light jog, but I could see he was itching to sprint, like his long legs were caught up in a tiny box next to mine. He'd slowed his pace for me.

What I wanted to talk about was the fact that this man had kissed me last night with enough passion to burn the entire house down. He'd lifted me up onto his countertop and had set me down with a brisk *good night* before going to his room and locking the door. I knew it was locked because about an hour later, when I eventually peeled myself off the counter, I checked to see if he was still awake and wanted to explain further what his mouth was doing touching my mouth in a way that was kind of concerning for feminism.

Our homemade pasta never saw a boiling pot. Instead, I freaked out and dumped the entire thing into the trash and told myself I would make more when I wasn't replaying a kiss in my head over and over and listening to my high school self's *in the mood* playlist.

Adam cleared his throat. "To get your mind off it."

It was a crime that he could get a sentence out without a hint of whining.

"Let's not talk at all," I wheezed.

"Has your mom tried to call you again?"

I could hear her shrill voice now, shouting about divorce rates and warning that a man like Adam isn't for me. *Pregnant.* I wanted to scoff, of course she would assume that. In her mind, no one would marry for the sake of love and happiness. Not that that was what *this* was. But it did make you wonder how she possibly could have managed to get with my dad, who was practically a tattooed, burly version of a butterfly.

"No." We slowed our pace downhill so I could catch my breath. "I don't plan on answering if she does. She can email me all the menacing thoughts that brew in her Wicked Witch of The 90210 brain."

Adam sniffed in amusement. We walked in comfortable silence for a moment. The sun was just peeking over the hilltops behind the tall buildings in the distance. Distant sounds of traffic and construction lulled in the background, but closer to us, was my newest running playlist. It mostly consisted of my favorite early 2000s hits that Adam claimed *showed my true age.*

The smell of dew on the grasses of houses around us coincided with fresh, clean air. It felt like being out here was a reset to your senses when you slowed down. Made you pay attention to the little things. A dog digging an escape under a white picket fence. A car starting. A man in a suit walking to it to go to work. Adam's consistent breathing. Adam's shorts swishing with every steady step. Adam's arms swaying front and back. Adam.

"And your dad?" He knocked into our silence. "Does he remember you telling him everything?"

"Surprisingly, yes." It was almost funny, really. The man usually didn't remember whether he had already eaten breakfast most mornings, so by eleven o'clock, he'd had four bowls of Honey Nut Cheerios. But somehow… "Every time I call or go up there, his first words are 'Hello, Mrs. Wells.'"

Adam smiled at the ground at that.

"It's like he's been truly waiting for this for years. Like it was somehow cemented in his brain."

Not to say it wouldn't leave again soon. The memories came and went for him, and I wasn't going to hold him to a standard that required him to strain more than he needed to.

"I'm glad. Maybe he just needed something to hold on to."

My lips curved. If he was going to grab on to something, me being married to Adam wouldn't be the worst thing.

Without asking me, because he was a torturous man who enjoyed seeing me breathless, Adam picked up speed as his house began to lift on the horizon. My legs burned with fire, but I kept what he told me before in the forefront of my mind. I wasn't doing this for health benefits. Though if I suddenly got legs like Simone Biles, I wouldn't be complaining. I was doing this because Dad *couldn't*. It was for him, whether he knew about it or not.

I steadied my pace with his, ignoring the throbbing in the balls of my feet and the sharp ache in my chest as my lungs begged for more air. My body screamed at me to stop, requesting an extra-large beanbag chair and a can of Diet Coke.

"What song are you thinking of?" Adam asked beside me, his eyes focused on me with this tinge of concern.

"What?" I huffed.

"The song you're thinking of. What is it?"

I considered for a moment as his house looked less and less like a blurry dot. A smile began at my lips, pulling from my chest.

"'Holding Out For A Hero' by Bonnie Tyler. But *I'm* the hero. Just in my training stage. I'm wearing my fighting leathers, and the whole squad is underestimating me. The part of the movie where they have the montage of them working out and drinking egg smoothies, and then in the next scene, they're jacked and ready to take on the dragon. Or an evil curse or whatever dark thing I have to face at the end of this."

"I like that."

My lips curled. "Yeah?"

He nodded. "'S cute."

My cheeks warmed at that. But it was also the precise moment we were coming around the curve of his driveway, and my whole body was lit in a flame. Adam lifted his wrist, pushing a few buttons on his watch and calculating our mile average.

I grabbed the water bottle I'd left resting by the tire of his covered motorcycle, which he *had* named Toothless after resisting the nickname for years.

"So how far was today?" I exhaled against the lip of the bottle.

Adam twisted his head back and forth with a squint. "About a third of what you need to do."

A third? If that was only a third, then just the biking and swimming to work on. That meant I could wrap this up fairly quickly and have time to—

"Of the running portion." He winced at what must have been some form of relief on my face. "A third of the running. So more like one-ninth of what you need to do."

I tossed my head back with a groan. "No wonder Dad never did this. This sucks."

We walked through his front door, taking our shoes off and making sure they were straight before settling on his couch. I could see it bothered him that neither of us showered first, but he had no complaints.

"At least I'm doing it with you." Adam shrugged.

My eyes scaled his body, from the shorts clinging to his big thighs, up to his chest and shoulders. His height was a natural advantage. His physique was one you could see he worked on, though.

"You could run a marathon tomorrow without even thinking." I bent over and pressed my thumbs firmly into my calf, raking through the shooting pains. "So does it really count?"

My amusement turned to a wince as my thumb dug into a particularly sore spot on the higher area of my calf. Adam set down his water and reached for my leg. "Let me see."

I happily propped it up on his thigh, and his hands got to work. His long fingers pulling and pushing my muscles in all the right places, lighting me up with this sting that somehow felt like the perfect concoction of pleasure and pain. My eyes crossed at some point, my head dipping back to the throw pillow behind me, and a soft groan left my lips. His fingers dug harder.

"How's the store?" he mumbled, but my mind had a smoke machine inside of it like the beginning of a Fleetwood Mac concert.

"Hmm?"

His legs shifted as he puffed an amused sound. "The record store? How's it been?"

I smiled with my eyes shut. That was one area of my life that was going swimmingly. It wasn't how it used to be, of course. That was to be expected when it was anyone other than Arthur owning it. It needed updates. The manager who'd started a couple of weeks ago swore he would get right to it as soon as he could get the funds approved by the new owner. But it was still my place.

"Good." I scrunched my nose. "Really good. Art came by the other day."

Adam's fingers slowed. "Yeah?"

I nodded. "I told him we were going to rip up the floors and find a similar pattern with better quality, and I mentioned the new light fixtures that I showed you too. He said they were too funky, but I think it fits perfectly."

Ever since he sold the place, Art would pop in about once a month. He never bought anything, but he would walk in and look around like it was a Walmart in a foreign area, where you knew the gist of it but could still easily get confused.

The new manager was a guy from the south side of Philly, but he was cool. He came once a week to check in on things, but for the most part, I had the place to myself. And since the new people had liked the slideshow I made a couple of years back, I managed to convince them to hold more author/artist events.

"Sales seem to be good." I grinned as my eyes peeked up at Adam, who was focusing in on my legs, back to his pushing and pulling.

He pulled his lower lip into his teeth, biting down on it. I sat up a little, my mind racing back to his lips against mine the previous night. A kiss full of stardust and flour while Karen Carpenter's sweet, slow voice buzzed in my ear. It felt like he was unthawing me. Slowly and surely, this warmth that started in my chest reached all the way down to my hips where his hands pressed since moving their way up further.

"That's good, I—"

"Adam." I interrupted instantly, because thoughts of the record store drifted away from my mind, and his lips were taking the center stage.

"Yes?"

"Yesterday...when you kissed me..."

He looked up at me, eyes dancing across my face, looking for an answer. "Mmm?"

"Did it..." I sighed. This was ridiculous, but I needed to know. "Did it mean something to you?"

His laughter surprised me, and I pulled my feet back into my own area of the couch. I reared my head back. Maybe it was a little more ridiculous than I thought. I had slept in the same bed as the guy. We'd done who knew what in Vegas and the night we met, so was it that unbecoming of me to ask what a simple kiss meant?

Adam reached for my leg again, his hands wrapping around my ankle and yanking me back down the cushion so my calves would rest on his lap again.

"You're my wife. Yeah, it meant something to me."

My brain let that soak for a moment. And then two. "Yeah, but I'm, like, your fake wife."

His hand left my foot and reached for my hand, his thumb brushing against the ring that I had grown so fond of. "Is this ring fake? The papers we signed?" His eyebrows dipped at me. He looked like an artist explaining his final piece before someone to review. As though these were the facts, and he wasn't going to waver from them. "You're in my house, on my couch, in my shirt. Is any of that fake?"

Maybe in my mind it was, because I decided in that moment to look around us, as if this were a hallucination. "Well, no."

"Neither is our marriage, then."

He said it as if he was entirely sure. Like he was reading the Bill of Rights or instructions on how to make Hamburger Helper. Clear as day, that's all it was. Nothing left to be argued. His wife, in his house, on his lap.

I sputtered. "Adam, but we're—" I huffed out an amused breath. "I mean, we're, you know." Us, I wanted to say. A completely undefined *us* that couldn't be put into one box. And his kissing me the way he did was adding about fifty more boxes to the list.

He dipped his chin. "Explain to me what you think this is."

I answered before I could think. "An acknowledgment between..." I paused, "...friends to reap benefits of a contractual agreement."

His lips, still smiling, fell slightly. "Then there you go."

"But when you kiss me like that, it doesn't feel like that."

"What does it feel like, honey?"

Warmth. Like being held by a friend you haven't seen in years, or like rewatching your comfort movie for the fiftieth time. The last bite of an ice cream cone. The crisp click of a needle on your favorite vinyl.

"Like I'm yours."

His smile melted over me. "Don't you think, in some way, you've been mine since the night we met?"

CHAPTER TWENTY-EIGHT

Adam / Then

Currently Playing: Golden Slumbers by The Beatles

***

It still felt weird that Rachel was connected to my family and friends in a way that wasn't through me.

But it shouldn't have come as a surprise that she was at Romfuzzled tonight, propped up in one of those tiny skirts, with two small pink bows tied in her hair and her head tossed back in laughter at whatever my sister was whispering to her. They sat in a large round booth in the back like normal, with Nathan on one side of Calla and Rachel on the other. My head swiveled to the bar to see Luke making drinks and Layla ringing up tickets. Crew was talking to a blonde at the bar, and by the look on her face, things were not going as he planned.

I opted for the bar first in an attempt to give my racing heart just one damn minute to calm down before going to our usual table. My fingers curled, knuckles tapping against the wooden bar top.

Luke looked my way, dipping his chin and readjusting his glasses. He set two beers in front of the couple down the row before heading my way.

"Whatcha drinking tonight?" he asked, but his hand was already reaching for a beer glass in a freezer below him.

"Water."

He looked up at me and curled a brow, but shrugged one shoulder and grabbed a bottled water from behind him before placing it in front of me. I knew better than to allow a drop of alcohol into my body while Rachel was around. It allowed my mind to share things that I didn't give it permission to.

The seat next to me swirled around, and I didn't have to look up to know who it was.

"Hiya, Sailor."

The number of times I told Rachel that I was rarely on ships and that I flew pretty much everywhere was insurmountable, but she knew it made my eyebrow twitch every time, so she kept it going. It was the same reason I called her Stevie.

"Hello." I dipped my chin and took a sip of water.

"How's the bike?"

"Good."

"Good."

Luke eyed us, looking back and forth before setting down the glass he was drying and slowly walking away without turning around.

"You didn't tell me you were coming tonight." Her finger twirled in a circle against a bead of water dripping off my glass.

"I didn't know I was until the last minute. Figured you'd probably be here too."

Rachel hummed. "Well, it's good you're here."

"Yeah?"

"Yeah, I was about to order straight whiskey, and I wasn't sure anyone was going to stop me."

I snorted, a small laugh rumbling through my midsection. "Yeah, probably for the best that I'm here, then."

My smile tilted up further at that, my eyes not leaving hers.

Sitting on the wooden bar top, her phone buzzed between us. Curiosity got the best of me when I saw *Graceful Care Nurse Line.* Rachel's hands scrambled to answer, almost knocking over both of our drinks in the process.

"This is Rachel Clarke," she answered in a rushed tone.

I couldn't hear the caller, despite how hard I was attempting to listen in. But her responses alone made it clear there wasn't any good news.

"How bad?"

"Is it the same as last time?"

"What is he specifically asking for?"

"Okay, tell him I'm on the way. Wait—no, don't. It may backfire, just...I'll be up there in a minute."

The call dropped, and I was already getting to my feet.

Rachel sighed as the phone fell to her lap, her shoulders drooping. "I gotta go."

I wanted to comfort her, wanted to say it was going to be all right and that she didn't have to carry the burden of taking care of her dad on her own, but I couldn't. My tongue held back, the words sitting right at the edge of it like raiders trying to break down a security wall.

"I'll drive" was all I managed to get out, reaching for my keys in the process.

She nodded without protest, and we ran out to the side door and over to my bike. I opened the extra storage, where the smaller helmet with a pink heart sticker—not my choice—sat.

"You had my helmet in there?" She pulled it out and twisted it around.

There were a handful of times in the past that Rachel had called me needing a ride, her tiny car breaking down after she pushed the limits of 'yes, my car is on E, but how far could I really push this thing?'. Now that I had the bike, I figured it was best to always keep it on me.

My hands reached to close the compartment, but it was too late. Her eyes had already caught sight. "And my favorite sweat-shirt?"

I wasn't aware that it was her favorite, not really. But the few times she had been to my house, she had complained that I must have been cold-blooded and that my apartment was "colder than the set of *Happy Feet*." This sweatshirt was the one she grabbed from my coat closet. She would settle it over her and let it fall around her upper thighs. I hadn't considered it mine from that first day forward.

I put on my helmet, closing the shield so she couldn't see my eyes. "Yes."

My leg swung over the bike and I settled on the seat as I started it. Rachel was silent behind me for a moment before I eventually felt her dip onto the seat, her thighs pressing against me and warmth climbing in my skin.

Once the motor was warm enough, I looked over my shoulder as she adjusted her helmet, making sure she tightened everything correctly. My right hand reached behind me and gave two firm taps to her thigh. She returned it with her arms wrapping around my waist and a quick squeeze to my stomach. It was a silent language we'd created over the several joy rides we'd been on before.

"*You ready?*"

"*Take me.*"

I dipped my chin and let my hand rest on the throttle. Rachel's hands held me tight.

I wasn't sure what exactly to expect when Rachel said her dad was having a rough day. When my grandmother's case of dementia got to be all-consuming, she was numb. Near the end, the only thing that changed her mood was music. My mom insisted on playing the soundtrack to the original *Cinderella* movie. Needless to say, it was a little awkward when nurses would come in to see me playing "A Dream is a Wish Your Heart Makes" by Nana's side table. Other than that, she was barely even awake, drifting in and out of conversation like it was all a simple daydream.

But Rachel's dad was younger, newer to all of this, and although you could see the confusion on his face, he was also strong. His military background was apparent. The guy was still built like a tank. Rachel claimed it was because he refused to sit still. She said that it helped him from focusing on the unknown too much. Apparently he was one of the very few in the complex who took advantage of the gym there. Said he usually had a few older people in the background cheering on his sets.

The odd part of it all was that every time I did come to visit her dad with her, Rachel always had this list of things to expect. She'd blabber about him not remembering names or asking how your day had been twelve times in a thirty minute span. How, depending on his day, he may have refused to eat anything and may look more drained, or he may be passed out on a recliner from overeating. She'd warn me about his eyes sometimes glossing over, like he was unreachable.

But this time, she didn't say a word about what to expect. I suspected it was because she herself had no idea what we were walking into.

I hopped off the bike once it was parked, setting my helmet in the case on the back. Rachel took hers off, her blond hair frayed and staticky at the ends. I reached for her helmet, placing it directly next to mine before closing and zipping up the storage.

Rachel's face was pale, her movements staggered and her eyes darting.

"It'll be okay." I nodded at her, needing some kind of reaction I'd recognize. She nodded back.

It wasn't enough to make me feel better. My skin crawled when I saw her like this, so helpless. Before I could fully process it, my hands reached for her, our fingers linking together. I squeezed. She squeezed back. It still felt distant.

We walked to his complex. One nurse was standing outside the door with a clipboard. His door was slightly cracked, and another nurse was holding it open. He was grunting, mumbling something in the distance.

"Yes, sir. We understand."

A rough groan fell on the other side of the door, and Rachel's fingers stilled before they dropped mine entirely.

She walked inside, nodding at the younger-looking nurse there with a tight smile.

"I'll be outside." The nurses gave us this apologetic look, and I followed Rachel inside.

Jack was sitting in the black recliner in the far corner of his living space, next to a stack of records and a player that looked almost identical to the one in his daughter's apartment. He leaned forward, elbows resting on his knees, with one leg shaking. His eyebrows were lowered, his lips in this deepened frown.

"Hey, Dad." Rachel walked around his couch, casually leaning against one arm as though this were any other visit.

Jack's eyes lifted to his daughter, and you could see them lighten for a moment, before going gray again.

He scoffed. "They called you?"

Rachel nodded, and his eyes scanned to me, looking me up and down in assessment. I wasn't needed here. I knew that. It was probably far too personal for me to even be around. But surely if she didn't want me here, she would have said that. Or she would have refused to let me drive her or forced me to stay outside with the nurses.

But then again, the anger in his eyes—the eyes of a man who'd witnessed far more than he deserved—was taking over. He wouldn't hurt his daughter. I knew that too. But a confused prior-service man was something I understood well, and I knew things could go south easily in situations like this.

Jack shook his head. "Ridiculous," he spat. "I ask a couple questions, and they start sending everyone in here like some kind of SWAT team."

Rachel mustered the smallest of smiles, this wavy grin that wobbled slightly. "I understand, I do—"

"Do you?" His voice raised. "Does anyone? I'm like an animal in a damn cage. No way in or out and people circling me all day. No one will tell me where my wife is, and they all treat me like I'm some kind of mental patient."

Her back straightened, and every fiber of my being begged to be beside her. To calm her tightened brow, to caress her hip and whisper to her that it was okay. She nodded. "Okay, well, give me just a second, and I'll come right back, okay?" Her whisper was just enough to make him nod at her.

She gave me a look and mouthed. "Can you stay?"

I nodded and went to sit on the couch as she slipped outside to talk with the nurses.

An animal in a cage. I knew how that felt. It was probably the only thing Jack and I had in common, other than the fact that we both cared for his daughter.

After deployments, trying to settle back into some kind of a normal lifestyle felt impossible. I thrived on routine and was hardly ever handed it. I needed instruction, a guide, anything. Without it, I felt lost, cornered and backed into a wall that left me no way out. It was suffocating.

"You gonna tell me the same thing too?" Jack asked, throwing himself back into the recliner with a glare my way. "Want to tell me to 'calm down'?"

I crossed my arms. "Wasn't gonna say anything."

"Good." He crossed his arms back.

We sat in silence, glaring at each other across the coffee table. Rachel's soft voice mumbled outside the door, low enough for her words to be unrecognizable.

A distraction. That would be good, right?

I looked over at the stack of vinyls, recognizing the one on top as the same that Rachel had played in the car before.

"You like The Romantics?"

When his eyes squinted at me, I dipped my chin to the stack.

He glanced at me, to the record, and back. His nose scrunched the same way Rachel's did when someone told her that Eric Clapton was overrated. "I don't care much for you being so nosy."

"Well, I don't care much for you making my girl cry, and yet here we are."

His eyes widened at the blow. And truthfully I didn't mean for it to sound so harsh. Jack *was* a good guy. He was confused and disoriented. I would be a grumpy ass if I was in his position too. It wasn't exactly his fault. That didn't make me any less upset at the small pool of water that had been forming in her eyes.

I didn't exactly mean for the whole *my girl* thing to slip either. That would probably only confuse him more.

Although Rachel *was* mine. I wasn't sure exactly how, though. Definitely not in that she was my girlfriend or really even what I would consider a friend. This was something more than that. As if her soul was tethered to mine. Even if she went off and married some rich golfer later on in life, she would still be mine.

Jack slumped his shoulders, looking out of his blinds to Rachel and the nurses talking outside. Whatever he saw must have shaken him a little, because the anger in his face was fading slowly.

He looked down at the pile of records and picked up the first one. He took it out of its sleeve and opened the player to set it on top. The needle slowly lowered, and a crisp guitar thrummed in the room. My shoulders relaxed a little. He wasn't yelling. Wasn't crossing his arms or glaring at me like I was his mortal enemy. That had to stand for something.

"Military?" he asked, looking at the tattoo on my upper arm.

I'd answered this before, of course, but I wasn't going to mention that.

"PJ. Used to know a lot of SEALs before. Never really wanted to be one. Cool guys, though."

He nodded and one lip curled slightly, his foot tapping against the rug as the music played next to him. "I miss that some days. The bond with your brothers out there and all."

I knew what he meant. People that went through what we had together always came out stronger. I wasn't a SEAL. That was an entirely different ball game. But I knew what it was like to be dropped into battle with only a few guys around you, not knowing if you're going to save a life or cost you your own. There's this bond that ties you together in a way that can't evolve in your day-to-day friendships.

And yet, whatever I felt for Rachel was different from that too. Not necessarily stronger, but different.

"Yeah, I get that." I nodded.

The song ended, and Jack picked up the needle, moved it back, and set it down to replay. "Rach loves this one." He smiled to himself, and I took note to make any attempt possible to find a record like it, or at least to see if she already owned it.

At her name, I craned my head to the window. Rachel stood there, nodding along to what the nurse was saying and wiping occasional tears from her eyes but never letting them fall.

"So, when are you gonna propose to her?" Jack asked from his chair across the room.

The question rang around in my head for a moment as I watched Rachel cradling her face in her hands, chest heaving quickly.

I took a deep breath and replied.

"As soon as she lets me, sir."

CHAPTER TWENTY-NINE

Rachel / Now

Currently playing: Burning for you by Blue Oyster Cult

***

Adam: No run tonight. I've got other plans for us.

I'll bring the candles, you bring the whipped cream?

Adam: Not those kinds of plans.

Go on…

Adam: Meet me at the house when your shift is over. I want to check off another bucket list item.

Are we going to get a chinchilla?

Adam: No.

Adam: They carry diseases.

So do most men.

Adam: Touché.

"A tattoo shop?" I gasped a laugh at Adam's smug grin as we hopped off his bike. "You're getting another tattoo?"

He shrugged a single shoulder. "Me and you both, honey."

I think he knew how well the whole *honey* thing was working on me because he'd throw it into a sentence when he didn't want me to say no. *Can you make me more of those sourdough bagels, honey?* I said yes every time.

"Wha—" I laughed with my head thrown back, looking up at the bright neon flashing sign. "I am *not.*" My smile couldn't go away, no matter how hard I tried to pull it down.

"Come on, Steve. You've been wanting one for years. Now's the time to do it."

I glared at his nickname for me. That one and *honey* definitely had the opposite effects on me. My teeth bit down on my lip, and it curled immediately. I had wanted one for a long time. I'd told Adam years ago, and he had apparently kept it locked in that everlasting vault that he called a brain.

He leaned in closer to me, whispering low. "Think about the list."

A snort left me. "Easy for you to say. You have like twenty tattoos. I'm an ink virgin."

"If it helps, you can pick out what I get."

I raised a brow at him. "Anything?"

"Anything."

"What about my name on your butt? In a very feminine font and lots of hearts."

He winced. "If that's what you want."

I would never truly ask for it, but Adam was a man of his word. That...left some interesting possibilities on the table. I glanced inside the large windows of the tattoo shop. It wasn't like any of the places I'd seen before, but then again, that was mostly on TV. I didn't see any burly men in leather jackets with mean scowls and clenched fists. No sign of the stereotypical framed skull paintings or tall, scary people with large holes in their ears and tattooed eyebrows that said *try me.*

No, this looked more like a casual coffee shop than somewhere to get a Care Bear permanently inked on your tush. Not that that's what I wanted. Though it was kind of tempting. Clean, crisp white walls with a multitude of plants scattered around the room. A brown leather couch on one wall, and a few chairs on the opposite side. Mirrors lined the wall behind the chairs. One girl had her back facing it, her neck craned to view a freshly inked tattoo.

If I *was* going to get a tattoo, this would probably be the place.

Adam's tattoos were always tastefully done. An array of flowers for his mom, his nephews' names in handwritten script, the tribal one, the plane, on and on. I had always been a *my body is a temple* kind of gal when it came to the thought of getting any ink. I assumed I would get something and regret it, but then I saw all of Adam's and my interest was suddenly piqued, and all previous assumptions dissipated.

"Do you regret getting any?"

"No. They are all what I needed most at the time I got them."

I looked up at Adam. He was smirking down at me. "Come on, you can watch me first if you want. Or we can do you first, to get it over with."

I still hesitated, and he sucked in a breath, dipped down to whisper to me. "I'll hold your hand the whole time."

That was enough motivation for me.

I reached a hand down to his wrist and wrapped my fingers around it, squeezing tight around his warmth. He nodded down at me and led me inside.

"Adam!" a low voice called across the room. A short older man with dark skin hobbled over to the front. "You did not call me—" The man's eyes looked from Adam to me, halting his movements.

I shifted, pulling my hand from Adam's wrist. The man's lips pulled in a slow smile, and he waved a shaky pointer finger at me. "Ah, you are Rachel."

"I am." I smiled, and Adam stiffened behind me.

The man had a small name tag on that read *Clyde*. He reached for my hands, his cold, wrinkled fingers wrapping around mine and giving them a firm shake. "Oh, you are prettier than I even imagined. Our Adam did not do you justice."

He dropped my hands and turned to Adam behind me. "What are we here for today? Want to add to your back?"

"Actually I was thinking about filling the last spot on my forearm." He twisted his arm to show one free space about three inches below the bend of his elbow. "Also, she's getting her first."

Clyde lit up like a child who'd been told he could see Santa at the mall. "Your first? Do we know what we're getting?"

Annoying as it was, Adam was right. I'd known what I wanted for a tattoo for years. I hadn't ever worked up the courage. I pulled up a Pinterest board named *One Day* and scrolled until the familiar image came up.

I twisted the phone to Clyde, and he pulled his glasses down and squinted at it. "How lovely. It fits you well." He directed a hand to an empty chair and a younger, gladiator-like man standing behind it on his phone. "Brendan, can help yo—"

"No," Adam interrupted, his baritone alone causing my skin to raise. "Felicity. She can see Felicity."

He gestured to the woman that was wrapping some kind of film around a girl's arm at her chair. Clyde smiled at him. "Sure, son."

After thirty minutes of signing waivers and getting a pep talk from Adam—which was more of a physical reassurance than a conversation—I felt ready. Ready enough, I guess.

Felicity laid me face down, and adjusted my shirt so she could see my back more clearly. She wiped me down and showed me a stencil of what I wanted.

It was exactly what I imagined, but custom tailored to me. A set of my favorite headphones, the ones that wrap around your head and rest on your ears like a couple of clouds, with a pink bow tied to each earpiece. Two of my favorite things, mixed into one tiny art piece. My love for music wrapped up in a perfect package with the cutest bow on top. It was everything.

I turned to get Adam's approval, not that I truly needed it.

"What do you—"

"I love it." He smiled, staring at my tiny ink patch. A real, truc smile full of pride. My chest felt weightless, and a tingling started at my head and spread down to my toes. My heart picked up speed, a *tap, tap, tap* on my chest, almost like an alarm going off. *Warning: you are getting way too excited over a single smile.* Yet it only made me want to hurry this process a little longer. Maybe sign up to get another one just to witness that smile again.

"You ready, honey?" Adam dipped his head to the chair, and I quickly nodded.

My excitement quickly turned to agony as Felicity, who I'd initially liked but was now plotting the demise of, stabbed me over and over again.

Truthfully, I'd always thought I had a pretty high pain tolerance. I'd broken my wrist in middle school and didn't even know until the next day because it felt a little sore. When my dad and I went to a Foo Fighters concert about six months before his diagnosis, in the heat of the moment—a.k.a. the drum solo of "One Of These Days"—it seemed like a great idea for me to crowd surf. It was more *crowd* than *surf*, considering I got trampled on by many grown men. My dad had to stick a hand out in the crowd and pull me up like a child drowning in the deep end without her floaties.

Even then, I wasn't this fazed.

Maybe it was the needle itself, or the fact that I had become more of a pansy the older I got, but this was torment. And if

Adam hadn't been here, chances were I would have jumped off this table the minute Felicity put that forsaken needle to my innocent back. Leaving with a single black dot that looked like more like a freckle than any sort of tattoo would be a lot less embarrassing if my husband wasn't right beside me. But he was, and considering he was entirely covered in tattoos, these must be worth it, right? Otherwise why would anyone get more than one?

"You're doing so good." He squeezed my hand, which was tightly wrapped around his, my fingers digging into the back side of his hand and forcing all pain to go away.

"Look at you, not even crying." He chuckled a bit. "You're better than Liam."

He didn't do good? was what I wanted to ask, but it came out more like "He didn't—Ah-—dogoo?"

Adam smiled at me, brushing one rogue tendril of hair off my forehead. This felt oddly like the birthing videos we were forced to watch in high school. "Cried the entire time. Had to take a break every two minutes. I think the artist was ready to kick him out. By the time we were finished he was begging for another though, and now he's got a sleeve similar to mine."

I laughed and immediately winced because Felicity took advantage of the opportunity to move closer to my shoulder blade. The sharp needle pain shuddered through me, a vibration forming the closer she got to the bone. And *not* the good kind.

"Why don't we go pick out a new vinyl after this?" He rubbed his thumb over my hand.

"Really?"

"Yeah. Or we can get that name tattooed on my ass if you're still interested."

I snorted. "That is very tempting."

About an hour of torture later, I had a tattoo. A real one. Not one of those fake floral ones that I'd gotten on a whim at PCB on Spring Break in 2010 that resulted in a fiery rash a week later. A real, life changing, forever there tattoo.

I turned my back to the mirror, admiring the outline art again and again. My cheeks hurt from smiling. I couldn't stop staring. It was absolutely perfect. And Adam's approving grin made it that much better.

Twisting on my heel, I reached for Adam. "I want another one."

I could totally see how people found these addicting. I was already envisioning a tiger on my thigh, or maybe a Bob Dylan lyric. The possibilities were endless. I could very well leave here in six hours looking like a children's doodle pad and still be this excited.

"Maybe let's just let this one heal first, yeah?" He reached a firm hand to my lower waist, slightly rubbing up and down, leading me in a trance.

I nodded and turned my back to Felicity, who had now worked her way back into my good graces, to wrap me up. She gave me a detailed list of instructions that were really hard to pay attention to due to the high I was riding, but I didn't have to even worry about it. Adam always made sure I was taken care of. This was no different.

When his turn came, he sat in front of the next free station, which was Mr. Gladiator—Brendan—from earlier. Adam ground his molars when he very politely introduced himself to me. Then he shortly explained to the guy what he wanted and settled in his chair, forearm up.

Since he was more accustomed to the process, Adam's tattoo didn't take nearly as long, and unfortunately, he didn't need nearly as much hand-holding as I had. Though he did wince at one spot, a quick sucked-in breath through gritted teeth that had me flying across the spinny chair fully prepared to deck Brendan. He assured me it was a more sensitive spot, but I still hated the sight.

With Adam's finished up, I pulled out my camera to take a picture to send to his siblings. Thankfully we hadn't had to tiptoe near as much around them, considering we were now married.

"Let me see it!" I squealed, but as the art came into view, my heart stuttered. The track in my head scratched, playing the same note again and again.

On the one free space of his forearm sat a thinly outlined record, on one side was a scripted *R* and on the other, an *A*. I stared at it for a moment, then two, frozen entirely, until his voice broke into my halted brain.

"It's not your name on my ass, but it's as good as I could get ya."

He shrugged a single shoulder as if the man had simply given me half of his side of fries or had agreed to split the cost of an Uber.

"Adam." My mouth dropped, closed, and dropped again.

They are all what I needed most at the time I got them. That's what he said before, wasn't it? Granted, that was years ago, but still.

"You just…it's beautiful." I hadn't realized my eyes were tearing up until I felt a single droplet on my cheekbone, slowly caressing its way down my face.

Adam's eyebrows lowered at it. "It's about time, you know?"

I smiled and nodded at him, because yeah, it was about time. Time for both of us after all we had been through together.

CHAPTER THIRTY

Rachel / Then

Currently Playing: The Way I Feel Inside by The Zombies

***

You know how sometimes you can have a bad day, then listen to happy music, and it helps? And how other days, you listen to sad music, and it helps even more? This was one of those days.

Sip 'n' Spin had officially sold. Arthur said the new owners were cool. The guy and his wife were out of state and wouldn't be in much, so I would have the place mostly to myself. They came by last week to say hello. The wife's name was Poppi. She had green and purple hair and told me I could call her auntie, to which I politely declined. She was nice enough, and her husband seemed like a bit of an odd ball, which wasn't too far off from our standard clientele. But still, they came in with a quick look around the place before discussing tearing it practically to shreds, ripping my heart out along with it.

It wasn't my place to say that this building deserved more than plain gray laminate floors and a landlord specialized in a quickly done white spray paint job, so I kept my mouth closed. And with keeping my mouth closed came pent-up frustration that's remained until today—closing day.

Arthur called me as soon as he left the attorney's office, giving me a quick *this isn't goodbye, kiddo* and reassuring me that I would still have a solid gig there. And all of that pent-up frustration, an overwhelming sorry, and that phone call came crashing down on me. Every weight I'd attempted to carry over the years sat on my chest as I lay flat on my back on my kitchen floor with Lionel Richie singing over me—a desperate concert for one.

It wasn't lost on me that I'd known this was coming up. I'd had seven previous months to mentally prep myself for that. But instead, I'd shoved all of that deep down in hopes that I would suddenly have a great-great-aunt reach out and say I was like her long-lost daughter and she was in her last days so she had to give *someone* her five-million-dollar inheritance. Turns out I didn't have that.

So, Lionel Richie it was. My newest best friend.

Three firm knocks beat outside my door, presumably my neighbor two doors down who liked to remind me regularly that my taste in music was, and I quote, "the gum underneath his shoe." Although the last time I'd seen him in the hallway, he was wearing a wife beater with cut-off overalls and an iron-on patch of Waluigi on his chest. So who was the real gum here?

"I'm not turning it down!" I shouted at my door, giving my unwelcome visitor a choice finger. He couldn't see it, but it was the thought that counted.

"I'd hope not." A call came back that was most certainly not my Waluigi-loving, music-hating stick-in-the-mud neighbor.

Adam?

I sat up and took in the space around me. The kitchen wasn't too bad. Probably because I had only eaten takeout for the last four days and didn't own more than five actual dishes. But there were two piles of laundry in my living room that weren't quite fold-worthy, yet weren't considered dirty either. Not to mention I still had Lionel belting out and an array of pillows spread across my floor.

"Uh...one second." I frantically crawled around, tossing all the laundry into the bathroom and sending up a quick prayer to the good Lord that the man wasn't going to need to pee during this visit.

"You know I don't care if it's messy," he rasped from the door, but it was a lie. He did care, he just wouldn't say it out loud.

I picked up my pillow fort remains and lifted with my legs, bending my knees in a halfway crab walk to my bedroom before tossing them out onto the open floor. A mirror caught my eye, and I took in the look I was sporting.

A black Snuggie—to portray my mourning—blond hair in a giant clip that had been up a little too long and was going to be a nightmare to brush out, and a face that had once had makeup on it...was that yesterday? Either way, the bags were out and the lips were gone and there was nothing left except this shell of a broken girl. If Adam ever wanted me before, he was going to change his mind now. It was a shame to wash away this level of mystique I had managed to carry this far into our friendship. Fixing this train wreck would require at least twenty minutes, and judging by Adam's hurried knocking, I had about twenty seconds before doors would be breaking down.

I sighed and reached for the door handle, locking my eyes on the floor as I opened it. "I know. Go ahead, spill it all. I look like Nanny McPhee before she gets all hot."

Adam shook something in his hands, and the sound of a wrapper crinkling forcing my head to lift up like a dog hearing their treat bag open. He gave me this sad tilt of his lips, sympathy spreading across his handsome face. In his hands was a sharing-size package of my favorite Sour Straws.

I met his eyes and dipped my head at the candy. "What are you doing?"

He looked down at the package and up to me, his eyebrows dipped low. "It, uh, took me a while to find the right ones. The worker had to go check in the back. They had red, but you don't like red. And even though blue raspberry still isn't even a real flav—"

"No, like what are you doing here?"

"You didn't answer my texts."

Texts. As in plural. I looked back into my apartment as if they would appear before me. I'd completely forgotten that I'd turned my phone on do not disturb, and I usually called Adam when I left work.

Before I could answer, he pushed the straws my way. "I thought you could use...company."

Was the candy supposed to be a bribe to let him in? As if he wasn't exactly what I needed anyway?

With his arm stretched out, I used the movement to take advantage and lean in, wrapping my arms around his body and pulling him close, my nose against his neck, breathing him in. Familiar and cozy. Warmth bloomed in my chest, and I sighed. I still felt like crying. Still wanted to be mad at the world. Mad at Art for selling, and mad at my ten-year-old self for sitting around listening to John Mellencamp instead of investing in real estate so I could have saved up enough to buy the darn place. But Adam's hug helped with most of that. His comfort washed over me like an internal Snuggie. How long could I potentially keep him here? He was like my emotional jumper cables embodied.

"It didn't go well?" He rested his chin on my head.

"Not good, but not bad. Just...I don't know. It feels like the end of an era."

More than that, it felt like one more thing I was losing.

My dad was slipping. My mother was off in California trying to make her life more than it was here. My sister hasn't so much as texted me a single *hello* in the last three years. My best friend got married to the love of her life and moved out, and now my favorite place in the world was being entirely taken over. How much longer until Adam left too?

"I get that. You have roots there."

I sniffled and nodded against his chest, my stray hairs getting all staticky. He pulled back just enough to look me in the eye. "Let's go inside, yeah?"

Adam settled on the floor next to me, staring at my ceiling fan circling around and around as the smooth, rich voice of Frank Sinatra blanketed over us. My sad girlhood playlist was really coming in handy. I finished up one sour straw, handed him one, and stole another for myself. This package wasn't going to last us ten minutes. I could already hear the voice in my head saying I was going to regret filling up on sour candy on an empty stomach, but my heart was slowly filling back up, and that felt more vital at the moment.

Adam chewed his straw with a scowl. "I just—make up your mind, you know? Blueberries or raspberries? What's with all of this concocted MSG BS?"

"You sound like the men at Dad's complex." I took on a lower, old-man voice. "*They don't make washers and dryers the way they used to.*"

He shrugged a single shoulder. "It's true. Everything is cheap now."

I thought back to Poppi, the green and purple Barbie who waved her hand around Sip 'n' Spin like it was a magic wand. *White wall here. Gray LVP here. Cover the old brick wall there.* Cheap was right. I was all for updates, but erasing history, erasing the stories in those walls, was a whole other thing.

A snort formed at the back of my throat. "You've got that right."

I gestured with my half-eaten sour straw, brandishing it in the air. "Even people. Places. Food. Everything is just cheap. Where's the authentic stuff? Where's the..." I searched for the right words. "Like the steady thrum of a guitar? Or a simple piano ballad? Now the world is full of artificial-intelligence remixes of songs we all once loved. Can't we make *more* originals?"

Adam sat up, his jaw flexing and his throat bobbing as he finished his own straw. "Are we actually talking about music?"

No. No, we weren't. Why was it so hard to find something real and genuine that didn't leave? That didn't lie, didn't steal or cheat. A real, tangible thing that wasn't bound to eventually crumple up like a used napkin and go flying in the wind. But was there something, or someone, just consistently there for you until...forever? Did that even exist? You hear all these stories about married couples who have lasted fifty-plus years, and yet I look around me and don't see a hint of that. Maybe for people like Layla and Luke or Adam's parents, sure. But did people like me ever end up in situations like that?

I couldn't help but have my mind immediately race to Adam. Adam, who was going to get married one day or get stationed in a foreign country thousands of miles away while I waited here for him, day by day. This fight-or-flight instinct in my mind shouted at me that he was like everyone else, that everyone, at some point or another, was going to leave. But then when I sat down and thought about it, truly thought about it, Adam wasn't like any other person in my life. This was the man who brought blue raspberry sour straws and records from the store to make me smile. People like that...did they also leave people like me?

"I don't know," I mumbled and quietly tested the waters. "I think I just want to try dating again."

"Oh?" His tone of voice gave me absolutely nothing. No hint of jealousy or shock.

I sniffed and raised my shoulders. "Yeah, I mean, don't you?"

Adam shrugged silently. We sat side by side, and I wondered if he could somehow feel how fast my heart was racing.

I pushed once more. "I like the thought of someone taking me out to dinner, telling me I'm pretty, and dropping me off back home with a kiss. I just miss that giddy first-date feeling."

"So...you're wanting to, like, *get back out there*?" Adam tilted his chin at me. The way he said *get back out there* sounded like he actually meant *you want to go get tetanus shots together?* Like he was absolutely disgusted at the thought.

In hindsight, it shouldn't have shocked me. The guy hadn't once—well, unless I didn't know about it—gone on a date in the two years we had been friends. And given how we met, I supposed it wasn't unrealistic for me to assume he could be meeting up with other women that same way and...I shook my head. No, no. The thought alone of Adam in bed with another woman was enough to make me nauseous.

"I guess." *No. Not at all.*

Almost worse than imaging him picking up a random woman to take home was the thought of me going on an actual date with anyone other than the man next to me. Thinking of someone taking me to the movies and not knowing how I liked my popcorn basically drenched in butter. Or going to dinner and having to explain to some random guy why I always order a sprite and a water—because I am thirsty when I am nervous. Worst of all, having another man's lips on mine and his eyes checking me up and down made my skin crawl.

You. I wanted to say. *I don't just want to try dating again. I want to try dating again* with you.I wanted to try hand-holding, opening-my-door, kissing-me-goodnight dates with Adam more than I wanted anything else. Because when I was with him, it was like all of those anxious little thoughts in my mind dissipated into thin air. He calmed my racing heart naturally, and finding someone else to do that for me was out of the question. There was no way.

"Stevie." He only used that nickname if he was desperate enough to really grab my attention. "Is there...I dunno, something I'm missing?"

How was I supposed to even word that? *Yes. I adore our friendship and everything about you, but I also crave more and yet am terrified of losing the last comfortable piece of my life.*

With a shrug, I settled with a small "I'm just scared."

He lay back on his side, facing me. His eyes trailed over me like a warm touch, yet I couldn't convince myself to turn to him. Everything in me was desperate to turn his way, to get any clue of understanding in his eyes. But the fear of rejection stood higher than any other desire I had.

"As long as I'm here, there is *nothing* that you should be fearful of."

That was true. Adam took care of me in a way no one else ever could. The fear wasn't anything when he was here. The fear was about what would happen when he wasn't. When he wasn't just deployed for a month or two, but when he was stationed who knows where. Out saving lives while mine crumbles away. He only had so much to carry. At what point was he going to drop the heaviest weight of them all?

"You make it sound so easy." I let out a humorless chuckle. His fingers reached for me, tilting my chin to face him.

Our eyes locked, and tiny fireflies lit up in my brain, like stardust dancing around us, or pieces of the city lights aligned together in one perfect art form. He had that effect on me. Probably on everyone. My silent giant. My loyal German Shepherd who was all bark and no bite.

"It *could* be that easy."

I looked down at his lips, recalling our last kiss in that dark, crowded hallway.

A moment of vulnerability for the both of us, a moment of giving in to the one temptation that had settled in this friendship from day one. It was meant to be quick, a small peck that I would blame on the romantic ambience of a wedding. But here I was, weeks later, with it still consuming my mind. How he held me, so gentle at the mouth but with such a firm grip. Like the kiss itself, we could take it slow. There was no rush. But then his hands on my hips, in my hair, down my back all kept me from sliding away. As if I ever wanted to. He kissed me like I was fully his, and for a brief moment, it really felt like it. It felt like the kind of night where you could go home with your date, take out the millions of bobby pins in your hair, and jump right into bed with your pj's on and fall asleep to reruns of *The Office*. For that brief moment, all I could imagine was the sense of comfort he brought me. He never once failed me, so how could I assume he would now?

"Adam," I whispered.

He swallowed, eyes searching mine. I had to know. It was going to eat away at me. Even if he left, even if he was to completely fall from my life and leave a giant rotting hole in his wake, I would have comfort in knowing the truth, wouldn't I? That if he didn't leave now, wasn't he at *some* point going to?

"Is...there something *more* here?" I kept my discreet tone, my eyes never leaving his.

He didn't answer. Not with words anyway. His chin dipped in a nod, a quick, painless confirmation to what sat in my gut. Everything in me shouted to just take the jump and go all in, to tell the guy that I had been crushing on him for almost two years and I didn't see that letting up anytime soon. But Adam never said a word he didn't mean, and I didn't know if I was ready to hear that answer if it wasn't exactly what I wanted.

"Then," I swallowed heavily, "what exactly is this?"

He opened his mouth, then closed it, as if he was carefully choosing each word in his head. "I...don't know. I like labels. I like to put things in boxes, and I can't quite do that with you."

Somehow that didn't help. Knowing he felt something more here too, more than just a friendship kindled through late-night phone calls and *this made me think of you* texts. Discovering that he didn't know what we were weighed me down even further.

But for now, it was an answer I was going to have to accept. I had no other choice. It wasn't like I had a box to check for us either. More than friends. That was all I knew.

CHAPTER THIRTY-ONE

Rachel / Now

Currently playing: Sunday Kind of Love by Etta James

***

The last month with Adam had flown by.

I was getting pretty good at running. Well, I thought so, anyway. Adam said I looked less and less like a baby deer the more we trained. I guess, somehow, that encouraged me. Either way, I hadn't hit that "runner's high" thing yet, but I was getting into a routine. We'd bike in the early mornings, watching the sun rise as a cascade of yellow, orange, and purple formed around us, his short hair barely moving in the wind while mine flew all over the place like it had a mind of its own. We'd both laugh going downhill and cringe going up. In the evenings, we ran. Before dinner, as the sun was setting, those same yellows, oranges, and purples from the morning dying before us. We listened to my *training to become a war hero* playlist, and Adam profusely reminded me that I should stop calling him sir when he gave me directions. To which I said *yes, sir.*

We had our routines. He made my coffee the way I like. I baked sourdough bread the way he wanted. I watched over his house when he would go help Crew with his truck. He would feed Myrtle when I didn't have the chance to. Eventually he volunteered to take over her care. The next day, he fed her and made his own discard protein waffles before I was even awake. Next thing I knew, he'd written her name in a scraggly font on the lid of the mason jar. When I asked about it, he said *in case we get confused*. Which was essentially the equivalent of the dad who never wanted the dog but was now buying the brand name food for it, along with an abundance of toys it didn't need.

We were still checking off other items on the bucket list. A couple of weeks ago, Adam went to the gym—because biking and running every day clearly weren't enough—and left a new Polaroid camera on the kitchen counter. Next to the white camera and several packs of film, he left a note. *Take more pics.* With a little check mark next to it. He was really, really cute.

I took a selfie with it, holding up the note and cheesing brightly at the camera, before sticking the photo on the fridge. I fully expected to come home from work and see it gone from the spotless stainless-steel appliance. Instead, he had added to it. A picture of my headphones sitting on top of my dragon romance book. The caption written below in black Sharpie read *Little weirdo.*

I cackled when I saw it, so I took a picture of his perfectly straightened shoes at the door and put it right next to hiswith the caption *Big weirdo.* We both laughed at it over coffee the next morning. Our fridge was now almost covered, and part of me was sad that we were going to run out of space soon. I'd need to get some kind of photo album eventually.

Summer was winding down as if it hadn't just started. The hot July mornings were now turning into cooler late-August evenings, and the smell of freshly cut grass was slowly being replaced with the smell of fallen leaves. Transitional as it was, Adam was always steady. My one constant.

This evening, I sat on the floor in front of his sectional, on a rug—which he claimed he had been meaning to buy for a while, when in reality, it bothered him that he didn't have one when I enjoyed sitting on the floor so much—testing various records. After my recent raise—thank you, Poppi—I splurged and bought some vinyls at an expo downtown. I dragged Adam with me, initially looking for things for the store, seeing if there was anything I could grab to display there. But I should have known it was more for myself than anything.

Adam didn't argue or complain, and every now and then, he'd ask a little question like *Why is that one so special?* Or *Do you have to have a certain kind of turntable for it to work? Is that what they're even called? Turntables?* He listened intently to each answer, a kid clinging to his best friend's words. The glimmer of innocence shined in his eyes, and it was utterly adorable.

I ended up with five records. Two Fleetwood Mac, one CCR, one Crowded House, and a final Alice Cooper single. Yet my mind kept going back to the one I left behind. Elton John's *Goodbye Yellow Brick Road*. The song itself was a classic, of course, but the artwork on the cover was what I needed. The pastels would have matched perfectly with my mahogany Fluance player, the perfect mix of dark and light.

I flipped the Crowded House vinyl between my fingers, settling for it instead, before placing it carefully on the player and letting the needle fall. "Mean to Me" strummed around me, and I settled in to it, my shoulders relaxing and my chest loosening.

The back door opened and shut. Perfect timing. Adam seemed to come home at the same time every day if he could help it. Occasionally he would get caught up with one of his brothers and come home, squeeze me like we hadn't seen each other mere hours before, and ask me how my day was. He was ten minutes later than usual today. His boots smacked the ground, followed by the sound of him immediately straightening them.

I smiled to myself. "I'm in here!" I called from my designated floor spot.

Adam didn't answer, but I could hear his slow steps approaching around the corner. He met my eyes, no slight pull of his lips, no quick walk to squeeze me. He didn't look upset or distraught, more so...distant. Like he hadn't slept well the night before.

"What's up?" I leaned my head back, grinning wide-eyed his way.

He stayed silent, eyes focused on the album cover in my lap.

"Uh-oh. The circus called. They want their lion tamer back," I joked, but he didn't even flinch. Just kept staring.

"Adam? You're freaking me out."

"I, um—" He cleared his throat and shook his head, taking a couple of steps toward me before settling on the chair off to the side. *Not* to his normal spot next to me on the recliner. He usually liked to sit behind me while I stayed on the floor. His fingers would brush through my hair, playing with the ends like a curious child. It almost always ended up with me falling asleep, head leaned against his spread muscled thighs.

His eyes lifted to mine, and there was something unspoken in them. Something that, by the droop of his shoulders and the corners of his lips pulling down, I wasn't ready to hear. I lifted my head up and tilted it to the side before he said the worst sentence I could have prepared myself for.

"I have to leave early for Hurlburt Field."

Hurlburt Field...as in Fort Lauderdale, Florida. As in he was leaving *me* early to go back to his job full of saving lives and constantly tossing himself into danger.

I blinked a few times and scrunched my eyebrows together. No. No, no, no. I still had three more weeks before he had to go back. We were supposed to keep training for the race. We still had to practice swimming. We still had things to finish on the bucket list. I was supposed to stay in this euphoric bliss for at least another three weeks.

"Oh." I sank into my seat as the "Don't Dream It's Over" began. I was too shocked to notice the irony. "Like...*leave* leave?"

He nodded solemnly. "They called me in early. One of the other guys got injured on the job, and they needed someone to cover. I'm the only one left on call."

It wasn't his fault. I knew that. But that didn't stop my heart from wanting to beg him to stay. Beg him to tell them no and to find some other job, find a career that meant we could wake up to coffee each morning and fall asleep on the couch each evening since neither of us wanted to be the first to say good night.

My jaw ticked. "So, so you're just going to leave me here? To go run off to Florida with the alligators and tan women in teeny tiny bikinis? Where you'll be wearing your hot uniform, and I'll be up here alone, running by myself with no one to make pasta for?"

His lip pulled a bit as he shifted forward, leaning over his bouncing knee. "I guess? Although I will avoid women in bikinis and alligators as much as I can."

I scoffed. Women were going to flock to him. He was a walking magnet. Even though he proudly wore my ring, that wouldn't deter some of those women. My face scrunched.

Adam sighed. "Please don't be mad at me, Stevie."

Mad wasn't the word for it. How could I be mad at a man who'd sacrificed so much for me and my dad? It was just...wrong to hear him say he had to leave. I wasn't meant to handle that part on my own. I was supposed to have a month to prepare for his departure and be able to dissociate myself in a mature manner. But I was far from dissociated. I was...associated? I didn't know the word for it, but we were there, and I didn't have time to turn back. I was far too gone for this man for him to up and leave.

I sniffed and slumped back in my chair. "I just really, *really* don't want you to go."

"I don't either. I really, *really* don't." He leaned forward, ducking his head so he could catch my eyes. "Most times, I'm not exactly excited to go out, but this time...This time feels harder. To leave."

This time *was* different. The last time he was in Florida, for one, I was mad at him, and two, we weren't...anything. Not really, anyway. Not like this. Before Vegas, it was never like this between us, so easy and natural. Fun, flirty, and yet...purposeful. Meaningful in the way that everything he did, he did with me in mind. Everything I did seemed to revolve around him. We were finding this new groove, or rhythm, or whatever you wanted to call it, and it was perfect. It was finally working for our good, and the cycle was going to break when he left. How hard was it going to be to get it back when he came home?

"C'mere." He opened his arms, and I gladly walked into them.

He cradled me into his chest and wrapped one arm under my knees, bending them into his lap as his other arm rested on my back with slow, smooth strokes of his hand. I rested my head just under his chin, my shaky breath against his collarbone.

"When do you leave?"

His hands stopped. "Saturday."

Two days. I only had two full days with him like this.

I didn't say anything. There wasn't much to say. It wasn't like he was leaving forever. I knew that. The other trips he took had flown by, and who knows? He may be sent home earlier than those last ones. There was no way for me to know, so it made sense for us to flip this switch and enjoy the time we still had left. But I didn't want to. I wanted to sulk. I wanted to sit in Adam's strong arms all night and never let him out of this chair.

My brain started rattling off all the things I was going to miss about him. His scent in the mornings, our chats over coffee, falling asleep on the couch together with our legs intertwined, taking pictures and putting them on the fridge, even running. Running...Was he going to miss the race?

I sat up from his chest alarmingly fast. His eyes widened at me. "When are you coming ba—"

"I'll be here for it. Two days before the race is when I should be back."

Should be. Because there was never any guarantee with him. He was trying to set low expectations now, when he should have done that months ago before picking up the role of world's best husband. I nodded and settled back into his warmth. He continued rubbing my back, and my heart rate came back down to a somewhat normal pace.

"I'll do my best to be there, honey. If I have to fly a plane there myself, I will be there," he gruffly whispered in my ear. "With a sign in my hand, and even if you wanted me to shout your name, I would."

I smiled at the thought. A loud Adam—which was an oxymoron itself—screaming for me at the finish line with a giant poster. He wouldn't, and I wouldn't make him. I knew where his comfort zone was, and I didn't like pushing him outside of it, but the thought was incredibly sweet.

"So." I sighed into his chest.

"So," he repeated.

"What do we do now?"

His hands froze at my back and then squeezed me closer, if that was even possible. "Let me hold you like this a little longer." His fingers flexed against my skin. "Just a little longer."

CHAPTER THIRTY-TWO

Rachel | Then

Currently playing: Be My Baby by The Ronettes

***

Adam's mom texted me this morning, asking if I could attend dinner tonight. I wasn't sure whether it was meant to be a compliment or not, but I was taking it as one. It made me initially wonder if she was asking on behalf of Layla or Adam. If anyone was going to find out about us being friends in that family, it would be her. She had this creepy, stealthy instinct that let her look into your brain directly. That or she could predict the future entirely. I hadn't figured out which yet. It shouldn't have mattered, really. Since we were just friends, but still, Adam and I had this unspoken agreement that whatever we had going on stayed between us. Neither of us strictly said it, but also, neither of us mentioned knowing each other previously to his family. Felt like it would...burst our friendship bubble I guess? The risk that Layla was an important shared connection to us both and if anything were to go south for us, the results would be unbearable.

Either way, pulling into the driveway full of cars and seeing Adam's bike to the side lit a spark in me, my pulse racing and fingers itching to turn off the car and run inside.

Stepping inside, I was greeted with a variety of *hello*s, the loudest being from Crew, who had two *Star Wars*–themed oven mitts on and was pulling something that smelled delicious out of the oven. I said a quick hello back as my eyes immediately searched for Adam. Maybe I should have texted him that I was coming here. At least to give some form of a heads-up. But we hadn't truly talked much since he'd come over after the store sold. I think we were both a little anxious about not knowing what exactly was happening here.

I locked eyes with Adam across the room, where he was sitting at the dining table with his dad, Calla, and Nathan. He glanced down at my overalls and back up. By the hint of heat in his eyes, you would think I was wearing something more provocative and not denim on top of my dad's old Jimi Hendrix tee.

"Hey, Rach. Come sit next to me." Calla patted the chair beside her, and I slipped into it.

"We were just talking about one of the guys at my work. He's a new player."

I nodded along, though I had no interest in baseball players in the slightest as long as Adam was staring at me across the table. Calla went on, telling the table about the guy, but my eyes were locked on Adam's. The slight curve of his dimple began to dip in as he smirked at me. I wondered if he was thinking the same thing I was. That no one here had any clue how close we were. How much he meant to me. How we'd kissed behind closed doors and how, in the grand scheme of life, a few tiny—okay, *not-so-tiny*—kisses shouldn't be that impactful, but they were.

"Rachel?" Calla elbowed my side, and I looked over.

"Huh?"

"So, are you single?" She raised her brows.

Everyone at the table was staring back at me, waiting for a reply I didn't have. Was I single? Truly? Adam's jaw clenched across from me. No. I wasn't, right? But then again, we weren't together either. Things felt...open, I guessed. The thought of Adam going on any sort of date had me wanting to stab an imaginary woman, so I could only imagine he must have felt the same back.

"Um." I kept my eyes on him, waiting for any kind of direction. If I said I wasn't single, questions were bound to arise. Questions like who and when and why had I never heard of this before? But if I said I was indeed available, where did that leave Adam and me?

"I'm not looking for anything" is what I settled on.

Calla's shoulders slumped. "That's a shame. He's a great guy. He takes his golden retriever to work sometimes. A real cutie." She leaned into me, talking through the side of her mouth. "Not just the dog, you know."

Nathan crossed his arms beside her and then shrugged. "You know, I can't even be jealous of that one. He *is* a cutie."

I looked back to Adam, but this time, he wasn't looking at me. His hands were typing away at his phone, a harsh line forming between his brows.

Layla walked into the room, carrying multiple glasses of water, with her husband trailing behind her. "My Rachel doesn't date. Not really." She plopped into the seat next to me, handing out glasses to each of us. "Not seriously. She's got a lot going on."

It was true. My life was chaotic. The store, my dad, my familial history, financial struggles, you name it. But somehow that didn't deter me or Adam from each other.

The conversation continued around us as my phone buzzed in my lap. I dipped my chin to read the incoming text.

Adam: You could have said yes.

My eyebrows knit together, something heavy and unsatisfying sitting at the pit of my stomach. I didn't want to say yes. I didn't want *him* to *want* me to say yes. I wanted him to stand here and now and tell me that we were more than friends. That I wasn't single, because although we couldn't label this relationship right now, I was still his.

It hurt, honestly. This was a different kind of hurt than I was used to. You expected people closest to you to disappoint you from time to time. You never expect them to cast you aside, though.

Maybe I will next time.

Adam coughed across from me, but I kept my eyes down.

I didn't like miscommunication. I didn't like the thought of leaving here tonight and having no idea where this left us. So whether I was going to get a harsh answer or not, dang it, I was asking the question.

Is that what you want?

Adam: No. But I don't like the thought of holding you back from something you want either.

Then tell me what this is.

He didn't respond, which was answer enough for me. It shouldn't have angered me as much as it did, but oh well. I'd never been entirely rational before. If roles were reversed and someone tried to set him up, without a doubt, at the very least, I would have begged him in private not to go. Or maybe I would have moved to his side of the table and clung to him like a koala, chanting *mine* over and over again.

Mama B and Crew turned the corner with trays of food, setting them down around us.

I wanted to smile and say thank you. I wanted to appreciate the good people around me and the quality time I had tonight, and yet I was so ridiculously stuck on a mostly silent conversation.

Normally, Adam's general quietness was something I liked. It was one of my favorite things about him, how he never said much and yet said everything at the same time. But this? This was the worst kind of silence.

This...indifference, or brushing off, or whatever you wanted to call it, wasn't going to work for me. It had always been so easy before, but it was like time was working itself against us, and the more we had, the thicker this unknown empty space got.

When I got back home that night Adam texted me a quick ***You all right?***

I didn't answer.

CHAPTER THIRTY-THREE

Rachel / Now

Currently playing: Until I Found You by Stephen Sanchez

***

I'd always hated the airport goodbye scenes in those cheesy rom-coms growing up. The crying at the gate, holding their handkerchief or whatever and watching the plane take off (which definitely had to be the wrong plane, in retrospect). The way she usually sobbed about their love and he would grab her, hoisting her up and spinning her with zero concern for those around them.

Pretty ironic that it was now my turn to do just that.

Adam and I had spent the last forty-eight hours hip to hip, minus showers and sleeping at night—though if it were up to me, those would have been spent together too. We kept our usual routines, though I requested time off so we could put in additional time to binge our favorite movies.

Layla offered to drive me home from the airport, which made me feel slightly guilty, considering I hadn't exactly been the best friend since we left Vegas. And kind of before Vegas too. But when I told her a hundred times that I could drive myself, she said, and I quote, "If you don't let me take you home, I will be sure to hide all your records where no one will find them again." She was a real friend like that. And now that we were here, where he was going to have to leave me, I was incredibly grateful that I wouldn't be driving home crying and screaming the lyrics to "Zombie" by The Cranberries. Actually, I may still do that, but at least I wouldn't be alone in doing it.

She parked the car and smiled at both of us. "Go on. I'll wait for you so I don't have to witness you two getting arrested for public indecency."

I clung to Adam the whole way. He hadn't had much to say the last couple of days, and neither of us had brought up the topic of his work or him leaving. I think, for both of us, not talking about it meant it wasn't truly real. As if we could keep each other the way we had without any end.

We stopped walking in front of the security check, as far as we could possibly go without being in the way of everyone else. My fingers slipped from his hand, and he reached for them one more time.

I turned to him, keeping my chin down to look at our palms facing each other.

"You know I don't want you to go." I sniffed to keep any rogue tears at bay. "You know that, right?"

His right hand freed his luggage, reaching for my back to pull me in for the tightest hug. “I know. You know I don’t want to go, right?”

I nodded, breathing in his scent and trying to memorize it. I wished I could bottle him up and take him home with me, giving the airplane a middle finger.

Adam’s chin moved against the top of my head as he spoke. “One month. That’s all it is. We’ve done it before.”

“It was different then.” I sniffed.

It was. The last time Adam was deployed, we were close, but not like this. Not where I felt like he was stitched into my soul. Where I felt like we were tethered together, and him hopping on that plane meant ripping those seams apart.

“Yeah, sweetheart.” He nodded and pressed a firm kiss to my temple. “It was. I’ll call you every night I can. Don’t go on a run by yourself without that pepper spray I left.”

“If I do, will you come back home?”

“Maybe.”

“Hmm. Tempting.” I attempted a wink up at him, but my eyes were cloudy with tears and probably looked pathetic.

He snorted in amusement, pulling back to look down at all of me. The snotty nose and teary eyes I was sporting kept me from looking my best, but Adam’s eyes trailed over me like I was the most striking sight he had ever seen. It wasn’t true. The man had seen me dressed to the nines before, and yet somehow, he still he made me feel the most beautiful here and now.

A hand reached to cup my jaw firmly, fingers spread to the back of my neck. I almost said it then. *I love you.* It sat right there at the tip of my tongue, ready to work its way out to him and cover him in the words he deserved. Because for so long, I hadn't known fully what this relationship was, and maybe I still didn't. But I knew I loved him. I loved him a lot, and wasn't that enough?

He must have seen it in me, sensed the words sitting right on my tongue, because he nodded. "Me too."

That only caused my tears to flow faster. His smile pulled back farther before he leaned in and planted a firm yet soft kiss on my lips. It wasn't a goodbye kiss. It wasn't a *this is the end* kiss. It was the kind of kiss that was left open. It had a cliff hanger, like all of my favorite cozy mysteries. One you knew would come back with the most satisfying ending. I wasn't getting that ending today.

I smiled against his lips, and he pulled me in closer, kissing me once more before pulling back. His big thumbs swiped under both of my eyes, drying my tears. "When I get back...we'll talk, yeah? About everything?"

I wasn't sure what *everything* entailed, but I was ready for it. For him and me, no barriers left.

With one more—okay, three more—quick kisses to my lips, he squeezed me tight around the neck. He whispered in my ear, "I'll miss you" and reached to grab his bag beside me. I wish I could hold it, and him, hostage.

I pulled at the sleeves of my sweatshirt to keep my hands busy as I watched him walk away, looking over his shoulder and smiling at me. I waited until he was out of sight to start fully sobbing. It didn't really make sense, I knew that, but I was going to miss him. A lot. Probably more than I had missed anything else in my life. And although a month didn't sound long, a single six-hour shift without Adam felt long enough.

My shaky legs wobbled me all the way back to Layla's car, where she looked up with the most patient, sympathetic smile that I'd ever seen. I sat down in the passenger seat without a word, reached for the aux cord, and immediately hit shuffle on the *Adam's gone* playlist I made the second I found out he was leaving.

"Annie's Song" by John Denver filled the car as the clouds above turned dark gray, the sky and music aligning with my heart.

Layla's hands brushed through my hair, getting caught on the tangled ends. "Oh, Rach." She leaned in to hug me. "I didn't realize it was so," she paused and came up empty, "between you two." I looked up and met her eyes and nodded. She pouted back at me.

"Come on. Let's get you home so we can watch compilations of Nick Miller, eat our weight in meat-lover's pizza, and cry together." She pulled her hands away and placed them on the steering wheel.

I sniffed. If someone had to be here to see me like this, I was really, really glad it was her.

When we got home, Adam's home, I was convinced every possible tear in my body had been poured out and my heart was empty, like a damp towel being twisted and strained of every emotion. He'd texted me several times already.

Adam: I'm boarding now.

Adam: There's a kid two seats in front of me that kind of looks like your dad minus the mustache.

Adam: A very large man is seated next to me, so you can stop your fantasy about me meeting another woman on a plane and mysteriously falling for her, as if you don't exist.

Adam: I have to put my phone on airplane mode. Gonna call the second I land. Miss you.

Each one twisted my heart more and more. I really did already miss him.

Layla and I walked into the house, a pizza in both of our hands, and set them on the counter. As we did, something caught my eye.

Sitting on the island was an unwrapped Allman Brothers Band vinyl with a yellow sticky note on top that said *For when you miss me* in Adam's handwriting.The tears that I thought had magically disappeared came rushing back like a tsunami washing out everything else in my mind. This man, I wanted to keep him.

He must have left it when I was helping put his carry-on in the car. I should have known it was weird of him to let me try, considering he barely let me lift a finger. That sneaky little wonder of a man.

Layla set down her pizza beside mine and looked over my shoulder to read the scraggly note. "Aw," she cooed. "Is that one rare or something?"

I sniffled. "No, but the one who gave it to me is."

CHAPTER THIRTY-FOUR

Adam / Now

Currently playing: Love Grows (Where My Rosemary Grows) by Edison Lighthouse

***

Voicemail from Rachel, 9:12 p.m.: "Hi. I miss you. You said to call you every night, but I got completely distracted playing rummy with some of Dad's friends. You should come to the next game night. These old ladies are really wild. One threatened to throw her dentures at me. Long story. Anyway, I miss you. I hope you're having...well, I don't hope you're having fun, because I want you here with me. But I hope you are having an enjoyable, normal work experience. I guess. Anyway, so yeah. Just wanted to say good night and stuff. I'm going to go wear out my record and eat the rest of your Pop Tarts. Be safe, please. I miss you. Nighty-night."

***

Adam: Thanks for the gift. I really liked it.

Rachel: Which part? The cards or the sour straws?

Adam: Both. All of it. The underwear too. All the guys were staring at me when I opened it. I don't think any of them have ever heard me laugh bef-ore.

Rachel: I love your laugh and I'm so glad you liked it. I thought the bacon boxers would make you smile!

Adam: They did. How's Jack?

Rachel: Really great, actually. He asked me where you were. Said he misses you. I agree.

Adam: Miss both of you. A few more weeks, honey. I'm counting down the days.

Rachel: You've gotten all soft on me now. Calling me honey and counting days. Where's my grumpy Adam?

Adam: He left as soon as you got that ring on your finger.

***

Rachel: So Luke and Layla are trying to convince me to go to a Star Wars convention with them.

Adam: They aren't.

Rachel: Layla told me I should wear Princess Leia's gold bikini.

Adam: I just looked that up. Please do not leave the house in that.

Rachel: ...so I should wear it in the house?

Adam: I won't tell you how to live your life.

Rachel: And you say I'm the perv.

***

Phone call: 11:39 PM.

"Hi, honey."

"Hi."

"I'm sorry it's late. We just got back."

"It's okay. You sound sleepy."

"Yeah, it's, uh, been a *long* day for sure."

"Save a lot of lives?"

"I guess. We had one guy...it, uh, wasn't good."

"Do you want to talk about it?"

"I can't, legally. Investigations and all have to happen, it's complicated."

"Oh, Adam. That's tough."

"It's just work. You get a little numb to it."

"Hmm."

"Tell me about the store. Are those managers taking good care of you?"

"Poppi and Ricky are...themselves. She told me that I was invited to their married couples' dinner, and after I politely declined, my coworker told me they were, in fact, swingers. So that was really dodging a bullet there."

"Gross."

"Yeah. But other than that, it's been good. I've been working up the courage to ask them if I could send them some other floor samples than what they're wanting to put in at the end of the year. I was gonna do it today, but then Poppi came in dressed like she was going to an anime convention, and honestly, it was far too distracting."

"That...sounds about right. You should still send it to them. Maybe they'll listen."

"Maybe. The flooring might actually be too much for some people. I guess it is kind of busy."

"Send me a picture, and I'll let you know."

"Ah, you *are* my honest Adam."

"Always for you."

***

Rachel: *attached picture of article about Adam saving someone at work*

Rachel: Your mom sent me this. My husband is a hero.

Adam: It's my job. Don't make me sound like I am so selfless.

Rachel: You are, though.

Rachel: Selfless, I mean.

Adam: Not really. I want you in all the selfish ways I can think of.

Rachel: You know I might consider that to be selfless too...

***

Rachel: Crew asked me to wear a fake mustache and hide out behind his competitor's food truck and distract them while he does who knows what in their kitchen. Just needed you to know.

Adam: Why is it that as soon as I leave, you end up in some kind of trouble?

Adam: ...did you say yes?

Rachel: of course I did.

Adam: and?

Rachel: it started raining. My colored-in brows and mustache started to melt away, and I looked like the matchmaker lady in Mulan. We ran back to your house.

Adam: And you didn't send me a picture of this because...?

Rachel: I need you to still think I am somewhat hot when you get back into town.

Adam: Don't think you could make that go away.

Rachel: I like flirty Adam. Does he only come out at night?

Adam: And bank holidays. And the occasional Friday the 13th.

Rachel: Those are my new favorite days.

***

Voicemail from Adam, 2:37 am:

"Hey. Sorry it's late again. I knew you wouldn't answer, but I still had to try. I am, uh, really missing you. Like a lot. I feel like I get how some of the guys felt years back when they'd get pissed when the time came to get back out there. I get it now. It pisses me off that I can't drive home to you now. But just one more week, right? We've survived worse. I have some things to tell you when I get back. I can't say it over the phone, but damn, I want to. I've got to go to bed. I'm rambling. Good night, sweetheart."

CHAPTER THIRTY-FIVE

Adam / Then

Currently playing: Close To You by Neon Trees

***

When I got a call from Calla with her screaming "*We need all hands on deck now!*" this was the last thing I pictured.

And yet here I stood, among all my siblings and their spouses, holding a drill, screwing together a working windmill for a miniature golf course. Over the last few weeks, Liam and Marigold had been working to put together a project for my nephews' school. Apparently last night during the storm, it got completely ruined. Which was what led Calla to abruptly calling me and shouting in my ear about "grand gestures" and "second chances."

I'd been working on getting this windmill going for about two hours. Crew cut out the wood for me, and I was making the logistics of it work. It wasn't like I could do anything electrical to make it move, but it was supposed to be windy during the festival, so if I positioned everything just right, it *should* seem legit enough.

Though I'd been dropping screws and staring off into space since Rachel's tiny car pulled in thirty minutes ago and she walked toward us in her denim overalls, lifting up her tiny portable speaker.

"I've got music and whatever is easiest." She held her speaker in the air and shook it, not looking at me. I turned my back to her, knowing good and well that if I was to face her while working on this thing, then I wouldn't get anything done.

Yet even my eyes weren't safe. Because her voice, that beautiful raspy voice that I knew better than my own was all around me. Hence, why I had to screw this last piece in approximately six times.

She was off to the side, painting animals with Layla and Calla, laughing away like this wasn't pure torment. Maybe it wasn't for her. Maybe to her, this was entirely normal. Maybe she was over our mutual silence and didn't care. That would make one of us.

After dinner on Wednesday night, we hadn't spoken much. It'd only been a few days, and I still called when she was getting off work. Our mixed emotions didn't mean I was willing to risk her safety. Her answers were always curt and dry. She didn't want to talk, that much was apparent, but she could be upset with me all she wanted, as long as it meant I knew she wasn't going to her apartment entirely alone.

"Speaking of *work*," Calla said with this suggestive tone. "Rachel, have you thought any more about possibly going on a date with Mason?"

My hands froze, and I had this immediate urge to rub between my pecs. Rachel was quiet for a minute. "I don't know." She was smiling. I could hear it.

"Who's Mason? Why haven't I met him?" Layla asked.

"One of the players I work with. He's so sweet. Here, let me find his Instagram."

I could hear them shuffling and some silence before Layla gasped. Loudly. "Oh my gosh. Look at those legs!"

Calla laughed. "Well, he does work out constantly, considering it's basically his full-time job."

I looked down at my thighs. My black athletic shorts covered most of them, but I still flexed a little. Did I still have muscled legs? Muscled enough for what Rachel liked? She'd liked them the night we met. I knew that much. Maybe it wasn't enough, though. Was I letting myself go? I was reaching my midthirties, but still. She was young. Young enough to be surrounded by muscled single men.

"Rachel." Layla's voice dropped in a serious tone. "You have *got* to at least meet him once!"

My mom chimed in. "Let me see this young man. Oh, wow. He is *something*. Do me a favor and bring him to family dinner sometime."

Wow. Thanks, Mom.

My dad grumbled a curse beside me, and she spoke up again. "Kidding, hun. I still love your legs."

All of my siblings and I simultaneously groaned.

"Well, Rach?" Calla egged on.

She said she didn't know. Did we have to do all of this pulling stuff out of her bull crap? Was no one listening? What was so great about a guy named *Mason?* How tall was he?

"I...I mean, the timing isn't ideal. Most guys don't like how much time I have to dedicate to my dad lately."

I loved that about her. It had been one of my favorite things about her from the day we met. She was loyal, even to her own detriment.

"Okay, I get that...but *one* night? Come on, I already showed him your picture, and I think I got him a little too excited."

"Calla!" Rachel scolded with a laugh. Layla and my mom giggled with them. It wasn't even that funny.

"Think about it. You haven't gone out in how long?"

"Almost two years." Rachel sighed. Exactly when we met. That was the last time she went out, same as me.

"Hmm. Yeah, it's time," my mom said. I was fully prepared to turn around and give her a death glare. She was *not* helping.

"Okay, yeah, maybe." I turned my head enough to look over and see Rachel staring right at me as she nodded. "I guess it's time."

My chest ached a deep pain down to behind my ribs, my palms itching and my mind racing. She was going to do it. She was going to go out. *You told her to, dumbass.* Not in so many words, but I guess, technically, I did push her away a bit.

It's just that I was easy picking for her. I was here and simple and knew her situation. It was the route of least resistance for her, and I wasn't going to be a default. I needed her to want me on her own, fully. Not as the guy next to her at the bar. Not as the guy walking side by side with her down the aisle of a friend's wedding. Not as the guy who was always there for her. I needed her to see this for what it was. I wanted everything with her, and I wasn't going to settle for less. If she wasn't ready for that, then I would be fine waiting. I'd wait forever if I had to. She could go on as many dates as she wanted, and still, in my head and heart, she would be mine.

We quickly finished up the majority of the project. Rachel did eventually sit next to me, sprinkled in glitter like she was made for it. After a few awkward moments—which in reality, were only awkward for me—she moved back to Calla and Layla.

Liam said the event wasn't until tomorrow night, so he would come and wrap up minor details in the morning. It was getting dark, and there was only so much work you could do while Crew was flicking two flashlights on and off and beatboxing as if we were at a rave.

I wiped my hands off on a spare rag, attempting to get any leftover paint out of the calluses on my fingers. Luke and Layla had already taken off. Calla and Nathan were right behind them. Crew yawned and said something about meeting someone at his food truck early in the morning, and my parents had left as soon as the sun was setting. Which left only Liam, Rachel, and me.

We hadn't said much to each other, other than an occasional "hey, can you pass that?" or me asking if she was okay when I heard her wince at one of the tools pinching her. I reached for my keys in my back pocket, turning to Liam. "You gonna stay here for a while?"

He nodded. "Yeah, gotta make sure it's perfect, you know?"

I didn't. Not really, anyway. But he had his reasons for winning over his ex-wife, and I imagined if I were in a similar position with Rachel, I'd probably be doing the same thing. I simply dipped my chin at him.

Rachel stood and reached for her speaker, turning it off and putting it in her back pocket. "I should go too. Not much I can do until this paint dries."

"Thanks, guys. I really appreciate it."

Rachel and I both nodded at him and started walking to her car and my bike.

The silence of the night fell between us, the only noise being our footsteps on the gravel and an occasional bird in the distance. My chest burned, aching to ask her any questions I could. I wanted to pull her close, drive her home, and kiss her good night, knowing exactly where we were leaving things. Every time I tried to ask her, though, tried to tell her the truth, my tongue got caught in my mouth. The words fell out of me like they never belonged there in the first place. She deserved to know everything, every piece of this, and yet I couldn't make myself do it.

We reached our vehicles, both of us fumbling with our keys.

"So, I'll, uh, see you later?" she mumbled, her voice wobbly and her throat bobbing.

I didn't answer back. Just dipped my head in affirmation. She sniffled, and I didn't look her way. I couldn't take it. One tear, and I was done for.

We turned away from each other, her walking to her car and me to my bike. I reached for my helmet, thankful to have something covering my face so she couldn't read me. She was always so good at that.

Her car door opened and shut, and I sighed in relief, knowing she was safe there. Or I assumed so until I heard her feet stomping against the pavement toward me. I turned my head. She wasn't crying. There was no sign of tears or distress. No, she was pissed. Nostrils-flaring, red-cheeked, nails-biting-into-her-curled-palms pissed.

"Are you not going to say *anything*?" She raised her shaky voice at me, and it was honestly relieving. I would gladly take anger over tears.

"About what?"

"You're going to let me go out with another guy?"

I bit back a smile. *Another guy*. As if we were actually going out.

My arms crossed. "I want you to be happy." Even if it meant me being on the sidelines.

"And me going on a date would do that?"

"You said before that you missed dates."

She let out a closed-mouth scream and stomped her foot. "You're supposed to tell me not to go. You're supposed to give me a reason not to."

"*Is* there a reason not to?" I asked.

Rachel lifted both hands to her face and palmed her eyes. "*Adam*." She sounded exhausted. "I give up."

"So you're going? On the date?"

"Give me one reason not to." She challenged me. As much as I wanted to take the bait, I didn't.

I shrugged, not replying. I had a million reasons for her not to go, each one ending with some form of *mine*.

We stood in the silence for a moment, until she scoffed a laugh and stormed off to her car, peeling out of the parking lot.

I waited an hour before texting her.

Are you home safe?

She read it and never responded.

CHAPTER THIRTY-SIX

Adam / Now

Currently playing: I Believe In a Thing Called Love by The Darkness

***

Every fiber of my being felt like it was electrified.

I was going to see my wife today. I was going to be able to hold her and kiss her and tell her every ridiculous thing I'd been harboring in my mind for the last four weeks. I was going to smell her, tangle my hands in her hair, and squeeze her tight against me until there was nothing left.

The ride back to Philly had been nothing short of a nightmare. The kid behind me kicking my seat, a young girl on my right asking for my zodiac sign, the guy on my left telling me his entire life story about losing his job as a zookeeper for "unscrupulous behavior." I didn't ask for details, but I was forcefully fed them anyway. For three hours.

None of that mattered, though. Not a single second of it, because I was finally going to reach my wife, my woman, and look into those round doe eyes and tell her I loved her. No holding back, no stuttering, no waiting, no last-minute backing out. I had no choice now. She was in charge of my body and soul, taking up every inch of my heart, and I had nothing left anymore. I was physically drained from not having her. Another week, and my fist would have been through a wall.

Right on my tail, zoo guy followed me. I think he assumed we were going to share an Uber or something.

"So, yeah. Essentially, I am not allowed within twenty feet of any petting zoos, regular zoos, or safari drive thr—"

I stopped dead in my tracks. "Look, my wife needs me, so I'm gonna pay you ten dollars to stop talking and go far, far away from me."

The patchy-bearded man squinted at me until I pulled out a twenty and waved it in the air. Turns out that was all I had. He shrugged and reached for it, grabbing his bags and walking the other way. Would've paid a hundred if it meant rushing over there any faster.

I passed through baggage claim, then rode the escalator down, facing the front door where we'd agreed to meet up. Looking down at my watch, I realized I was earlier than I thought. My hand reached for my phone, ready to call Rachel.

"Adam!"

I lifted my head, and across the platform, with about twenty people between us, stood Rachel in those cut-off denim shorts with that old ratty military shirt of mine she knew I loved her in and braided hair cascading down her tanned summer skin. Overall, she looked the same. It wasn't like I'd been gone long enough for either of us to change that much, and yet my heart started picking up pace, my blood pounding beneath my fingertips. She reached a hand up and waved excitedly at me. Me. My smile was slow, starting at the corners and pulling into a full cheesing grin as wide as I could. No sense in holding it back. The excitement I had to see her outweighed any care of staying emotionless.

We ran to each other at the same time, parting through the crowd like the red sea, forcing bystanders to step around us. Ten feet apart, she squealed and ran full speed, arms wide, at me. I set down my bags and opened my arms as she jumped toward me, her legs wrapping around my waist.

"Hey baby." Both of my arms swaddled around her body, squeezing her tight to me as her nose buried into my neck. I lifted one hand to the back of her head, my fingers pressing into her braided hair, kissing her temple.

She smelled like summer and rain and all things good in my life that I wanted to keep. And I *was* going to keep her. There was no doubt about it.

Rachel pulled back with a sniffle.

"Don't ever leave me again."

I chuckled, enjoying how the vibrations in my chest resonated against her.

"Yes, ma'am."

"I'm serious. I don't think I can go that long without you again. I might kill someone if they try to take you out there again anytime soon."

I smiled down at her, a swell of pride forming in my chest. "Yeah, that's my wife."

If only she knew. I wasn't going to tell her that I only had another two months here before I had to go again. She probably already knew in the back of her head. But this was a happy moment. One I never wanted to look back on with dread. So I kept quiet and held her as long as I could.

"Let's go home. I've made way too much food, and I need to feed you." She wrapped an arm around my waist, and I put my spare one around her shoulders, leaning in to kiss her temple.

She was right. My counter was covered in every kind of baked good, lasagna, and sourdough recipe you could dream of.

"I was anxious for you to get home yesterday and went a little overboard." I didn't think I'd ever seen Rachel look sheepish before. At most, her cheeks may get a little pink, but this whole hands-wringing-together, ducked-chin, and anxious-eyes thing was entirely new to me.

I set my duffel bag on the ground and took my shoes off, not bothering to straighten them at the door. I popped my fingers and cracked my neck.

She continued, not looking my way. "Myrtle's really been put into overdrive lately. Is there really such a thing as too much sourdough, you know? Probably good for your gut health. Not that your gut is bad. I mean, look at you—"

I cut her off with a hand to her jaw, tilting her up to press my lips to hers in a firm kiss. A silent promise of love and longing fulfilled lying between us. It was a kiss that spoke of the countless nights spent apart, of fears faced and battles fought, and this sort of unbreakable bond that held us together through it all.

In that moment, nothing else mattered. We were no longer separated by miles or duty. No longer wondering how much longer till I could lift her up and show the world she was mine. No more voicemails and texts. No more FaceTime calls that kept dropping when my signal was out. No. With our lips moving in tandem, biting, pulling, we were simply two souls reunited, finding solace and joy in each other's arms.

Rachel bit my lip and tugged before pulling back, breathless, chest heaving, her lips wet and eyes weighted.

"Adam. Do you love me?"

I put a piece of hair behind her ear. "You're my wife. Of course I do."

Rachel's head shook. "No. I mean are you *in* love with me?"

"I wouldn't have married you if I wasn't."

Her eyes rolled. "You know what I mean."

I smiled down at her. Yeah, I did. "You tell me. You are the one thing in my life that feels steady. You're the first thing I think of when I wake up and the last when I go to sleep. Everything I see reminds me of you, from the sunset to a pack of sour candy. It's like you moved into my head without my permission. I don't even know when it happened, but one day, I looked around me, and you were all I could see. You're like my little squatter."

She snorted in an attempt to cover her tiny sniffles. "All right, big guy." She planted a quick kiss on the corner of my mouth. "You know I love you too, right?"

A few months ago, my answer would have been a swift *impossible*, but that was then. Now? Yeah, I knew she loved me. I knew it in the way she left me sticky notes on my packed lunches, or how she tried her best to pick up after herself for me—somehow still always leaving a little Rachel trail. Or how she kissed me with no holding back, no barriers, no fuzzy unknowns. Just 100 percent her, and she gave it all to me, a guy who didn't deserve to ever call her his.

I pressed a kiss to her temple, pulling her into my chest. "Yeah, I know, honey."

CHAPTER THIRTY-SEVEN

Rachel / Then

Currently playing: Kiss Her You Fool by Kids That Fly

***

I would say I was currently packing, but packing was a very loose term for shoving articles of clothing into a suitcase that was enough to pass through TSA guidelines. With Dave Grohl's voice practically shouting in my room and me angrily shoving bras into a mesh side pocket of my yellow luggage, the overall mood of today called for a playlist that I would label *pissed because the man of your dreams is clueless.*

Or maybe he wasn't clueless. Maybe he didn't care at all. No, that couldn't be it. I mean, there was no possible way. Adam knew how I felt. I'd made it more than obvious over the last few months. Even the last year. He was my first outlet. My only outlet, really. And still he let me go out on a stupid date with a hot baseball player with thick thighs.

Okay, I didn't actually go. But I wanted to, just to spite Adam. I did ask Calla for the guy's number, to which she squealed and said she was going to start plotting romance book tropes with Layla for our children to read one day. I didn't exactly correct her, since I wasn't sure where to even start with that.

I texted Mason a brief, simple message that said I was caught up on a man who may or may not love me back and that if we did ever go out, it would solely be as friends. He was a sweetie. Calla was right about that. He came back to say that if I ever changed my mind, he would be there. I told him politely not to wait...and I may have said there was a hot young nurse at my dad's complex who would love for someone to take her out before sending her contact and a picture I stole off her Facebook. Win-win. Actually more like win-lose, because I still didn't have Adam. Not in the way I wanted.

A few days after finishing up Liam and Marigold's project, Adam was called out to work again. He didn't tell me where he was flying to this time, or when he would be back. Part of me hoped he wouldn't be back in time for us to all get on the flight to Vegas for the wedding. The other 75 percent was begging him to hurry home.

I was still irritated, though. Still pissed that he either knew what this was and chose to ignore it, or he didn't actually like me that way. Either way, I was really sick of feeling like I was being dragged along without any form of explanation.

Three sharp knocks came from my door, booming down the hall into my bedroom. I trudged along, stepping over mountains of probably clean clothes and assortments of makeup bags to get to the main entrance. I opened the door to see Adam standing there with a furrowed brow and shaky hands holding his helmet.

"Uh..." I trailed off.

He walked beside me into my kitchen. If I wasn't so relieved to have him back in the states, I would have probably kicked him out. But I was relieved, so I kept my mouth shut.

"I just left Calla's. She said your date was yesterday." He didn't look mad or necessarily disappointed, but...lost. Like he was asking a question more than making a statement.

I wasn't going to tell him that I hadn't gone. Mostly because I was feeling petty, and a small part of me would have loved to see Adam all jealous with his stupid man muscles and heaving chest. I liked caveman Adam. Even when I wanted to strangle him.

So I crossed my arms. "Yes, it was..." *supposed to be.*

He ran a hand through his hair, pulling at the ends. "Did he kiss you?"

"And if he did? Does it matter?"

"*Does it matter*? Rachel, I rode here going a hundred and twenty miles an hour, running four red lights to see you."

When I wasn't so fired up, I was going to have to remind him to never in his life do that again, especially not for me.

I shrugged. "You do that, but you can't simply tell me how you feel about me?"

"I know, okay? It's just, you said you wanted to date again. I didn't think it would be this soon—"

"You, Adam!" I practically shrieked, not caring if I sounded just like my mother. "I wanted to date *you.* When I said that, I was hoping you would pick up on the fact that I've been caught up on you for months, you big, dumb—" I growled in the back of my throat, not having the words in my state of anger.

I breathed through my nose and did my best to continue. "If you're jealous, say that. If you want more with me, say that. If I mean absolutely *anything* to you, *say that*. You can't expect me to hop along this relationship forever, having no clue what I mean to you or what this is." My voice was rising higher and higher. I knew I was bound to get a complaint from my crappy neighbors any minute now, but I couldn't seem to make myself care. "I can understand your silence most of the time, but I'm not a freaking mind reader, Adam. Help me out here. I mean, are we anything at all? Friends? Part-time lovers? More? *What*?"

I could see the moment he was pushed too far. I hated that I was the one who'd done it to him, but I couldn't be expected to stay in the dark forever. Or maybe I wasn't in the dark entirely, but it was dim. All I could make out were shapes and colors that didn't give me any sort of answer to the big picture. Not when it came to him. His eyebrows dipped down, pupils gazing up and down, as if he was memorizing this moment.

"More," he declared in that low baritone of his. He walked toward my door, a hand on the frame and looking back over his shoulder to the floor below me, not even at my eyes.

"I can't—I don't know what, and I don't know how but...more."

This time, it wasn't enough for me.

CHAPTER THIRTY-EIGHT

Rachel | Now

Currently playing: I Will Survive by Gloria Gaynor

***

"You ready, sweetheart?" Adam asked with a rough hand on my lower back.

"No." I smiled warily. But I was here anyway, wasn't I?

Granted, I was doing the "sprint" triathlon and not the regular one I had foolishly hoped to sign up for. After the last couple of days of running and swimming with Adam at his parents' house, he so kindly told me I wasn't quite ready for the full thing—mostly because of the swimming. He said it in the same way a parent tells their kid the park is closed or that the store didn't have their favorite ice cream. As if I was going to be entirely heartbroken over not having to run an additional five miles or so and who knows how far for swimming.

I was a strong swimmer. We had a pool at my house when I was growing up, and I was pretty good at making laps, but it was speed that was against me. Adam said I used too much energy in the swimming to focus on the running or biking portion. At least now it was only a half-mile swim, three-mile run, and then twelve and a half or so miles on a bike. It wasn't going to be easy. It was borderline impossible for a reformed couch potato such as myself. But Adam, Layla, and the entire Wells Family were here to support. How could I not give it my best?

Everyone was starting to line up. Mostly men in their midforties stood at the white line. It was a little intimidating, everyone in their tight black wet suit–running combos and their tiny pouches of energetic goo. Most of the people here seemed to do this professionally. Their equipment was all name brand, and they all had runner's bodies with lean muscle and zero percent fat content. Meanwhile, my swim cap had come from Target, and it wasn't until last week that I truly understood how to hold my breath and push air underwater. Growing up with a pool meant mostly me sitting out on a float, lounging around to work on my tan and taking maybe a lap or two to cool off. I certainly never trained for the freaking Olympics.

But none of that mattered. I wasn't here to win or to claim a medal like a lot of them. I was here for my dad, and I'd told Adam to be sure to grab a picture at the end so I could rush to show him as soon as my legs weren't flabby Jell-O.

"You're going to do incredible." Adam kissed my forehead and squeezed my arm.

That was a stretch, but I had gotten a lot better at running over the months, and if I could make it across that finish line, what else in life could I do? The world was my oyster and all that.

With a shaky hand, I squeezed his wrist, turning my head to kiss his cheek. "I should go line up."

He nodded. "Be careful. Don't push yourself too far, and take a break if you need to."

My smile grew wider. He was such a dad without even realizing it.

"I love you," I whispered up to him, and he shook his head at me, pinching one of my cheeks. "I love you, little squatter."

Calla stepped up behind Adam, her fiancé hot on her trail. "Good luck, Rach!" she shouted, two hands around her mouth despite the fact that I was three feet away.

Behind her were Marigold and Layla, holding up signs that said *Run, Rachel, Run!* with a Forrest Gump figure on one side. Layla's had a cute hand-drawn Yoda on there that said *May the course be with you* in a cute *Star Wars* font. I loved them all so much. And they were mine, technically speaking. My sisters-in-law. But prior to that, they were the best girlfriends I could have ever asked for. I smiled at them softly with a head tilt. I still felt a twinge of guilt over never telling them about Adam before. But that would change soon too. We were supposed to meet up for a girls' day on Monday as a celebration of me, hopefully, not being dead. I would catch them up on everything then. After that, all circles of my life would finally be put back together again. My little mosaic of a life. Broken here, shattered there, but put back together by the most wonderful glue, making the prettiest art around me.

"Thank you guys so much, really." I gave them each a hug, then gave Adam one more kiss before taking my spot toward the far end of the line, since I knew my boundaries.

Marigold whistled and Layla shouted between her hands. Adam's lips twisted in a smile at his family before he looked back at me.

The guy at the front with an orange flare gun raised his arm as the crowd counted down. I looked down the crowd to the side, my eyes instantly catching on my tattooed husband in a black tee with a small smile on his face.

He mouthed, "You've got this."

And that was all the encouragement I needed.

Bang. We were off, diving into the water.

Twenty-seven felt like an awfully young age to die from exhaustion, but I wouldn't put it past me either. I'd made it out of the swimming portion now, although I was currently the very—and I do mean *very*—last person in this race. There were a couple of women in front of me, one who was quite pregnant and the other who was at least eighty. So that was that. But somehow, I was still alive. That felt like a win.

I ripped off my wetsuit, leaving me in my one-piece running suit as I slipped on my race belt for the biking portion. The bike with my number on it was up and ready at its station beside me as I started grabbing my helmet and glasses. The glasses were a last-minute addition that Adam forced on me, but now that I felt the wind, I got it.

"Come on, Rach!" I heard one of the girls shout, but I didn't up to see which one.

If I timed this right, I could use the time on my bike to make up the time I'd lost on the swimming portion. I was fairly good on a bike, and the running itself couldn't be too much, right?

I tossed one leg over the seat as my hands gripped the handles, squeezing tightly around them. Unlocking the brakes, I took off to catch up with the people in my far view, my feet hooking to the pedals.

"You've got it, Stevie!" a husky voice shouted loud and proud behind me, and I smiled down at the bars in front of me. Oh, he was *so* going to get any kind of sourdough treat he wanted after this. Well, after I didn't feel like my lungs were being squeezed out by an evil giant.

My bike and I cut through the wind, the supportive shouts around me slowly dwindling as I began leaving that crowd behind and heading down the path through the streets of Philly.

Two miles in, and the muscles in my legs were already beginning to heat up, this deep, dull burning sensation that started at the root of my calves and was slowly creeping up. But that didn't matter. I was still going. I'd gotten the worst part over with, surely. Swimming was done, and now the biking and the running were just...cherries on top. Sure. My legs continued pushing as I worked to catch up to the other racers, my newest goal simply being *don't come in last.* Foo Fighters "Monkey Wrench" began to play in my ears, and I smiled to myself, looking down at my feet pedaling.

I was wrong. About swimming being the hardest part. Maybe the breathing in the swim section, sure. But keeping up pace on the bike's incredibly thin tires, which I still wasn't entirely used to, as well as trying to focus on how I was going to do my next transition was at least twice as difficult. We were reaching the end of the biking portion. The paved road was surrounded by temporary walls with rows of people—family, friends, loved ones, volunteers holding signs and shouting individual's names. I hadn't seen Adam and the rest of my people in a few miles. I assumed they were rushing to the next viewing spot after the transition.

The once somewhat narrow path was now becoming wider as we reached the area to hang our bikes up and transition into the running portion—the last portion. Rows of bikes were hung up before me, their handlebars caught on these metal stations labeled with each contestant's name and their correct shoes and running materials.

Swinging one leg around the side, I hopped off my bike a little too harshly, considering my knees buckled at the movement. My calves were wobbly blobs of Jell-O and the soles of my feet ached a deep, red-hot pain. But my arms settled over the bike as I pushed it down the alphabetical lineup, all the way to the *W*s. The *W*s. Because I was a Wells now.

I wasn't sure how I was going to manage to finish this race, not with the ache in my calves and the acidic burn that was building up in my muscles. But I had to do it. This was about much more than me proving to myself that I could. Although, selfishly, I was extremely excited to take a picture and post that I did it to look back on for years to come. Regardless, it was for my dad. The training, the race, the shortened breath, and sore muscles—all of it was dedicated to him. With that, and the thought of giving Adam the sweatiest hug after this, I kept pushing forward. My sign finally came into view. The familiarity of my running shoes almost made me sigh in relief.

I hooked my bike up, making sure the wheel was positioned to not knock over any of the other bikes. *Breathe.* Adam's voice rang in my mind. *Slow down on transitions. There is no need to rush putting on your shoes or stretching.* My chest rose as I breathed deeply in through my nose and out of my mouth. I closed my eyes, turning my neck from side to side to pop it. Then I grabbed my socks and shoes and quickly, although not too quickly, changed into them. I shook out my shoulders, bouncing and stretching a little before putting in the earbuds I had stashed in my running shoes and started my *running fast, kicking ass* playlist.

The comfort of my socks no longer being pooled with sweat, mixed with the feeling of being entirely free from a bike—just me and my legs here to finish up this race—was euphoric. I never in my life thought I would say *Thank God, I only have to run three miles.* And yet there I was. My neck craned, searching for my own people down the rows of spectators cheering on each person approaching with their bike. I would do absurd things to hear Marigold's whistles or hear Layla shout *nice butt, Rachy-poo* like she swore she was going to. But my eyes couldn't find them in the sea of mixed-up people holding signs for their loved ones.

I stretched my legs, pulling one with my foot touching my butt and then swapping, all while attempting to steady my breathing. I shoved down any possible disappointment that I hadn't seen Adam or the others since the last transition. It wasn't like they could run the entire thing with me. Plus, who knows? Maybe I'd passed them without realizing. I did have my AirPods volume turned up pretty high.

Feeling ready, I shook out my shoulders and began in a slow jog with two other women right beside me. I smiled—attempted one, anyway; it may have come out looking more like I was going to throw up—at both of them, and we steadied our pace together to keep pushing through to the steady track ahead of us. That was one thing I had noticed about this race so far. The people around me that seemed to do this kind of torture for fun all encouraged each other as if this was a group effort.

It almost reminded me of being on a road trip and you and three other cars are all matching speeds down the interstate. Though you might not even make eye contact with them, you still felt like they're your buddies for those couple of hours. Until one of them betrays the pack and veers off to their assigned exit.

I kept their pace as long as I could. They were both a little older than me but had running bodies. Tight calves, smaller thighs than mine, toned stomach muscles shining underneath their tight crop tops. I wasn't in their league in the slightest. But they hung around for about a mile when I knew they could have taken off without me at any moment. The encouragement was definitely helpful for as long as I could keep up. But whereas they were saving their energy by going at my pace, I was using all of it to keep up with theirs. Each step was getting harder. Blood pounded in my ears, my breath becoming louder and louder over my music. My throat begged for water despite the fact that I'd chugged down two cups from the volunteers about three minutes prior.

My body ached for rest, for a couch to magically appear to fall back on with a giant glass of water in my hand while an Adam-shaped figure rubbed my feet. My joints, mostly my knees, begged for me to stop, my chest filling with this icy-hot pain that somehow felt like all of my organs were shutting down. Everything in me screamed to stop then and there.

I really did try to keep in mind why I was doing this. Why I'd signed up for this in the first place. I wanted to see my dad—as soon as I chopped off these legs and magically grew new ones—show him the pictures, and say *look, I did it. I did it for you.* He wouldn't remember it. In fact, maybe thirty minutes later, he would ask what I did over the weekend, and I would probably just shrug and say not much. The point wasn't so he would remember. It was to see his reaction and know how much it would mean to him. The old him and this new transitioning one as well.

I kept that in the forefront of my brain as I pushed farther and farther. One mile down, two miles down, two point five. Each mark was a reminder of what the goal was here.

My body was betraying my mind. I so, so badly wanted to finish. I wanted every bit of my spirit to be there, but my feet relented. Just when I thought I wasn't going to make it, that my legs were going to give out and I was going to have to army crawl out of this nightmare, I heard the familiar deep rumble of a shout in front of me. On the horizon, beyond about ten other racers, was Adam.

Two hands around his mouth, yelling my name in that baritone that was sure to scare off anyone in a twenty-foot radius. Maybe it was because I hadn't seen him in what felt like ages, or maybe it was because I was past the point of exhaustion and was borderline delirious, but I started crying. I slowed my pace to a stop, forcing racers behind to veer around me. My head slumped down, shoulders shaking as the tears flowed out of me involuntarily. They rushed out one by one as I cried, bent over with my hands on my knees.

"Come on, honey!" he shouted, and I looked back up, not caring the slightest that I had to be the least attractive person on the planet while my Adam was practically Superman in civilian clothing. The finish line was right there, in perfect view, like pearly white roads leading to a golden gate. I shouldn't have even stopped, but hearing him, seeing him, made it feel like my entire world had stopped on its axis.

I sobbed, my chest aching and tightening. I sniffed in an attempt to not look like a four-year-old throwing a tantrum, but I couldn't keep this in. Even more so when I heard another deep voice shouting at the sidelines.

"I didn't come this far to not see you finish."

My eyes shot up again, because this time, I was surely, *surely* hallucinating. Behind Adam, in his distressed red Phillies tee and long khaki shorts, stood the man who had raised me to be everything I was.

My bottom lip wobbled, and I rubbed my eyes. "Dad?"

He chuckled, his eyes looking clearer than they had in weeks. He looked like the man who'd taught me to ride a bike. The one who used to sing Hootie and the Blowfish to me when I couldn't sleep. The same man who was left behind by almost everyone in life and yet had never once given up on me. There he stood, smile wide and laughing loud enough for me to hear over the crowd.

He pointed at my face before turning to Adam to say something in his ear. Whatever was said caused Adam to bust out laughing. That dimple that I wanted to write an entire dissertation on flashed for everyone to see.

They were here for me. Right in front of Calla, Layla, and Marigold, as they whistled and shouted my name. Crew was beside them, crying, which somehow turned my sobs into laughter.

I spread my arms wide and ran full speed to my father, pulling him into the tightest hug.

"How are you even here?" I asked against his chest as his hands wrapped around me and patted me hard on the back. It felt like I was being transported to the moment I fell off my skates as a kid, scrapes covering my scrawny knees with blood pouring to my ankle. My sister pointed and screamed, which freaked me out even more. Dad held me, told me crying was okay—that he cried all the time—and brought me inside to clean it up. Mom yelled at him for not watching me better. Ironic, since she was sitting on the couch watching the news. He didn't answer. He just cleaned me up and wiped me free of tears before hugging me with a firm pat. *You're so strong, little Stevie.*

The memory shuddered through me as my sobs grew louder. He was the best, best dad there ever was. There was no doubt about it. Even in this state, he was still the best.

"My son invited me, of course." He sounded so bright, and I smiled into his shoulder. What a good day for a good day.

His son. What a little softie my dad was becoming. I remembered visiting him last week, talking about Adam coming home soon and my excitement. He smiled over at me. *I always wanted a son. Closest thing I got was a girl in pigtails that shared my love of ACDC and* Jurassic Park. He'd ended up with both now. As long as Adam was mine, he was going to be Dad's too. And I had a feeling he was going to be mine for a much, much longer time than any of us anticipated.

I pulled back to look at Adam, who was smirking down at me with that dimple that I wanted to crawl into. I knew I looked awful, but not an ounce of me cared as I leaped for him, my thigh muscles magically feeling a burst of energy that only he could cause. Chuckling, Adam reached for me and picked me off the ground, squeezing me tight.

"You okay?" he asked low in my ear.

I nodded. "I can't believe you did this for me."

"You're my wife. You know I'd do anything for you."

I sniffled and pulled his face to mine, planting my lips on his, tears and all. Ignoring the wolf whistle from who I assumed was Calla, I wrapped my arms around Adam's neck, squeezing tight and shaking against his lips.

He pulled back and set me back on my feet. "Let's finish this, yeah?"

No more motivation needed. I could have flown to that finish line if I willed it. I nodded enthusiastically and readjusted my race belt so you could see it more clearly.

My feet turned to go to the finish line when I stopped myself and turned back. "Dad!" I shouted.

"Yeah?" he asked with a head tilt.

I waved a hand over. "Come on!"

He deserved this. Chances were, he wouldn't remember it tomorrow. That was okay. I would remember enough for the both of us. He chuckled and waved a hand to brush me off, something he did regularly when he didn't want to admit he was confused.

Adam dipped down a little to his height, speaking in his ear as he separated the temporary fencing enough to leave a gap for my dad to join me. Dad's eyes looked from Adam to me as I reached a hand out his way for him to grip.

"Your bucket list," I explained. "Let's cross one off together, okay?" I smiled at him through the ache in my chest.

He smiled, wide and proud, and stretched his arms out before taking his hand in mine. I pulled him into the path with me while Adam and his siblings walked down to congratulate us at the finish line.

"You ready?" I asked.

He shook his head with a smile. "Let's go, kiddo."

I got into a running stance before stopping. "Wait!" I reached my hands down and unclipped my race belt with my dedicated number on it.

Turning to him, I clipped it around his waist. This was his race to finish, not mine. He deserved every bit of credit he could take.

The crowd around us cheered loudly for him as we clasped hands and gave one more quick hug. I knew my mom didn't deserve to see him for a second, but part of me wished she was here to watch this. To see him glowing under the crowds cheering. To see him smiling brighter than I ever had. He had his bad days, of course, but this? This was my dad. And I had never been prouder of that than right at that moment. If he forgot it all tomorrow, so be it. I would never let this memory slip from my own mind.

"Let's finish this together." I smiled as we took off, right toward the other man I loved with all of my heart, who stood at that finish line, clapping away with a single tear in his eye. We ran at a slow enough pace to get to the finish line. Cameras flashed all around us, but all I could think was *run to his arms. Hug him, kiss him, be with him*. Adam was all I saw in my tunnel vision. Dad could enjoy the attention all he wanted, and believe me, I knew he wanted to. That man loved any excuse to brag, and who could blame him?

Adam wrapped an arm around my waist and lifted me up, wrapping both of my legs around his abdomen and settling them on his hips. I kissed him, long and hard, whispering *thank you* again and again against his lips.

If I hadn't already been married to Adam Wells, I would have dropped down on one knee right here.

CHAPTER THIRTY-NINE

Rachel / Then

Currently playing: I Miss You, Blink 182.

***

The last thing I expected on the flight to Vegas was to have Adam sitting next to me. But it was either him or Crew, and Crew was in front of me, asking a random lady if she wanted to play cards with him.

I stole the window seat, partially because of my potential motion sickness but also because I was petty, and it felt like another way to deny Adam something I knew he probably wanted. He wouldn't tell me he wanted it. He wouldn't even make a passing comment. But still. I knew it bothered him, and that was enough for petty old me.

As soon as we were allowed to, per the flight attendant's instructions, I stuck my earbuds in and cued up one of my three road trip playlists. This one was my emotional version. Full of Stevie Wonder and Billy Joel. As opposed to my more upbeat travel playlists that mostly consisted of Dolly Parton and Rusted Root.

Adam's leg shook beside me, his knee bobbing up and down and his hands shaking. For someone who flew often, he was pretty anxious for a pretty average flight. My initial instinct was to ask him what was wrong, but he was on the top of my irritation list at the moment, and I didn't want to voice my concern.

Instead, I pulled out a single earbud, handing it to him before switching the song over to "How Are You True" by Cage the Elephant. The darkness in his eyes lightened up as he reached a hand to my phone, searching for a song to answer with. The familiar music filled my ears as I registered his song choice. "I Miss You," Blink 182. My heart dipped.

Screw him for knowing me so well. For knowing I had such a soft spot for the guys and...dang it, I missed him too. A lot. The last few weeks hadn't exactly been easy. Not talking to Adam felt like losing a part of myself. It was awful, but I was still upset and confused. I deserved that, didn't I?

Adam pulled out his earbud, reaching over and yanking mine out too. He whispered low in my ear. "I'm sorry I'm not good with my words."

That alone made my chest go tight. The skin around it felt almost itchy, like I had this undeniable urge to rub my hand over it. I knew he wasn't good with words. I had always known. It was what I always said was a part of him I loved so dearly. And somehow, I ended up using that beautiful part of him against him. Damn.

I lost the battle in my head. The war between wanting to stay mad and the not wanting to fault the guy for not being able to find the words in a situation I couldn't exactly read myself. Looking up at those puppy dog eyes he didn't even know he had, I knew that battle was bound to be lost any moment.

I sighed and leaned into him, placing my hand over his. "It's okay, really."

He looked up at me with hope, and I smiled at him before breaking my own heart. "Maybe we were always supposed to be friends."

Adam reared back like I had physically hurt him. It was almost enough to make me take it back. But no. One of us had to be strong enough to see this for what it was. And if it had to be me, then that was all right. I would shoulder that burden for the both of us.

His head shook. "That's not—I don't—"

"I know." I gave him the best smile I could form as my hands reached for the earbuds. I put one in his ear and the other back in mine.

Reaching back for my phone, I pulled up the only song I could think of.

"I'll Be There for You," by The Rembrandts.

Adam's head dipped into his hand, covering my view of his face so I couldn't read him. With nothing left to say or do, I dipped my head to his shoulder and rested on him as the *Friends* theme song played in our ears. Looking back now, I think that was the exact moment our hearts broke in silence together.

CHAPTER FORTY

Adam / Now

Currently Playing: The Rain Song, Led Zeppelin

***

This was the third time I'd woken up to Rachel's hair spread out on my pillowcase, and I was so thankful to know it wouldn't be the last. For so long, I just knew I had no chance of having something as sweet as her in my life. How often could you find a woman who tasted like butterscotch and smelled like daisies? Once in my lifetime, apparently. And I wasn't going to let her slip. Not like I almost had before.

Warm sunlight poured out from the sliver of open space between the curtains in my room, turning Rachel's blond hair golden on my shoulder. I twisted to breathe in her hair, all floral and pretty and right there, begging for me to run my hands through it. She shifted beside me, stretching and humming, before turning into my side and throwing an arm around my abdomen.

"Morning," I rumbled.

"Morning." She took a deep breath and pulled me closer to her side.

"How are you feeling?"

Watching her race yesterday felt like there was a rollercoaster in my chest. A part of me wanted her to keep pushing faster, harder, to reach the potential I knew she had in her. The other part, the biggest part, wanted to scoop her off that track and carry her the rest of the way. To spoil her and hold her and take on the pain for myself. But yesterday meant everything to her and Jack, and I knew there was no way I could take that away, no matter how protective I felt over watching the pain strike across her face with each step.

She groaned. "I hurt. Everywhere. But probably better than I would have if you hadn't rolled me out last night."

"You're welcome." I snorted.

Her eyes rolled with a smile as she pinched my side.

She wanted to come home instantly and have me take her to bed. I believed her exact words were "Take me to your room and cuddle me until we die." I did half of that. I did take her to my bed, tossing her up and immediately reaching for the muscle roller I'd bought for her months ago and rolling out her shins. She screamed at certain areas. It broke me, but anytime I stopped, she swore to keep going. So we both suffered through the pain until she passed out, in her running gear and all.

"What are your plans for today?" I asked and took one hand to her back, rubbing up and down.

"Shower, sleep, eat, repeat until I feel normal again."

I chuckled. "Whatever you want, honey."

Rachel hummed and leaned farther into me, placing her head on my bare chest and settling into my hold on her waist. "Or we could do something else."

She waggled her brows like the little deviant I knew she was.

"Absolutely not, Stevie. You need rest."

"I always feel well rested after being with you."

I snorted. Yeah, me and her both. She once said I was like a wild panther, but I'd kissed the woman enough times to know she was the untamed animal in this relationship.

"Just one kiss?" she bargained, knowing well and good that saying *just one kiss* was the same as saying *I'll eat just one chip out of a fresh bag. I'll just get one tattoo, and never do it again.*

But denying her wasn't something that came naturally, so I leaned in and pressed my lips to hers. She hummed happily and leaned farther into me, her leg swinging over my abdomen as my hand lightly caressed her bare thigh under the line of her shorts.

She had no clue, not a single one. She was out there taking care of everyone around her, not realizing she was simultaneously healing every tiny crack in me. She was warmth and sunlight and reminded me of fresh watermelon on the hottest August days. Refreshing and so sweet. Too sweet. Much, much too sweet for me.

My phone buzzed obnoxiously against the nightstand beside me, and I pulled back enough to whisper against her mouth. "Let me turn it off."

She smiled, slow and sweet and so inviting that I almost decided to chuck the phone through the wall. Her lips moved from my mouth to my cheeks, to my jaw, planting soft kisses as she went.

I grabbed my phone and flinched when I saw the name. Sitting upright, I carefully pulled Rachel off my lap. He only called when there was an emergency. We'd made an agreement that anything he needed, I could handle over email.

I looked back at Rachel, who was staring at my phone and back at me with a head tilt. Guilt coursed through me. I could only imagine what I would feel if I saw someone calling her, and she reacted the way I had. But today was the day I was going to tell her. I couldn't do it the moment I got home. She had the race coming up, and I didn't want to break her high if she didn't take the news well.

"One second, baby." I stood and answered. "What?" I asked, my tone low but sharp.

"You need to go up there now," the crotchety old voice answered.

My free hand reached for my hair. I couldn't —it was more complicated than...

I looked back at Rachel, who had never looked more lost. I wanted to brush my thumb over those furrowed brows and kiss her pursed lips and put her right back to sleep.

"What happened?" I asked in a hurry.

"The store's flooded, bad. Several pipes burst last night from the water pressure above it. A lot of the merchandise is ruined. Almost all of it."

My chest ached, and pain shot through my palms. I knew I was going to have to break two pieces of news to my wife today. Both that could potentially break her heart.

I hung up without a goodbye and dropped my phone.

"Who was tha—"

"The store is flooded," I rushed out, heading for a pair of shoes in my closet. "We need to go now."

I didn't provide further details. I wasn't planning to tell her this way. I had points to make, explanations to give. It wasn't meant to be some last-minute, forced, hurried confession.

"My—*My* store?" Her lower lip wobbled, and in that moment, I would have done tremendous things to take myself back six months and start this marriage over. Start it right.

I nodded and rifled through my closet, to avoid her eyes and to grab us both T-shirts. We ran out the door in little more than pajamas, her with those bunny slippers she wore around my house. I attempted to make her stop and slide on real shoes, especially considering she needed arch support desperately right now, but she ignored me, pushing right out the door and to her car. I insisted on driving, and truth be told, I think the only reason she accepted was because her brain was working so fast right now, putting puzzle pieces together. There was no way she could focus on the road.

She wasn't supposed to find out that way. This was never meant to go this way. Why did he call me right when I had her happily in my arms? None of it could be blamed on anyone but me. I knew that. It would have been nice to chalk this up to some simple mistake, but it wasn't just one mistake. It was hundreds of chances that I'd lost—no, that I volunteered to give up. Time and I were in a race, and it had won.

The ten-minute drive was silent, the streets of Philadelphia around us still mostly asleep as the sun rose in the distance. My mind raced to piece together an explanation, but did that even matter now? Just when we had things figured out, I had to go and screw it up all over again.

I knew what the risks of marriage were when you didn't love someone enough. I knew that lost connection meant divorce. But no one ever warns you of the risks when you love someone *too* much. When you love them to the point of causing pain to them. Because right now, that felt just as heavy on my heart.

We pulled onto the street. The streetlamp lit up enough of the store to see standing water inside. The power was fully out, the brand new neon sign on top now blacked out.

Rachel opened her door without a word and walked toward the entrance as if she was in a trance, her eyes glazed over. She leaned into the glass, two hands cupped around her eyes so she could see in. Her fingers shook, but still, she didn't say anything. She didn't cry. She didn't yell or shout at me. Just stood there silently watching.

I reached into my pocket and pulled out my keys, searching for the one with a yellow cap before putting it into the door lock and twisting it to open. Only then did Rachel look up at me, and that's when I saw a mixture of fury and confusion swirling in her eyes.

CHAPTER FORTY-ONE

Rachel / Now

Currently playing: Someone's Gonna Break Your Heart by Fountains Of Wayne

***

Adam was the other investor. The "out-of-state" one. That was the only explanation. The only reason Arthur would call him directly when the place flooded. It was why he suddenly had a key to the front entrance. Why he hadn't heard from Poppi or her husband, I had no idea.

My arms wrapped around my abdomen. I was going to be sick, truly. My stomach cramped, twisting and turning at the thought of looking Adam in the eye right now. My vision was blurry as he opened the door, burning hot sensations pushing at the back of my throat in a lump that I refused to acknowledge. I wasn't going to cry. Not here, not in front of *him*.

I had an overwhelming urge to throw something, specifically at Adam Wells's face.

All of the memories came rushing through me as I stared at the ruined checkered floor that I loved so dearly, each one hurting more than the last. The night where I cried to him over the thought of losing the store. The slideshow I showed him, asking for his opinion of each sentence. The time I told him my feet hurt from being at the counter all day and then the following week, when a cushioned pad appeared right where I stand. The way he listened to me every time I talked about how much I loved the store. And never once did he decide to tell the truth.

I was *not* going to cry.

I walked through the entrance, ignoring Adam's protests.

"It's not safe, and you're not wearing proper sho—"

My bunny slippers stomped on the floor, sloshing the muddy water. The pain in my feet from yesterday felt like nothing compared to this growing ache in my chest.

Betrayal, lies, deceit. Each word flung around in my brain as I searched for any reason for him to not tell me. Did I give him a reason not to? I shook my hair out, pulling at the hair tie in it. No. Even if I gave him a reason not to tell me, there was no excuse. This wasn't on me, and I wasn't taking the blame.

I turned to Adam, my gaze shooting daggers at him as my fists clenched at my sides. "You bought it."

His eyes stayed on mine. "I just invested in i—"

"You bought it," I corrected. Technicalities meant nothing here.

"I did."

"Over a year ago?" My question came out almost whiny as I fought to hold myself together.

"Yes."

I sucked in a shuddery breath and knew my tears weren't going to stay in for much longer. I was an angry crier, no matter how badly I didn't want to be. I wore my heart on my sleeve. Adam used to say he loved that about me. But even that memory felt burned too.

"Why, Adam?" I hated how upset I sounded. How weak. "Why couldn't you just tell me?"

I wanted to ask how too. When, exactly? I wanted to ask every question that bounced around in my head, but the biggest one was *why.*

"I was going to." He moved closer to me, reaching a single hand out, his forearm tattoo peeking out at me, then one with our initials on it with that stupid record. God, I was an idiot. I flinched back, and he winced, dropping his arm. "I had plans to tell you and to give you time, I just—"

"Had to wait over a year?"

"No, I just thought it would—I don't know, Rachel. I thought it would ruin things. I've never exactly been open with how I feel, and it kind of backfired in a way I didn't expect."

A loud, booming, sarcastic laugh jumped out of me as I crossed my arms.

He continued. "I needed to help. I didn't want to make things weird for you."

"You lied to me for almost our entire friendship and our entire marriage because you thought telling me the truth would be...weird?"

"Not our entire friendship, just the last six months of it. And I didn't lie. I —"

"Lying by omission is still lying," I spat.

It was too late for me to stop them. Fat, heavy tears started falling down my cheeks, and even as I aggressively wiped them away, my hands shook in anger.

"These are angry tears." I pointed at my face to clarify. "*Not* sad ones."

"I know, hon—" He cut himself off abruptly, knowing his little *honey* trick was useless.

"So you are this *out-of-state investor* that I always heard little comments about?" I used my fingers to make quotation marks.

He dipped his chin. "I was technically *out of state* when I bought into it."

"So when I came complaining to you about our out-of-date systems and then they magically got replaced a month later?"

He stayed silent, eyes laser focused on my collarbone.

I gasped as the next thought barreled into my head. "And my raise?" My voice was breaking, shattering into tiny pieces, too tiny to pick up and put together again. "The one I was so, so proud of. That was *you*?" My hand covered my mouth, my fingers shaking against it.

Adam stuck a hand out in defense, and a line formed between his brows. "No, I just—"

"What? Signed off on it?"

His eyes fell to the floor, and his lips formed a tight line. That was a yes, then.

I sniffled as my tears fell harder, my heart breaking again and again as I looked around the shell of the place I loved so dearly. The place that now just felt like...a facade. A movie set where nothing was ever real. It felt like a twisted version of *The Truman Show*.

I stuck a hand out to him. "My keys."

I hated that I even had to ask him for them. It was my freaking car.

He stuck a hand into his sweatpants pocket and froze. "I don't think you should drive while you're upset."

"And I don't think anything of your opinion right now. Keys."

He flinched back. A part of me wanted to take it back so badly, but the damage was done. Good. Maybe he'd feel an ounce of what I did.

He handed me my keys, and I walked right out of the door, only feeling slightly guilty that I was leaving him without a ride. He had siblings, family, friends. I'd lost all of that in an instant. Did they know too? Layla? No. There was no way. She would have told me. Someone, one of them, would have told me.

But wasn't this what I knew was going to happen all along? I'd sat there, waiting and waiting for that shoe to drop with Adam. I only had myself to blame for letting that reminder go.

People leave you in life, and there was nothing you could do to prevent it. Adam was just another one of those people. So why did this hurt more than the rest?

CHAPTER FORTY-TWO

Adam / Now

Currently playing: Homesick by Noah Kahan

***

After checking the back of the store for further damage and locking the place up, I reached for my phone to call Nathan.

Technically, he wasn't my brother. Not by blood, anyway. But he was as good as. Plus, any of my siblings right now would pester me with questions about why I needed a ride and what I was doing outside the record store. Nathan was a good enough guy to keep his mouth mostly shut and not press on the harder questions.

"Hey, man," he answered after two rings.

"Hey, any chance you could give me a ride?"

There was a silent pause between us. If he couldn't, I wasn't above getting an Uber. This seemed easier.

"Yeah. Where are you?"

I rattled off the address. I could hear his brain putting the pieces together, but he didn't question me. He simply just said, "I'll be there in twenty."

When he pulled onto the street, I hopped into the passenger side, swinging the spare key for Sip 'n' Spin around my fingers. As suspected, he didn't ask questions.

As we were approaching the highway exit that would lead me to home, Nathan kept driving. I tossed a thumb over my shoulder. "Turn's that way."

"What?" he asked, looking behind him and then turning back around, shaking his head. "Oh, no. We're going to Romfuzzled."

I shuddered. The last thing I needed was all of my family members jumping me at nine in the morning.

"It's not open."

"It's always open for us. Besides, Luke asked Crew to help with some food truck event thing, and I'm bored. So you're coming."

My head rested against the seat. "I'm not good company right now."

"Are you ever?" He snorted. "Kidding. Well, kind of. But either way, Calla gave strict instructions to bring you back so that when she's off work, she can come by, and I can't say no to that girl." He said it with this dreamy voice that was comparable to a thirteen-year-old talking about his neighborhood crush.

I groaned. If my baby sister had to marry someone, I guess Nathan was as good as we could get in this family.

We pulled into Romfuzzled and entered through the side door, finding Crew and Luke arguing while Layla sat at the bar with a laptop, typing away. Marigold sat beside her, leaned back in the chair with two hands on her barely swollen belly.

"Luke, stop moving and listen to me. It's swing, two, three, four and turn, two, three, four—"

"I didn't sign up for dancing when you said you were going to make a TikTok for the bar."

"Oh yes you did."

"Where?"

"In the fine print right next to where you need to be better at lip syncing and cutting out your millennial pause—" Crew stopped and looked over at me, eyes squinting.

"Adam." He tilted his head. "Whoa. What happened?"

He set down his phone and ran over to me, passing Nathan and putting the back of his hand to my forehead—which I promptly smacked away. "Did you get in an accident? Oh no, where's Rachel?"

I scrunched my eyebrows together and opened my mouth to answer, but he kept going.

"Are you guys getting divorced?"

"Divorced?" Liam shouted across the bar.

"Oh, Adam." Marigold pouted and then promptly started tearing up—I assumed because of the pregnancy hormones. Liam put an arm on her shoulder.

I squinted at all of them. "I haven't even said anything."

Crew pointed at my lower body. "You asked Nathan for a ride, and you're wearing sweatpants in public. And you definitely have not showered today. This is full-on crisis mode."

Luke adjusted his glasses. "You do seem kind of off."

I felt it in my instincts to brush it off, to dip my chin and keep quiet and move the conversation past me. But wasn't that what had gotten me here in the first place? Keeping everything to myself had gotten me nowhere. Actually it had gotten me less than nowhere. It had gotten me ten steps away from the woman I loved more than anything else on this earth.

My fingers raised to pinch my nose. *Force it out. You need help. You can't do this alone.*

"I screwed up."

That was an understatement for how much guilt was sitting on my chest because I'd made Rachel cry. How everyone around her has somehow messed up and worked their way out of her good graces when I *swore* I never would.

Marigold twisted the chair beside her my way, patting the empty seat as an invitation. I accepted and moved to sit down while my siblings gathered around. Crew sat beside me and tried to rub my shoulders, but I shrugged him off.

"What happened?" Luke asked, still wiping down glasses.

No more holding back. No more avoiding the subject or brushing it off. They were bound to find out at some point, so I couldn't beat around the bush.

"Do you remember how I sold my portion of Romfuzzled to Liam a year and a half ago?"

They all nodded.

"I used it to invest in the record store."

It was silent for a moment.

"Rachel's record store?" Crew asked.

I confirmed with a nod, and then it got quiet again.

"And...you never told her?" Liam asked, his hands still resting on his wife beside him.

"No."

Marigold looked between all of us and stood up as quickly as a very pregnant woman could. "This seems like something I shouldn't be here for, so... I'm gonna walk outside."

Layla quickly closed her laptop and followed. "Mmm me too."

They both slipped out, and with them gone, I felt a little more relieved to share, considering they would probably rather hear Rachel's side of things.

When the door shut, I continued.

"When she told me that the store was for sale years ago, I felt like I had to do something to help. The old owner needed a certain amount out of it to retire, and I tried pulling strings, but I couldn't make it work."

I left off the part where I searched for two weeks to try and find Arthur's number without Rachel finding out. Or the fact that when I couldn't get the right number, I showed up at his house and nearly gave the guy a heart attack until I mentioned wanting to buy the store. He said he thought I was coming to rob him—I would assume because of the tattoos that he eyed like they were going to jump off my skin and attack him.

"I told him I wanted to invest at least. Make it better for her. She'd call me and complain about her feet hurting from standing all day or say how there was a spider infestation in the back room and she was scared to go in there. Stuff like that. I wanted to help. I offered him the cash up front to fix what he needed, but he refused. I left him my number in case he changed his mind, and I waited. Eventually he called me. Said that there were some investors new to town that wanted to buy it. They didn't have all the cash for the building and renovations. That was where I came in. I loaned them the rest of what they needed and used the leftover money for essentials."

Liam tilted his head. "So you were an investor then?"

"Right. But then I started suggesting different things, and they started listening and implementing and..." I closed my eyes and flared my nostrils. "I didn't see it as a bad thing back then. Not really. I thought I was doing her a favor. Then she was being so overworked when business started doing good again, and even though they hired help, I knew she deserved more. So when the other investors mentioned raises, her name came up, and I...well." I avoided any of their staring gazes. "What was I supposed to do? Not sign off on it?"

Crew spoke up next to me. "I don't see anything wrong with it. You bought her a record store. Got her a raise. Cool to me." He shrugged.

Nathan, Luke, and Liam all shook their heads.

"Nah, don't listen to him. You did screw up," Luke said.

Nathan snorted. "Yeah, to be fair, Crew hasn't had a real relationship in...forever, so he doesn't get it."

"Screw you guys. I could have a real relationship tomorrow if I tried hard enough."

None of us fought him on that one. Crew was good-looking—maybe the most good-looking of us, objectively. But he also was a walking train wreck, and most women realized it about two minutes into a conversation. About the time he started talking about his obsession with different kinds of cheese.

"Look." Liam leaned in. "Trust me. I lost Marigold by keeping stuff to myself. You *did* screw up. Own that shit. Don't play it off as something it wasn't. You can't expect to keep her close without actually letting her in. She's gotta know everything from beginning to end."

Luke nodded. "We've all done it. Being vulnerable with her is the only way you can ensure your marriage stays intact."

"Is that what you want?" Nathan asked. "To stay married, I mean. Calla made it seem like you guys were doing it for, like, a temporary thing."

I nodded. "We agreed to use the extra money from my work to help her with her dad's bills and then to get them both good insurance. Plus, I needed extra money for the renovations. But I knew going into it that I didn't just want that."

I pulled a deep breath in through my nose as I worked up every bit of courage to force out the next bit. "We've been friends for...years. I met her before I even knew she was Layla's friend, and then we felt weird because we hooked up once, so we agreed to stay only friends and then," I paused, remembering every step that led us here. "And then we just kept hanging out. When I realized I was in love with her, it felt like it was too late to go back. Buying into the store, securing it for her, felt like a way I could keep her close."

"Like a safety net?" Luke asked.

I nodded. "Yeah, basically. I was going to tell her a long time ago. I had plans to tell her about the store and the whole love thing, but just when I was starting to work up the courage, she was going on a date with that baseball player—"

"Oops," Nathan said, and I glared at him.

"It felt like I needed her to want me for me, and not because I'd bought her a store. So I thought that, after her race, I'd tell her for sure. When I knew without a doubt that she loved me. I had plans today to take her on a ride to her favorite mountain and do a whole setup and just...spill it all out for her. But my phone rang, and the store was flooded. So she knew when they called me about it first."

"Ouch." Crew chuckled. "I mean, that is some rough timing. Seriously, what are the chances—*Ow. Quit it, Nathan.*"

I sighed and leaned back in my chair, raising my hands to take off my hat and run my hands through my hair before putting it back on. "I just don't know what to do from here."

"Give her some time. Then, when the opportunity comes, go talk to her," Liam answered.

Luke nodded. "Yeah, listen to him. He somehow managed to lock Marigold down twice. He knows what he's doing better than the rest of us."

Liam smirked, looking out the window to his pregnant wife as she waddled up and down the sidewalk.

Time. I could give her that. If I was going to do this, and I really wanted to, then I'd sacrifice wherever it took. Even if that meant leaving her to herself for a while.

CHAPTER FORTY-THREE

Rachel / Now

Currently playing: With a Little Help from My Friends, The Beatles

Adam: I'm going to stay at Crew's for a few days to give you some space. I do love you. I'm sorry.

It was odd when you knew the exact moment a new emotion had entered your brain. At that single text, I felt boiling rage, and yet I also felt this tinge of guilt alongside it. Because I was basically—temporarily—kicking this man out of his house. Plus, I felt grief. Grief for the loss of what we had before. Back when I was ignorant to the giant red flag sitting in front of me.

The logical part of my brain knew Adam wouldn't purposefully hurt me. Grumpy as he was, that man was a teddy bear. And over the years, he'd shown how he cared for me in all of these little actions. And I believed in them with my whole heart.

I just didn't know there were secrets behind those little actions, whether they were meant to be good or not.

I tried to calm my racing heart, tried to casually toss my phone to the floor beside me and not dissect every word in his text. I tried to turn on a record—Snow Patrol, specifically—and lie back on the hard floor in my Snuggie and drown out all of my bewildering emotions. But every corner of this house was haunted with memories of him. Our Polaroids were still stuck to the fridge. His shoes were aligned at the door. Myrtle sat in her jar in the cabinet, practically begging me to tell her where her dad was. Not really, but I imagined that she would be. But above all, right on the kitchen counter, sat my race belt with my number still attached.

I hated that he'd taken that away from me. That this beautiful core memory was now going to forever be associated with this morning. With the lies and the deceit. No, maybe he hadn't lied to me outright, but he'd hidden things from me. Big, giant things that were life-altering. *I have an investment with too many monthly expenses.* Gosh, I was so stupid. An investment. What did I think he was investing in? Watches? Sour straws? His favorite old western films? Come on.

With my head on the floor, I heard four firm knocks at the door, and I shot up.

Adam wouldn't knock at his own house...right? Whether it was just me here or not.

I turned the volume down on my record player and listened, waiting for anything additional. I was met with silence. Maybe it was just USPS dropping off self-help books to guide Adam through what keeping secrets does to a deeply rooted friendship-slash-marriage. One could dream.

"Rach?" a familiar voice called. "You in there?"

My heart rate slowed back to a somewhat normal pace, and my shoulders relaxed. Layla. Thank God.

I ran to the door, even more grateful when I pulled it open.

Layla, Calla, and Marigold all stood there smiling at me, and I swore that at that sight alone, I was fully prepared to break down crying all over again.

"We thought you might need some company." Layla smiled.

I sniffled and nodded, talking in the most wobbly I'm-def-about-to-cry-all-over-you-guys voice. "Please."

"Oh, Rachel." Marigold's brows dipped sympathetically as she leaned in for a hug. Only her tummy got in the way, so we did more of a belly-bump than an actual embrace. She moved behind me, and Calla and Layla each hugged me too. That alone instantly made me feel better.

We all settled in around the couch. Calla opened a bottle of wine and handed us each a glass—except Marigold. She was drinking coconut water out of a wine glass so she could feel included.

"We were at Romfuzzled earlier, and Adam came in. I didn't stay to hear the story, but he looked absolutely torn apart," Marigold said with a sip of her drink.

Why didn't that make me feel better? If I was upset with him, beyond upset, then I should've been over the moon at the thought of Adam Wells looking a mess. But deep down, my love for him outweighed my anger, even at this moment.

That only made me angrier, because that made my heart a really inconsiderate turd.

"What happened?" Calla asked.

My shoulders slumped as I shared the story. Or at least as much of the story as I could. Wasn't like I'd given him any time to explain.

"Let me get this straight. Adam basically bought the store for you before you guys were even actual friends?" Layla asked. All three of them were on the edge of their seats, staring at me in bewilderment.

"Well, not exactly." I winced. This was the part that made me entirely hypocritical. I hated how much Adam had kept from me, but hadn't I just done the same to them? In their eyes, Adam and I had gone from practically strangers to married in a single night. Then we'd stayed married for government benefits. I'd kept this huge secret from every single one of them. Not only that, but any time he came up, I purposefully changed the subject to avoid the talk at all costs.

My eyes started to tear up at the reminder of how wrong I'd been for the last few years. How awful of a friend that made me.

"I knew Adam before I met him through you guys." I sucked in a breath and spat the rest of my explanation out like a podcast put on 2x speed. "We actually hooked up like almost four years ago, and then he came to the record store like a week later. I was going to ask him out, but Layla, you came in, and I realized you knew him through Luke. It immediately felt weird, so we agreed to not do anything about it. Then I got his number from your phone, and we started texting and hanging out without your family. We ignored our attraction for a while, which was really hard, 'cause that man is so fine—sorry, Calla. And then at Layla and Luke's wedding, when I was supposed to go grab the touch-up bag, I met him in the hallway, and he kissed me. Like a lot. I knew it was because my boobs were all huge in that bridesmaid dress, but I didn't want to tell anyone, because it was your night. Then in Vegas, we somehow ended up getting drunk and then at a chapel and things went from there and now—"

"Rachel." Layla put a hand on my knee and leaned in. "Breathe, girl. It's okay."

My chest shook as tears were quickly falling down my face. "It's not okay. I've been a really awful friend to all of you."

All three girls started shaking their heads, each saying some form of "no, you aren't" or "why would you think that?" But I shook my head back at them.

"I am. I haven't been there for you guys in years. Not in the right way. I think, deep down, it's because I felt so guilty about the whole Adam thing. But there wasn't a good way to tell you guys."

Marigold handed me a tissue and tried to sit by my feet. But then she groaned about her sciatica and sat on the couch.

I sniffled and continued. "Layla, I'm really sorry I made out with your new brother-in-law at your wedding."

She laughed, but there was sadness behind it, like she was holding back her tears too.

"And I'm sorry I've lied to you guys. I just liked him a lot, and I thought it would make things weird here. And then we told my Dad, and now he calls me Mrs. Wells, and I can't imagine how confused he would be if we get a divorce—"

"Divorce? Oh, Rach." Calla scooted her butt closer to me, lifting a hand to twirl my hair. "Is that what you want?"

When I thought about it, truly considered it, no. Not at all. These last few months had been some of the best in my life, and I could only contribute that to Adam. Getting a divorce would be taking all of those things away from me, physically and mentally. But I was just so...mad. I felt played and wronged in every type of way. And I still couldn't wrap my brain around why. Why, why, why?

"No. Not really," I said honestly. "But if he doesn't actually love me, then what other choice do I have?"

Layla snorted on the other side of me. "You think that man doesn't love you?"

"No. Not when he lied to me for so long. I don't know how he could."

They stayed quiet, clearly disagreeing with me, but I still felt in my bones that it was wrong. I was mad, but mostly sad, and I wanted to cling to old memories that now felt meaningless. It sucked.

"I think," Calla slowly started. "He had good intentions. I mean, the man sold his partnership with Romfuzzled to buy it. For you. I just think he went about it the wrong way. Maybe if you guys could sit down and talk, he could explain."

I nodded. "Yeah, I'm sure it would help to talk. But honestly, the last thing I want right now is to see him." Maybe not the last thing, but still, it was low on the list.

Marigold leaned her back against the couch. "What if you go visit your dad tomorrow? Get out of this house and just hang out with him. It seems to always help you."

A corner of my lip pulled up. "Yeah, I think I will."

"Well, until then, let's go un-organize Adam's closet and hide all of his left shoes." Calla stood, and we all laughed and followed.

That night alone made me realize that maybe some people were bound to leave you, but the ones who stuck with you were the only ones worth having. So maybe I'd done something right in life after.

CHAPTER FORTY-FOUR

Rachel / Now

Currently playing: Cats In The Cradle by Harry Chapin

***

I settled on Dad's couch with a mug of what I thought was coffee. It tasted really watered down, so I just set it on the coffee table and pretended like I wasn't interested. Meanwhile, my dad was bent over, flipping through his records, looking for the perfect one. I never had to wonder where I got that from.

He eventually landed on Tom Petty and set it in before taking a seat next to me on the couch.

"How's my baby?" he asked, patting my knee.

His eyes were clear today. Not as great as Saturday at the race, but you could see he was more here than not, and I was grateful for that.

I chuckled. "You know I'm twenty-six, right? And married?"

Dad pulled his head back in surprise before looking me up and down and furrowing his brow. "What happened to my fifteen-year-old?"

"She grew up." My chest shook a little. "And unfortunately had to take on responsibilities."

"Bah." Dad waved a hand. "Absurd. You're still my baby."

I smiled softly at him, not feeling like delving into that further. Maybe in his eyes I was always going to be a baby. It was probably that way for most parents. But nevertheless, this baby was in charge of taking care of him. And that meant death to my personal life so that I could take on the challenges of this new life. This life where I woke up at three a.m. in a cold sweat, wondering if he was all right. This life that had me growing gray hairs at twenty-three from the abundance of bills piling up.

Not that he needed to know about those things. He was happy. And as long as he was, I could take on the rest.

"Twenty-six," he scoffed. "Man. I missed out on so much."

I shook my head. "You didn't miss out on a single moment. I've been here. I'll always be here. I know as you get older, things become fuzzier. Everything is harder to remember, but I want you to know I remember everything. I remember the way you cared for me, the funny voices you took on when you read books to me, how gentle you were when I got in trouble. I remember how much you taught me and how loved you always made me feel."

I sniffed, my vision turning blurry. "I'll remember enough for the both of us."

Dad lifted a hand to my cheek and patted twice. "I'm so lucky to have you as a daughter. You are just...so special to me." I smiled softly, and his face shifted.

"But, my little Stevie, you can't take everything on by yourself. Especially now that you're married." I avoided his gaze as he kept talking. "That Adam boy, he's good. Real special too. You can't carry all of this by yourself. Lean on him. He'll help you. I know."

My shoulders were shaking the more he went on. Here I was again, avoiding the topic just to get by. I sniffed again. "I don't know. We're...struggling." That was the best I could muster.

Dad hummed. "Yeah, I would think so. Most new marriages do. But you two are good as gold. I see it in both of you."

"You think?"

"I know. People like you two? The more it hurts, the more love there is. Uh-uh, don't give me that look. I know your mom and I didn't work out, but that's different. We got married because she was pregnant and we felt forced to. This?" He pointed to my ring finger. "Is real. About as real as it gets, I'm sure. That man wanted to marry you long, long ago."

I understood that Dad could easily be confused and could be pulling from false memories his brain had made up for him, but since it was exactly what I wanted to hear, I clung to it.

"Really?"

"Oh yeah." He nodded. "He showed me the ring way before. I forgot about it after a while, but then he'd show up, remind me he was marrying you, and show it to me again. A bunch, actually. Took a while for me to really get it."

"Adam...had the ring before Vegas?"

The store...the ring...*Did* he actually love me before we even signed papers? I mean, I was halfway there before everything fell apart in our friendship. I knew deep down there was more there. Maybe he did too. But the ring came from Vegas, so there was no sense in that. I just needed Adam. I needed my honest, truthful Adam, who only ever said what I needed to hear, not what I wanted. That was why I needed him most.

I stood up from the couch, ready to research, and gave my dad a hug. "I gotta go. Love you." I kissed him on the cheek and was about to walk right out the door when his voice stopped me.

"Rachel. Remember, by birth, you're my daughter. But by choice, you're my best friend."

CHAPTER FORTY-FIVE

Rachel / Now

Currently Playing: Thank you by Led Zeppelin.

***

I had an idea of what to expect when I walked into Sip 'n' Spin once I saw Adam's bike outside. The other manager's car wasn't here, and I didn't see Poppi's car, so I was walking into this entirely alone.

It had been two days since I'd last seen him, and it was almost—actually no, it was entirely pathetic—how much I missed him. Even with the anger raging inside me, even while sleeping in his bed and sobbing on his pillow at night, I still missed him. A lot.

Opening the door, I instantly heard the sound of something loud slamming into what sounded like the floor in one of the back rooms. I walked over, setting my keys on the dry countertop and moving past the still somewhat wet parts of the store.

My wedges clicked along the peeling linoleum down the hall and into our storage area, where Adam was sitting on the floor with a crowbar, attempting to lift up flooring that had been glued down sometime in the seventies.

He turned around when he heard me, eyes looking up and down my outfit, his neck turning slightly red. I was still in a pretty sore mood this morning, despite wanting to see the man, and nothing made me feel better than dressing myself up. Even if I was only leaving the house to get the mail, I always felt better dressed up.

His eyes eventually left my skirt and lifted back to my eyes. Neither of us said anything, but you could see the apology in his eyes. See the sorrow in the bags underneath. He looked like he hadn't slept in two days, and if I knew Adam—which I did—he probably hadn't. He'd probably stared at his phone, waiting for the house alarm to go off so he could run to my rescue. That's just who he was.

My mouth fell to a flat line. He looked down in his hands and lifted the crowbar toward me. "Want to take your anger out on these floors?"

Only he could make me smile in this state. As much as I wanted to say no, I couldn't. So I accepted the tool and sat down on the dirty floor beside him.

These floors really were glued with some kind of twisted magic, because after twenty minutes of silence—other than me groaning when I got to a particularly rough spot—I'd only pulled up three pieces. I could practically hear Adam thinking, holding himself back from asking what I thought and if I was still pissed. He knew I was upset, but he didn't know where that left us. Truth be told, I didn't either.

After some time passed, and I gave up on digging up these fossils that some would call flooring, I leaned my head against one of the shelves on the far side of the wall. Adam sighed and moved to sit next to me, making sure to leave a good bit of space between us. Probably because he was concerned I might deck him.

"Are you okay?" He broke the silence.

"No. Not really."

He nodded. "I miss you a lot. It's been a weird couple of days."

I snorted, imagining a living situation that included Adam and Crew. "How's Crew's place?"

"Last night I woke up to him making empanadas at two a.m. because he couldn't sleep. He was also playing Taylor Swift loud enough for the neighbors to hear."

That had me chuckling even more. I could picture Adam coming into the kitchen and shouting at him, with Crew acting all innocent.

"How's home?" he asked.

"Not the same."

He hummed and leaned closer to me. "I know you're mad. I'm really sorry I screwed up. I should have—"

"Where did you get my ring?" I cut him off, asking the question that mattered more than any of the others bouncing around in my cranium.

He stayed silent, with his mouth slightly ajar.

"Because I talked to Dad yesterday. He said you showed it to him before Vegas. I figured he remembered it wrong, of course, but then I googled the chapel where we got married. There wasn't a jewelry store within three blocks of it. And the one I found wasn't open that day."

Adam dipped his chin before looking up at me. "I got it before we left. Before you even went on that date. I had plans for it, for us, and then I got jealous and felt stupid holding a ring for you while you might be interested in other options. So I thought I should let you go, let you have fun on a date with that random guy in hopes that you'd come right back to me."

He stopped, like I would actually want him to not go further, so I gestured for him to continue.

"My original thought was that I'd get the ring, get your dad's blessing—whether he remembered or not—and take you on a ride. I wanted to go to that mountaintop you loved so much, lay out a blanket, and lay it all out. I was going to surprise you with keys to the store—tell you it was mostly yours if you wanted it. That we could spend a few years saving and buying my partners out so it could be fully yours. That I'd gotten it started, but we could finish it together. That you could have your own work in it too, so it wasn't like some pity gift. At the end...I was going to pull out the ring and just go for it. If you said no, I was willing to accept it and let go. Probably wouldn't be hanging around you much anymore, but I would've been okay as long as you were happy. I was going to do it the weekend we got back from Vegas. When we were still riding a vacation high and still felt calm and relaxed. I thought maybe it would make you want to say yes. I was genuinely terrified."

He puffed a breath out. Meanwhile I was holding on tight to mine. "But then...we started drinking, and you mentioned wanting to get married, and I had the ring, and apparently drunk me thought it was genius to ask you there. And...yeah. I screwed up, Rach. Bad. But I *was* going to tell you. I was going to make it a gift to you. It ended up being harder to explain the more time went on. I didn't even know how you felt about me until I was leaving to go to Florida and you were almost as upset as I was. I knew as soon as I got back and your race was over that there would be no more beating around the bush. I love you. I have for years, and that's one thing I won't apologize for."

My eyes stayed locked on his, my mouth ajar and tears blurring my vision. That was all the answer I needed, wasn't it? It was everything I had to hear. My Adam didn't do anything spontaneously. He was meticulous, thoughtful—overly thoughtful, really—and considered every outcome before diving into something. You would think my past self would have realized that when I woke up in that hotel room with a ring on my finger.

"Adam." I leaned closer to him, placing a hand on his jaw. "I am honored. So honored to be your wife."

A breath shuddered through us both. His hands went to my waist as his head dipped low.

"I'm sorry I got so mad. I was hurt, and I didn't want to hear you out, but...I should have known you never meant to hurt me. You protected me, time and time again, from any pain. I should've realized this was eating you up too. I'm sorry."

His long arms wrapped around my waist. He pulled me to him and breathed me in. "Thank you, Adam. For everything, you incredible man."

He pulled back enough to plant a kiss on my forehead before leaning down to kiss me.

His lips met mine in a kiss that was both tentative and passionate, a mingling of apologies and forgiveness. *I'm sorry,* it said. *I love you,* it practically shouted at me. He started soft, a gentle exploration of my lips, testing the waters as if this could be any different for us now. And maybe, in a way, it was different. We were both different. But in the best possible way. Growth, that was what we each had. Separately and then together.

I poured every ounce of all my pent-up emotions into that kiss, a silent promise to never let anger or pride come between us again. It was a kiss filled with years of shared memories, of laughter and tears, of the joy of being together and the pain of being apart. A kiss that made promises on its own. Promises to not let something this good slip between us. Never again.

Adam pulled back from me, his hands brushing through my blond hair. "I have one more thing for you." He stood and went around the desk, pulling out a gift box with a poorly wrapped bow. I eyed it curiously, and he shrugged. "I can't wrap very well, but I thought you'd appreciate it anyway."

I reached out for the gift and opened it like a wild raccoon, which made him smile. Opening the box, I slumped. "Oh." I sniffed. "Oh, Adam."

Sitting in that perfect square box was what I'd searched for for years. David Bowie, *Prettiest Star*. In pristine condition. Exactly like the one my dad gave me before my mom destroyed it. My tears fell hard and fast as I looked up at him. "How?"

"I called Arthur when I was in Florida, asked if he could track down the original owner."

So that was why he'd randomly come up here to dig through files from nearly ten years ago.

"He found the guy's number, some dude living in a mansion off a hill. I called a hundred times and eventually got through to him. This was supposed to be a part of the whole...will you marry me thing..."

I squeezed the record gently to my chest and rocked from side to side. This man. Oh, this man. He was every bit of mine as I was his. He was in my veins and my heart, pushing and pulling me back to life.

"This must have cost a fortune."

"Ah, it was worth it. Been saving for a while."

My nose sniffled and I walked toward him, carefully setting the record on the countertop. I leaned into Adam, wrapping both arms around his neck and pulling him in for another kiss.

He pulled back and looked down at me. "Before we went to Vegas, I told you we were more, but I didn't know what it meant. I know now. Husband and wife. That's what we're meant to be. What we were always meant to be."

I smiled up at him. I couldn't agree more.

EPILOGUE

Rachel | Now

Currently playing: You Get What You Give by New Radicals

***

"So, how big is too big?"

"Is there really such a thing as *too* big?"

I considered it for a moment, looking out at the miles of rows filled with Christmas trees, any and all sizes to pick from. "Mmm, no."

My hands fell to Adam's, and our fingers locked together while we wandered through the aisles, searching for the perfect one.

I wasn't kidding when I told Adam that I was going all out for Christmas this year. Our house was covered in bows, scented candles, tiny village houses, and fake snow all over. I kept waiting patiently for Adam to tell me to knock it off, but he never did. It almost made me want to take a bet with Layla on just how much glitter and tinsel I could add in this house before he gave up and asked for me to stop.

We passed some small Charlie Brown kind of trees that Adam didn't even look at. He knew I was here for the minimum ten-foot showstopper trees. The crisp winter air filled their lungs, invigorating them with a sense of excitement and joy as they searched for the perfect tree.

Our breaths formed tiny clouds in front of our faces as we laughed and chatted, our cheeks flushed with the cold. With my hair half-up and half-down, tiny strands (my angel wings, according to Adam) kept flying in my face. I could fix them myself, but every time the wind blew them into my face, he'd brush them away, his touch gentle against my skin as we strolled through the rows of towering pines and fragrant firs. I just wanted an excuse for him to touch me. I think he did too.

"I think this one might be too small," I eyed the medium-sized tree in front of me with a critical gaze. Too short and a little too wide.

Adam smiled down at me. "Pick whichever one you want, honey."

I smiled so brightly to myself, and a little to him, that I swore it felt like a light echoed through the quiet forest around us. We kept walking down farther until I stopped in my tracks, eyes widening in awe as I beheld the majestic tree before us.

At ten feet tall, it stood proudly amidst the woodland around it, a beacon of comfort in the heart of the forest. Its branches stretched outward like open arms, welcoming the soft caress of falling snowflakes and the gentle whispers of the winter breeze. Our tree. For our house. For us.

"It's perfect," I breathed out low.

Its top reached toward the sky, as if yearning to touch the stars themselves.

Adam came up behind me and wrapped his arms around my waist, pulling me close as we stood together beneath the towering evergreen. "I think you're right," He murmured, his voice soft with wonder. "This is the one."

I smiled and leaned into his embrace, feeling the warmth of him enveloping me like a cozy blanket. At that moment, surrounded by the winter forest, I was so grateful for that night years ago. A night of stupidly ordering straight whiskey and somehow expecting to enjoy it, when I got so, so much more out of it.

We may have waited a long time to get to where we were, but it was worth the wait. I breathed in Adam's scent and swayed with my back to his chest. So worth it.

With every book I write I always wait until the very end to write acknowledgments. Mostly because I am ready to pull my hair out about 50% into the book and my acknowledgements would be more of a jumbled thank you's squished together instead of actual words. So now, as I finish formatting very last minute, I am listening to It's Raining Men by The Weather Girls and I feel *ready.*

The relationship between Rachel and her Dad were based off of my own with my father, minus the early set dementia. My Dad, Alan Renfroe (who's real first name is Jackie...AKA Jack), is without a doubt the coolest guy on Earth. He plays music live in Gulf Shores, AL area almost every single night and I am absolutely his biggest fan. (Fun fact: he actually opened for taylor swift in Saks, AL way back before the ERAS tour and to this day it is my biggest flex) But really, Alan Renfroe is this giant teddy bear with the biggest heart and the coolest style (Hawaiian shirts have *never* looked cooler) with the best music taste. Rachel and her dad are so near and dear to my heart, just as my relationship with my dad is. So the times where she talks about singing her best of 80's karaoke mix? That was all me and him. The performing for their families? That too. Rachel's first concert was The Eagles? So was mine. Down to the song choices, every single piece of this is covered with fun little stories of me and my dad, and I am honored to include him in this. So first off, thanks to my dad for raising me in a house with excellent music taste. And for my love for Planet Of The Apes that has recently resurfaced.

Secondly, my family. My one and only's: Justin and little Saylor, without you two I really wouldn't be able to write more than a single chapter. You both constantly encourage me to become better, and I thank you daily for it. You are the greatest loves I have ever known.

My knee slappers (yes i just decided to name us that): Mads and Kels, okay seriously. What would I ever do without you two? I have never had friendships like I do with you guys. That being said, I hate you both for refusing to come move to Alabama so we can live out our dreams of being old ladies on our back porches sipping on sweet tea and reading Elin Hilderbrand. But you make it worth it. I love the guts out of you two!!!

My editors: Mel and Beth, thank you for always taking my sloppy work and somehow always pulling it together. You two are professional turd shiners (this is your newest official editing title, sorry I don't make the rules)

Last, and never least, my readers: Oh boy, here comes the water works. What would I even be without you guys? To keep it simple and sweet: you guys give me purpose in a way I have never felt before. I love all of you and your reviews, support, and never ending love my way. Please go buy a slice of cheesecake if you're reading this. You deserve it.

Crew, we will see you soon!!

9 798330 337378

Printed by Libri Plureos GmbH in Hamburg,
Germany